Macworld
Music Handbook

Macworld is the UK's most popular magazine for the Macintosh. Each issue includes news, reviews, lab tests, "how to" features, expert advice and a buyer's guide, plus a cover-mounted CD-ROM that includes full-version software, top demos and trial versions, games, shareware, fonts, icons and much more. You can subscribe to **Macworld** magazine by calling +44 (0)1858 435 304 or by visiting www.macworld.co.uk.

Printed in the US by Edwards Brothers Inc and in the UK by Biddles Ltd

Published by: Sanctuary Publishing Limited, Sanctuary House,
45-53 Sinclair Road, London W14 0NS, United Kingdom

www.sanctuarypublishing.com

Cubase VST demo CD provided courtesy of Steinberg. © Steinberg Media Technologies AG. All rights reserved. Made in Germany. For more information, visit www.steinberg.net

While the publishers have made every reasonable effort to trace the copyright owners for any or all of the photographs in this book, there may be some omissions of credits, for which we apologise.

ISBN: 1-86074-319-6

Macworld
Music Handbook

Michael Prochak

acknowledgements

At the risk of sounding like an insincere Brit Awards speech, there are a number of people I'd really like to thank for their help and assistance in making this book possible. I'd particularly like to thank Tony Tyler for all of the useful tips and smokes, and for the last-minute, hands-on demos; Jake Wheery and the whole crew at Ninja Tune for being especially helpful, interesting and inspirational; and my son Tim, who's the real wizard with this stuff and the one who makes sure that I still listen.

I'd also like to thank Zia McKie at Time & Space for her interest and prompt response to my request for sample CDs, Keven Renshaw at Midiman for the last-minute audio-card and break-out box, Oliver Wenger at Steinberg for finally getting me a copy of Cubase VST version 5.0, Yasmin Moledina for chasing that copy of Cubase for several months and for providing the various add-ons I wanted to play with, Mark Porter and Risto Sampola at Steinberg for at least trying to get me some artist and industry contacts to interview and, of course, Penny Braybrooke and Alan Heal at Sanctuary for being so patient about the slipped deadlines. Also. a special thanks to Simon Jary, Mandie Johnson and everyone else at **Macworld** UK who helped with various bits and pieces.

This one's for Tim and the evolving magick of White Visitation

"The music business is a cruel and shallow money trench, a long plastic hallway where thieves and pimps run free and good men die like dogs. There's also a negative side."
– Hunter S Thompson

contents

introduction

"In dreams begins responsibility."
– William Butler Yeats

few tools actually transform their culture. The Macintosh, however, did just that, and as the first true personification of McLuhan's vision of the computer as a medium, not merely a tool or a vehicle, its very *raison d'être* had to be to do nothing less than to change the thought patterns of an entire civilisation. What's significant about the Macintosh is that it broke down that modal barrier between words and pictures, sound and motion, and allowed a whole new community of people to confront their own artistic and creative abilities. The original Macintosh had its own distinctive character and slightly anarchic demeanour, which was a direct result of human effort and the creativity of the artists, musicians and techies who created it. Apart from being dynamic and brilliant, most of the original Macintosh development team were atypical of their ilk, because they actually had a life outside the arid, wirehead world of computers. For example, Andy Hertzfield could talk for hours about James Joyce, literature in general and rock music to complement a degree in maths and physics. Joanna Hoffman originally specialised in an obscure corner of Persian archaeology before she decided to change careers after the Iranian Revolution closed off all relevant digs. The frighteningly talented Alan Kay was a child protégé, distinguished musician and all-round renaissance man before becoming a virtuoso computer programmer. And Jef Raskin – who had degrees in computer science and philosophy – was also a painter (with work exhibited in the Museum of Modern Art), a musician and a former conductor of the San Francisco Chamber Opera Company. And the list goes on.

So, with that sort of pedigree, it's not surprising that the Macintosh has long been the choice of professional musicians, due to the close integration of hardware and software for the recording, manipulation and playback of digital audio. And although Steinberg's Cubase started life on the Atari ST, its natural home in the evolving digital world is undoubtedly the Mac. With the launch of Cubase VST version 5.0, Steinberg has provided Mac users with a powerful and accessible integrated music software environment, where within nothing less than a "virtual studio" you can record, edit and process MIDI and audio data in a creative and affordable manner. Furthermore, Apple's adoption of USB and FireWire technology means that Mac users can instantly connect digitisers, MIDI devices and DAT storage drives in order to capture high-quality 44.1kHz audio tracks at ultra-fast speeds.

To paraphrase Douglas Adams' definition of the universe, Cubase is big, mind-bogglingly big, and it's got more power and functionality than most of us know what to do with. Likewise, the whole craft of recording, sound, mixing and production is equally big and even more impossible to examine in any detail in one single book. That's why this book focuses on the creative process, and is aimed primarily at musicians and Mac users interested in creating and recording their own music. It's not an unabridged compendium documenting in mind-numbing detail all of the features and functions of this wonderful creative tool. Instead, I've tried to make it read like it was written by a musician rather than by an engineer, techie or producer, and hopefully I've provided enough practical details and tips, at the right level, to allow you to start recording and mixing your music as simply, quickly and painlessly as possible. This book is designed to introduce musicians to the skills and techniques required to use the essential elements of Cubase VST, whether they've read the manual or not. It's also designed specifically for Mac users, who traditionally hate manuals and prefer a more heuristic approach. The idea is to familiarise the musician and the Mac user with the essence of Cubase on the Mac so that you're free to create the music you hear in your head but have been unable to realise in a recorded form…until now.

With the availability of easy-to-use music production software like Cubase VST version 5.0, the Macintosh is changing the way in which music is made. What used to be done by a team of people in an expensive editing studio can now be done by one person at home. All it takes is the right equipment and a bit of knowledge about the basics of digital recording and MIDI. When making music on the Mac, you can use two different processes for creating sound: audio and MIDI. The ideal production scenario integrates both capabilities in one powerful package, such as Cubase VST.

To input audio into your Macintosh, you first need to convert acoustic sound into a digital format that your computer can read. This process, known as *digitising*, is performed by an analogue-to-digital converter. Most Macintosh computers have a built-in stereo analogue-to-digital converter, allowing you to plug a microphone directly into your Macintosh and record.

Unlike audio, which needs to be digitised, MIDI instruments – such as keyboards and MIDI guitars – generate digital data. To input MIDI data to your Macintosh, you can plug your MIDI instrument into one of several available MIDI interfaces and plug the interface right into your computer. With the addition of music-production software, your Mac will then become a fully functional digital-audio workstation.

Audio editing is performed in the same way that you would manipulate text in a word-processing program – in composing music, you can cut, paste, delete and insert what you need to create your song. All of the fine-tuning and editing of the MIDI data takes place in software such as Cubase VST, which is known as a *sequencer*. Here you can correct rhythmic errors, print sheet music or change instrumentation (changing one part from flute to oboe, for instance), even after you've recorded your song. Using integrated music production software, the Power Mac makes editing audio and MIDI easy. While the characteristics and functions of each are distinct, the editing process is virtually the same on the Mac.

Once you've created your music, there are a number of ways to share it: you can save your song as an SMF (Standard MIDI File), which other MIDI musicians can then play back on their own MIDI systems; you can burn your own CDs; or you can convert your files to a format such as MP3, which allows you to send your music as an email attachment or even stream it from a web site, using QuickTime.

Because this is a book focusing on the Macintosh, I'm assuming that readers will already be familiar with the general conventions and operation of their computers and their operating systems. I also haven't gone into a lot of technical detail about add-on audio cards or peripherals, since these will vary considerably depending on your own personal studio set-up. However, when it comes to add-ons and MIDI devices, I can't recommend reading the manuals and documentation strongly enough. Yes, it *is* boring, but in these instances it's the only hope you have of getting everything working together in a reasonably harmonious fashion.

Ultimately, the magic that is music always depends on that indefinable something that turns a riff, break or chord sequence into something transcendental. A good Mac running Cubase VST version 5.0 can cater for nearly all of your creative studio-recording needs, but it won't write your songs for you and it doesn't come with creativity and talent plug-ins. As clever and as powerful as a Mac/Cubase digital studio may be, try to remember that, generally, musical perfection does not exist. And even if it did, a MIDI sequencer – however powerful and accessible – isn't what you should use in order to search for it. As we'll see, some level of technical involvement is inevitable, and even though it offends your Mac-oriented sensibilities, you'll need to at least browse the manual and peripheral documentation. But the real secret for musicians and Mac users alike is simply to know the limits of the software and to be properly equipped before taking the musical plunge. Luckily, with Steinberg's Cubase, you can always choose how deeply you wish to go. The user interface and level of functionality can be adapted to each individual's needs, but it's you, the musician, who needs to know how to enhance that power and add the essential element of magic. So feel free to dream…

chapter 1

the digital revolution

"Ego keeps the music business going, and promoters – including myself – are very good at making excuses."
    – Vince Power, Mean Fiddler Organisation

As Jerry Garcia once said, it's pretty clear now that what looked like it might have been some kind of counter-culture is, in reality, just the plain old chaos of undifferentiated weirdness. For your typical struggling musician, songwriter and producer, the music business can be one of the nastiest and ugliest businesses in the world. It's crawling with con-men and ruthless, unscrupulous tricksters chasing the money the way a junkie chases the dragon. Let's face it, when you come right down to it, an A&R man is nothing more than a parasitic groupie with a chequebook. And even the chequebook isn't really his. Fortunately for the cause of creativity and struggling musicians everywhere, digital media and the Internet could be sounding the death knell for huge rip-off record companies and manipulated music retailing. In the last year or so, traditional record sales have plummeted, acts have been dropped from labels and a plethora of concerts and festivals have been cancelled. Even MTV has begun to worry, because there is a steady shrinking of interest in all those self-indulgent videos that groups and record companies feel so obliged to produce to distract attention away from the fundamental fact that what generally passes as popular chart music is…well, crap.

But the beat goes on, as they say, and home or "DIY" recording – the digital desktop studio – is currently one of the fastest-growing and most creative industries in the music community. Similar to the effect that digital video has had on the television industry, cheaper and more powerful audio systems now offer composers and musicians more direct control over the creative process and are making them less dependent on large studios, engineers and producers. Four-track MiniDisc recorders are almost as cheap today as four-track cassette recorders were a few years ago, and can now double as a mixdown deck, providing many aspiring bands with the ability to produce professional-quality demos, if not complete albums. And computer-based digital studios providing 16- or 24-track mixers, hard-disk recording and unlimited audio effects are becoming the mainstay of home studios and professional producers alike.

Best of all, you don't even need a top-of-the-range Mac to produce professional-sounding audio. Down my way, people like Claire Hamill and Andy Warren have their own digital studio driven by an extremely early Power Mac. South Coast Studios – who also run the Underground Music label – still use a Power Mac 8600, and are beginning to exploit the Internet for the sale of music and CDs in a "just-in-time" fashion, thanks to affordable CD burners and the tumbling prices of blank CDs. Veteran *NME* editor and Mac pioneer Tony Tyler does absolutely amazing things with a beige G3, Cubase and some stunning keyboards and outboard effects, and real-time dot-coms like MPM 24/7 claim to offer a hybrid of online managed and unsigned acts, a virtual record label and full-service management and promotion for those who still want to chase the record companies' carrot. What it all means – apart from unimaginable artistic control – is that even unsigned bands can now record albums, cut out the middle-men and the record companies and actually deliver their music the way they want to, directly to potential fans at a cheaper price, and still make a reasonable amount of money in the process.

upsetting the record industry

Frank Zappa said that most rock journalism is people who can't write interviewing people who can't talk for people who can't read. I suppose something similar could be said about a lot of bands that get signed (or manufactured) by promoters and major labels: they can't sing, they can't play, and you just have to listen to realise that they can't write. And yet, out in the land of the Yahoos, they still manage to make money, and when you're a major international record label merged with any number of other media, publishing or high-tech companies, that's really the only thing that matters. As twisted TV "documentaries" like *Popstars* continue to confirm, it's a kind of reverse Darwinism, where it's all about the survival of the unfittest. Traditionally, unknown, unsigned or unconventional musicians have tended to remain that way. OK, perhaps a Mac with a Cubase-powered digital studio, a CD burner and an Internet address won't kill off that side of the record industry just yet, but if you're a singer, songwriter or new band with talent, you can actually sing and play your own instruments and you simply want to be heard, make money and retain your artistic integrity, a digital desktop studio could provide the plain old chaos of undifferentiated weirdness that makes getting signed – and the power of big record companies – look increasingly irrelevant.

In the past, the rationale behind musicians struggling to secure a major record deal boiled down to one thing: money. Record companies had it while musicians usually didn't. Unfortunately, what most musicians discovered to their cost was that, even after they'd managed to secure a deal, the equation didn't really change all that much. Record companies always rationalised this inequity by pointing out that mounting an effective global marketing strategy is expensive. Record companies also tend to be hulking great slack-jawed behemoths with huge overheads and staffing costs. Despite the hype, however, success rates can be quite low, and on a very good day you can almost understand why major labels ensure that they control every aspect of their artists' output, from copyrights to distribution to actual pricing. (Well, then again, maybe not.) One of the consequences of this gluttonous approach has been a bland music scene that's nothing more than a dilution of a dilution of a dilution, which over the past few years has resulted in over 30% of bands signed to major labels being dropped and nearly as many employees made redundant.

Nowadays, however, that sort of greed-inflated, cost-based, business-speak drivel simply doesn't hold water. The ubiquitous digital revolution has levelled the playing field more than the music business likes to acknowledge. Accessible technology now means that, whether you get a major record deal or you simply produce your own stuff on a Mac with Cubase, actual production costs are relatively minimal. Once you've mixed down your master, you can produce CDs – usually with jewel cases and inserts – for under 60p each.

In terms of the music business in general, I have to agree with Bill Hicks: the Britney Spears, boy bands and Billies that clutter the current charts really are the spawn of Satan. Not that the music charts actually mean anything these days, of course; at the end of the last century, good old Cliff proved once again that carefully orchestrated sales can get almost anything in at Number One, no matter how rancid. And the beauty of the chart system is that you don't even have to sell that may copies to hit the top of the chart. But while record companies and radio stations continue to churn out and promote video-driven pap, out in the creative wasteland, away from the goat-boy glances of A&R geeks that wouldn't recognise a decent song if it came up and hit them on the arse with a can of Diet Coke, real music is still being produced, and lots of it. Very shortly, all those middle-men, parasite scum with their posy, egocentric awards ceremonies will become a global anachronism scraping the shrinking, bottom-feeding retail slime of what's left of a less-then-lucrative, brain-dead, pre-teen market. Well, one can only hope…

making it on your own

As a musician, I've always appreciated the Mac. Equipped with high-quality integrated sound, it was born to rock from day one, and it's always had the best music-production applications – such as Cubase – and is still the easiest platform for handling sound, integrating with live instruments and even burning your own CDs. For example, the new version of Toast is a joy to use, and it even lets old freaks like me copy ancient vinyl or dub four-track tape masters directly to CD with little or no effort. And everyone knows that the Mac is still the best and most accessible platform for creating Web sites. So, for creative musicians and producers everywhere, the tools are there and the magic is just beginning.

MP3, the technology that allows music to be downloaded directly from the Net, has actually knocked "Sex" off the number one spot of being the word or phrase most commonly entered into search engines, and despite efforts to kill off sites like Napster and its ilk, it's MP3 and whatever comes next that could help revolutionise the entire music industry. Perhaps in the not-too-distant future, musicians will feel even more confident about asking whether or not they really need a traditional record deal and the whole record industry may be forgotten, like some bad music-hall joke. For now, though, be aware that the music business can be a particularly ugly money trench when it comes to contracts and small print, and in the real world the great rock 'n' roll swindle isn't just a figure of speech. For too many traditional companies, it's a way of life. Not everyone who signs a major deal gets what they want, and that illusory road to fame is paved with too many artists – some of whom have hugely successful back catalogues – who end up living in poverty after generating billions for the record industry.

The poet and artist William Blake noted that the labours of the artist, the poet and the musician have been proverbially attended by poverty and obscurity. However, he believed that this condition was never the fault of the public but, instead, was the result of "a neglect of means to propagate such works as have wholly absorbed the man of genius". In his time, Blake was a pioneer in developing printing and engraving, and was a great advocate of self-publishing as a means of reaching a greater audience. Today, desktop digital studios, cheap CD production and the Web are generating the same kind of hope and excitement in music as printing and self-publishing did in Blake's day, and for a lot of very similar reasons.

According to Alan McGee, the man who mistakenly discovered Oasis and set up Creation Records, within five to ten years the future will see the death of most of the record companies. To back up that belief, McGee recently quit as head of Creation Records and set up an Internet venture, Poptones. With increasingly sophisticated and accessible tools, like the stuff already in common use on the Mac, it will be a lot easier and sexier for bands to maintain artistic control, create their own albums, upload them to the Net and deliver them straight to their customers at a cheaper price, with no A&R geeks to please, no record companies and no middle-men.

For example, right now, a new band can record in their sitting room with a four-track or a Mac, or in a local studio with any of a dozen mix-and-match permutations. A final mix can be mastered to MiniDisc, DAT or CD, or simply saved as an MP3. Instead of slogging to get signed by some record company that's more concerned about how you look than how you sound, musicians can create a "virtual label" via a Web site and upload MP3 files for fans to listen to or download, then giving them the option of either receiving the whole album online or ordering a CD directly from the band. At the moment, for under £4,000 you can buy a duplicator that will copy 100 CDs at a time, which also eliminates the need to shell out for large numbers of pressings in order to keep down the unit cost. In this way, "just-in-time" production becomes a very easy option.

Before you start to salivate over reports of huge record deals being offered to various bands, try to keep in mind the fact that advances are effectively loans, and they have to be recouped before their recipients get any further royalties or payment on sales. On top of that, record companies will try to pay artists 90% of what's sold, rather than the 100% you might assume they'd get. Deductions can be frightening and extensive, and as an artist you'll probably end up paying for minuscule things, like packaging and promotional material, as well as footing the bill for video production, studio time, etc. If you're lucky (or unlucky) enough to secure a record deal with the Sonys or EMIs of this world, even with a particularly good contract you'd probably only make around £1 on every CD of yours that was sold. However, there are plenty of cases like that of Toni Braxton, who was forced into bankruptcy in 1998 after selling $188 million worth of CDs, because her label paid her less than 35¢ per album. Based on current costs, if you recorded and produced a CD on your own and sold it directly to the customer for, say, a tenner (which is a lot cheaper than buying a CD in the shops), you could still expect to make at least £6 on each CD after all expenses had been met.

And that includes the costs involved with mastering and pressing, the production of inserts and jewel cases and some sort of distribution deal. So, for every 10,000 CDs you'd sell for a major label, you could expect around £10,000, while for every 10,000 CDs you sold on your own, you'd make £60,000. Which would you prefer?

The reason why McGee believes there will be no record companies in five to ten years' time is because it will be sexier for bands to upload their music onto the Internet and deliver straight to the fans, for a cheaper price. Perhaps when the major labels have lost enough money we'll see what's currently growing into a healthy underground coalescing into something to which the general public can once again relate.

online distribution – a world market

The beauty of marketing music directly to listeners via the Net is that nobody dictates who your audience is or should be. The consumer has full control over what they want to listen to and how they go about obtaining the sort of music they want to hear. All musicians have to do is make it easily accessible and target their demographics. OK, Web-based music won't improve the public's taste, but it could democratise the market. After all, the fact that somebody like David Hasselhoff can sell millions of crap albums in Germany, or that the Nolans are still big in Japan, does tend to suggest that there's a market out there for almost any kind of music. And as more of the world goes online, the Web could be the way of finding it…provided that you have a system for selling your stuff via credit card.

In many respects, the Internet is the most frightening phenomenon to hit the music business since the whole thing began. Gone are the days when the sale of music was wholly dependent on the movement of physical and almost always over-priced product. Gone are the days when global marketing was exclusively the province of fat, multinational record companies. Thanks to the Internet, unsigned musicians who are producing music in every conceivable genre are already beginning to gain substantial benefits, both in terms of money and notoriety, and the more this forum grows, the more the anachronistic, bloated record companies will struggle.

Although, deep down, record companies hate the fact that musicians can now build a direct relationship with their audiences, many established labels are now working in a much more co-operative way with artists' own sites and even independent "fan" sites. Out in record land, established labels have also been rushing madly to launch their own Web sites and market new releases and back catalogue in a downloadable format. Some of the bigger players, such as EMI, have recognised the writing on the wall and have announced that they will be switching focus from manufacturing CDs to delivering music to customers on the Web. Even Our Price has launched a site selling downloadable music files. EMI also joined the dot-com gold rush when it bought Musicmaker.com, which now offers the ability to create compilation CDs from some of the parent company's massive warehouse of tracks. Besides this, there's also a plethora of "unsigned" sites promising the world to gullible wannabes, and big boys such as Universal are launching sites like Farmclub.com in order to entice new artists with the promise of a proper recording deal.

Technology and online access is no substitute for talent and imagination, however, unless it's your life's ambition to become one of the legacy-less legions of sterile, manufactured pop artists wallowing in the muck of commercial mediocrity, where "most successful" certainly doesn't mean "most talented" and where money is more important than music. Effectively, the Internet and burgeoning digital technology can offer an alternative for musicians and unknowns by which they can produce and promote their own music and potentially make it available to a global audience. However, once you get out on the Net, you'll discover that cyberspace is a wild, noisy and twisted place, and that it's all too easy to get lost in the virtual crowd. If in space no one can hear you scream, as they claimed in *Alien*, then in cyberspace no one will hear you unless you do. Current NEC research estimates that one and a half billion Web pages are available, and that these are increasing by two million every day. This means that even the best search engines (which in itself is an oxymoron) have enormous difficulty in plucking the musical needles from this cacophonous haystack. So, even with the advantages of the Internet, co-operation, promotion and creativity are the only things that will prevent cyberspace from being over-run with the same old sludge that clogs our airwaves and high-street record shops at the moment.

Other new beneficiaries of Web-based music – apart from the musicians themselves – may also be a new breed of facilitators that can offer services that complement desktop studios, such as honest, music-loving management, cheap mastering facilities and fast servers to host and market those emerging virtual labels. This significant evolutionary progress will be made by those with both an ear for production and the ability to get their heads around the fact that marketing on the Net isn't the same as marketing through traditional print or broadcast media, while never forgetting that playing live and working the real world still counts. But we'll talk about that later. As it happens, I've left the G3 on and I've got an album to finish…

chapter 2

why professionals prefer the Mac

"In terms of multitracking actual audio, I've only ever used Macs. I had more problems just trying to use a PC."
– Guy Fixsen, Music Producer

I find myself more and more in agreement with another philosophical tenet of one of my favourite dead rock stars, Frank Zappa, who suggested that people will agree with you only if they already agree with you. You don't really change people's minds.

One of the things about which a lot of people already agree and probably don't need their minds changed is the simple fact that the Macintosh is a superb platform for music. Unlike PCs, whose audio capability has always relied on plug-in cards, every Mac motherboard has always had built-in audio-processing capabilities as standard. And of all of the machines out there, none is better than the current crop of G4s, which is why over 90% of recording studios and a growing number of serious home studios use them instead of PCs. OK, digital sound has generally come a long way since the early analogue synthesisers of the late 1960s, and today most desktop PCs are capable of reproducing CD-quality sound or working in conjunction with a burgeoning range of digital audio and sampling technology, including digital hard-disk recorders, digital sampling instruments, digital sample players/synthesisers and audio device controllers. That is, of course, provided that you can manage to get your assorted sound cards and various other add-on gizmos to work properly in the wacky and wonderful world of Wintel.

Apart from some of the early Mac PowerBooks, all Macs have 16-bit stereo audio in and out as part of their basic hardware configuration. You can't do that on any PC unless it's got an extra sound card or some other audio interface. This means that, although media hype has conditioned most people into believing that PCs are generally cheaper than Macs, by the time you buy all the extras you need to bring them up to Mac standard, you're probably not really saving all that much. As it happens, a complete, mid-range G4 system with a monitor, a fat hard drive and ample memory will cost less than £2,000 and will provide anything from 16 to 24 audio tracks, or even more, if you get a really fat hard drive. Twenty years ago, you'd have paid more than that for an eight-track tape recorder. This same Mac system allows you to run a number of virtual samplers with your audio software and loads samples as fast as changing synth patches on dedicated samplers. As an added bonus, the Mac also provides you with on-screen graphical editing and mix automation for your MIDI tracks and all of your audio tracks, and even virtual instruments.

So, whether Uncle Bill likes it or not, when it comes to music, the Mac is still easier to set up and use than any Windows PC, and contrary to public ignorance it really isn't that expensive. Think about it: if you're a musician who's simply interested in creating music and getting it recorded, the last thing you want to be doing is struggling with the arcane evils of a PC. If you want to run games, surf the Net and run spreadsheets in the discomfort of your own home for cut-rate prices, then go ahead and buy a PC; but if you're a serious musician or producer and you want to make real music, don't even think about it. Today's Macs are still the easiest computers to use, and easily have more punch, when it comes to music and digital audio, than ever before. Sequencers and plug-ins are expanding to exploit all of this power to the full, and if you're using a G4, or whatever comes after, audio latency is less of a problem, and matching suitable audio cards is much less hassle, generally speaking. And if you don't want to be desk-bound, the latest crop of PowerBooks are more than capable of providing excellent mobile studio facilities for bands on the run.

Nowadays, even old standards like MIDI are facing competition from new technologies, such as FireWire, an interface standard developed by Apple that offers better bandwidth and accessibility for the digital transfer of music and sound. So, despite Apple's usual lack of panache in promoting itself as *the* ultimate creative solution for music and audio, the Macintosh is still the favoured computer within the music industry for all aspects of digital audio production. Major studios, like Abbey Road, have installed Power Mac systems, and a plethora of composers, musicians and producers – both signed and unsigned – now work exclusively on Macs.

Steinberg recently upgraded its flagship sequencer, Cubase VST/32, for the Mac. This sequencer, like this book, is aimed at the creative musician who wants to write and/or record original songs and arrangements and doesn't need hugely sophisticated mastering tools. However, despite all of its new features, version 5.0 does seem lean heavily in the direction of the more technically minded producer/engineer types. As a matter of fact, some of the new features and interface "improvements" may actually irritate some creative musicians, who may have been more at home with version 4.1. But don't worry, you'll get used to them.

Cubase VST version 5.0 – new features

Although version 5.0 was a real step-up for PC users, many of the "new" features were already available in version 4.1 for the Mac. The most striking difference you'll notice, when you upgrade to version 5.0 on the Mac, is the overall look of the program. The Arrange window has had a *Changing Rooms* done on its colour scheme, and the virtual mixers and effects have been redesigned. Effects such as reverb have been greatly improved, and the default plug-in interface has been modified so that you can see every parameter at once. For example, in the EQ window, you can draw EQ curves with the mouse, although unfortunately you still have only a one-step undo function. However, the latest version of Cubase VST pushes the boundaries even further, and now all Cubase versions support 16- and 24-bit recording modes. An all-new equalisation algorithm brings unprecedented performance and musicality to the onboard equalisers, and a new set of plug-ins provides an uncluttered professional aspect to the plug-ins that you need every day. All of the Cubase 5.0 plug-ins are written by Spectral Design's DSP professionals, including CubaseVerb, which sets new standards for onboard effects quality. In addition to all of this, Steinberg has added high-quality dithering options to all versions of Cubase in order to optimise the reduction of the number of bits to the 16 used with CDs. This means that, apart from being the perfect digital-recording studio, Cubase VST is now a perfect mastering tool as well. The new version also includes the Apogee UV-22 dithering algorithm, which is widely seen as being the absolute best-sounding dithering program in the industry.

With Cubase VST 5.0's InWire, you can also sign up for free Internet studio access and take part in real-time sessions with Cubase VST 5.0 users around the world. Your changes are streamed to the other users each time you "actualise" the project you have open, just as their changes are delivered and integrated seamlessly into your version. Additionally, the Universal Sound Module (a special VST instrument included with Cubase VST 5.0) means that you have access to a common sound palette shared by all other studio members, even when you're on the move. While you're working, you can use the built-in Internet chat services, or even an Internet audio and video stream, to interact with the other studio musicians. Cubase's InWire is supported by the Rocket network, and offers enhanced support, including all VST parameters and dynamic mix and effects automation data.

With the arrival of the new multiprocessor Macintoshes, such as the G4 MP series, not only have multiprocessors arrived on standard machines but the latest OS (Operating System) versions support it in new and more comprehensive ways. Steinberg has used this new functionality to greatly increase the amount of power available to the VST audio engine. With the previous multiprocessor scheme, the maximum processing power available to the audio engine was one CPU, as the complete audio process could only exist on one processor or the other. Now, the audio-processing load can be split much more evenly between the two processors. There is still only one processor doing the MIDI, file-handling and user-interface work, but its remaining processor bandwidth can be used to support audio tasks also. Techie geeks estimate that this new MP model brings about a 50-60% increase in processing power over a standard single-processor machine, and around a 20-30% increase over previous multiprocessor performance. The improved timing of Cubase VST 5.0 for the Mac offers MIDI timing that is mainly limited only by the CPU and its OS. Interference and delays are minimised by a new technique that allows a better internal connection between MIDI engine and audio engine.

All versions of Cubase VST 5.0 now support 16- and 24-bit recording. Cubase VST/24 is replaced by Cubase VST/32 and supports the recording, mixdown and export of 32-bit floating-point files. Cubase VST 5.0 also imports MP3 files and converts them to AIFF files directly on import. With the optional MP3 encoder plug-in component, Cubase VST can also export directly to MP3. The auto-crossfade feature ensures smooth audio playback. This function can be activated independently for each audio channel and automatically crossfades between consecutive audio segments for smooth, click-free transitions. With the new "generic" remote control device, you can set up any MIDI control device to control the VST mixers, the MIDI Track Mixer or the Transport controls. Yamaha DSP factory support is also now available for all three versions of Cubase VST.

The new version of Cubase continues to support AltiVec and multiprocessing, and adds a new option for "extended" multiprocessing. When using a dual-processor machine with this option turned on, Cubase assigns all odd-numbered events (tracks, effects, etc) to the first processor and all even-numbered events to the second processor. It's been estimated that this will enhance performance by at least 50%. Additional features for Cubase include "true-tape" emulation, which lets you overdrive audio while recording without introducing digital break-up artefacts, thus allowing a much stronger signal, and a software version of Apogee's UV22, which will allow you to dither tracks down to 16 bit/44.1kHz for CD mastering. Not only that, but the release also includes the 24-bit LM-9 drum machine, and for around $99 you can also get the LM-4 (described as the LM-9's big brother), which comes complete with 400MB of sound that is "sample-accurate, and clocks itself from the audio engine". Great stuff, if you're a bit of a sad techie, but if you're a musician first and an engineer second then all of that big science could start to get a bit tedious.

Incidentally, PC users had to wait for nearly two years to get most of the improvements that version 4.0 already had on the Mac. With the Wintel version of Cubase 5.0, PC users are still playing catch-up, although they now have things like a dedicated MIDI Track Mixer, a new Controller editor, an enhanced toolbox, a user-definable toolbar and key commands, along with improved dragging and dropping and Transport bar display options, etc.

For me, the greatest advantage of the whole so-called digital revolution is that anyone can play. Like multimedia, digital recording can be as complicated or as simple as you want to make it. And, like multimedia, you don't always have to have the most expensive, top-of-the-range kit and accessories to produce interesting and original music. You just have to be interesting, original and creative.

system set-up

The nice thing about Cubase is that you don't have to have a particularly flashy system to get things up and running. Once you've got the hang of how things work, you can either continue to build up your system gradually from scratch, or you might want to opt for one of the many digital audio "bundled" offers that can found in adverts in magazines such as *Sound On Sound*. However, if you can't afford the latest and greatest Mac system, don't be afraid to shop around for a second-hand kit. Older Power Macs can be found for reasonable prices, and you'll find that most of them are perfectly functional and generally upgradeable. And don't forget, you can use Cubase with iMacs and PowerBooks, as well.

budget systems

The great thing about using Cubase on the Mac is that, even with a bog-standard budget system, you can still produce great-sounding music. I know of several musicians who actually produced their own compositions with a demo version of Cubase and, although they couldn't save their files, still managed to burn mixed-down tracks onto CD – but don't tell Steinberg! The minimum system for running Cubase 5.0 is:

Processor:	PowerPC 604e processor
Processor speed:	200MHz
RAM (cache):	64MB
Operating system:	Mac OS 8.5 or later
Drives:	CD-ROM drive
Other components:	256K second-level cache, MIDI box

You can actually produce excellent results with this sort of set-up, but you do have to have a lot of patience and determination. Everyone in this industry suffers from "processor envy", and we all drool over the newest and fastest machines. But if you're operating on a budget, keep in mind that, a few years ago, people were producing magazines on Mac Pluses, and I know of a couple of studios that are still running all of their sound gear with the aid of a Colour Classic. So, if money is tight, you can still afford to put together a reasonably effective digital recording studio without spending thousands. However, if you can spend a bit more, the minimum recommended system for running Cubase 5.0 in a much more effortless manner would be something like this:

Processor:	PowerPC G3
Processor speed:	266MHz
RAM (cache):	128MB
Operating system:	Mac OS 8.5 or later
Soundcard:	approved MME- or ASIO-compliant sound card
Drives:	CD-ROM drive (external floppy for VST plug-ins)
Other components:	suitable for Power Mac G4s and iMacs

Obviously, you want to get the fastest system with as much memory and with the best audio card you can possibly afford. You should also go for the largest and fastest hard drive that you can afford, preferably one of the newer AV models. For the best results, you should always defragment and optimise your hard disk before recording, and particularly before you actually install Cubase. Before you do install Cubase, you should also:

• deactivate File Sharing and Virtual Memory;

• disable AppleTalk;

• select an audio input in the Monitor and Sound control panels, if you're going to be using built-in audio inputs and outputs;

• disable all anti-virus software;

• install the MIDI interface and its drivers.

Another important thing to do is to minimise your extension set. Digital recording can throw up some weird conflicts with other applications and their extensions, and often the cause won't be all that easy to track down. So, in order to avoid some of these hair-ripping annoyances before they start...

1. In the Control Panels folder in the Apple menu, choose Extensions Manager.

2. Choose Mac OS [system version] base set.

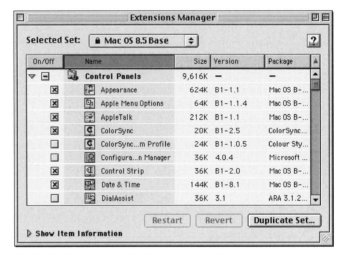

3. Choose Duplicate Set. Rename the set "Cubase" and then switch off any other extraneous extensions that may cause conflicts.

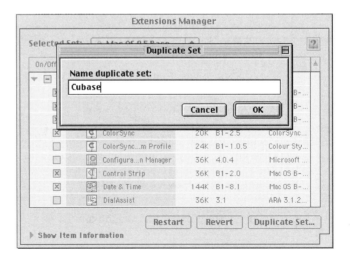

4. Restart your machine. Use this extension set whenever you're using Cubase or any other digital audio applications.

pro systems

If you've got the budget, the sky's the limit for a truly professional Mac-based digital studio, and a number of specialist dealers will configure custom-built digital systems to suit your particular recording requirements. For example, for just under £15,000 you can have a G4 Mac, a 24-channel mixing desk and all the add-ons you need to set up a complete digital studio that would rival many existing commercial studios. Or, if that's a bit too ambitious for your wallet and your bank manager's ulcer, you could still get a very competent high-end system for between £2,000 and £3,000. A typical mid-pro system might include:

Processor:	Power Mac G4 with 1MB level 2 cache
Processor speed:	266MHz
RAM (cache):	256MB
Operating system:	Mac OS 8.5 or later
Soundcard:	approved MME- or ASIO-compliant sound card
Drives:	30GB internal system drive, 15GB optimised internal audio drive, CD-ROM drive (external floppy for VST plug-ins)
Other components:	MIDI box, SCSI card, 17" monitor or larger

If you can afford cutting-edge technology, Apple has recently launched the most powerful and expandable G4 Macs ever, which include easy-to-use power tools for creating movies, music CDs and even DVD videos. Features include:

• Fastest-ever PowerPC G4 with Velocity Engine and a processing speed of up to 733MHz;

• Optional dual 533MHz PowerPC G4 processors;

• New on-chip level two cache and backside level 3 cache (667MHz and 733MHz systems);

• New, high-performance graphics cards and AGP 4x slot, 133MHz system bus and PC133 SDRAM of up to 1.5GB;

• PCI throughput of up to 215MB per second;

- Personalised music libraries and custom CDs;

- CD-RW drive for creating music CDs and archiving data files;

- iTunes software for managing digital audio collections and creating music CDs;

- Start-to-finish movies and DVDs;

- FireWire for connecting DV camcorders and digital-audio peripherals;

- More expandability than ever;

- Four high-performance PCI slots (64 bit/33MHz);

- Easy access to built-in expansion bays and slots;

- Two 400MB per second FireWire ports for connecting up to 63 devices;

- Two USB (Universal Serial Bus) ports for connecting up to 127 peripherals;

- Optional AirPort wireless networking.

Models include 733MHz, 667MHz, 533MHz and 466MHz single-processor configurations and the dual-processor 533MHz Power Mac G4. The Power Mac G4 is a phenomenally powerful computer, and this is especially evident when it performs processor-intensive tasks in creative and scientific applications. In fact, at speeds of 5.5 gigaflops, the new 733MHz PowerPC G4 processor with Velocity Engine is up to 57% faster than a 1.5GHz Pentium 4.

As the ideal "studio in a box", the new Power Mac G4 has an improved system architecture, featuring a new, 133MHz system bus, which can move data at speeds of over 1GB per second. And with five slots – one AGP 4x graphics slot (loaded with a graphics accelerator) and four high-performance PCI slots – plus an AirPort card slot, FireWire ports and USB ports, the massively expandable Power Mac G4 lets you pursue your musically evolutionary ideas on an even grander scale. Most models feature the state-of-the-art Nvidia GeForce2 MX accelerator, complete with 32MB of SDRAM for blazing-fast 3D performance, but you can choose the ATI Radeon or GeForce3 cards instead, if you prefer.

band on the run

Out on the road, G3 PowerBooks already offer a viable alternative to desk-bound digital studios, but the latest PowerBook G4 is just too sexy for words. Just one inch thick and weighing a mere 5.3 pounds, the PowerBook G4 is the world's first notebook computer made of 99.5% pure-grade, CP1 ("Commercially Pure") titanium.

At the core of this new mobile system is the PowerPC G4 processor with Velocity Engine. With speeds of up to 500MHz, the PowerBook G4 packs a tremendous punch, crunching through digital, audio and video and rendering huge audio files faster than ever before. And the 100MHz system bus (the pipeline between memory and processor) and the 1MB of backside level two cache (with speeds of up to 250MHz) make significant performance-enhancing contributions, as well. The result? The PowerBook G4 outguns all Wintel Pentium-III-based notebooks by up to 30%. And with an industry-leading battery life of up to five hours between charges, you can keep outshooting your PC counterparts long after their batteries have given up the ghost.

However, unlike PC notebooks, which either shed features or compromise performance (or both) in order to achieve modest weight reductions, the PowerBook G4 is a robust, full-featured system with everything you need to do your best creative work on the move – up to 30GB of hard-disk space, room for up to 1GB of RAM and a slot-loading DVD-ROM drive, plus ATI RAGE Mobility 128 graphics, FireWire, USB, PC card slot, VGA output and S-Video output, along with a built-in microphone and stereo sound output. All that's missing, in fact, is the excess weight. With its 15.2" mega-wide-screen format and 1,152-x 768-pixel resolution, this display is perfect for laying out your audio, video or graphics projects, tools and palettes simultaneously, or for keeping multiple applications open while you work. Meanwhile, the DVD-ROM drive allows the playback of DVD video and DVD-ROM discs, as well as music CDs.

peripherals and add-ons

How you actually configure your Cubase system and what peripherals and add-ons you might need will vary enormously from user to user. There's a huge range of samplers, microphones, keyboards, monitors and effects that can be used in conjunction with your Cubase digital studio, and frankly it would be impossible to cover even a fraction of them in any detail in a book like this. However, there are some items (ie microphones) that are probably an essential part of any digital studio and which do need some further comment. Also, unless you're happy listening to your playback through headphones, you'll probably want some sort of monitoring system, including an amplifier and speakers. For MIDI-based recordings, you'll also need some sort of input device, such as a MIDI keyboard/synth, but we'll look at issues like this as we get further into the recording process. The "Working Practices" section in Chapter 4 will provide you with a more detailed notion of what you'll need (apart from your Mac and Cubase) to complete your digital studio set-up.

missing the bus

One thing you'll notice, when you start using the newer Macs for music, is the fact that a number of buses and interfaces that have been standard on every Mac since its inception are now missing and presumed gone. These include the designated modem and printer serial ports, where you used to be able to attach your MIDI interfaces; the ADB (Apple Desktop Bus), where you used to connect those horrendous software-protection dongles; and the SCSI ports, for connecting high-speed hard drives and facilitating high-speed SCSI transfers to sample-editing packages. Apple has done away with these, ostensibly to drive the development of new interface standards and to force third-party developers to create devices for new interfaces, such as USB, which in theory will take the place of both serial ports and the ADB port. The upside of this is that Macs can now utilise peripherals developed for the entire computer industry. However, for musicians, it also means that there is nowhere to plug in traditional MIDI interfaces or dongles. However, a range of cards and adaptors is readily available to deal with these issues, and there are plenty of good solutions that don't cost an absolute fortune.

The other thing that's missing from the new Mac is the traditional floppy drive. Generally, this isn't too much of a problem, but if you want to use the range of VST plug-ins that Steinberg provides on floppy disk, then it's worth investing in an external USB floppy drive. These are also readily available and quite reasonably priced.

using Cubase 5.0 – the OMS dilemma

A primary consideration, when using Cubase for the first time, is whether or not to use OMS (Open Music System). Steinberg's manual comes down firmly on the fence, leaving the choice to the user, but in fact, if you're using a modern Mac (ie one equipped with USB rather than serial ports) and don't wish to spend money on a PCI card containing serial ports, there is no choice: OMS is obligatory.

OMS is the creation of Opcode Systems, and was designed to break the "16-channel barrier" that normally constrains MIDI operation. It also allows you to use "librarian" software, which stores every single patch (voice) within an

OMS-compliant sound module inside a database, which can be accessed directly from within Cubase, making the selection of patches a simple matter. Put simply, whereas normal MIDI operation restricts you to a maximum of 16 MIDI channels, OMS allows up to 16 channels per out port on your (OMS-compliant) MIDI interface. So, if you have an interface with four outs and a 16-channel multitimbral sound module connected to each of these, with OMS you can have 64 MIDI channels at once.

The ongoing problem with OMS is that, two years ago, its creator company, Opcode, was purchased by the guitar company Gibson. Since then, it has more or less gone to sleep – that is, it now lags behind badly in terms of software development, being still written in so-called 68K (ie pre-PowerPC) code, which makes it slightly uneven in performance on Power Macs. Worse still, since the advent of the blue-and-white G3 series – on which the old serial (modem and printer) ports were finally dumped by Apple and replaced with USB – OMS has become more important than ever before, since the USB channel won't accept anything else. And yet there are acknowledged problems with USB/OMS which are still being investigated, problems which are made worse when the USB channel is asked to carry audio signals as well. However, it's perfectly possible that you'll never encounter any problems, especially if you route your audio in/out via a sound card.

Put in a nutshell, you should use OMS:

• if you're running a USB-equipped Mac;

• if you're running a serial-equipped Mac but want more than 16 MIDI channels at once.

Consider doing without OMS:

• if you have a serial-equipped Mac but a low MIDI requirement (ie 16 channels or under);

• if you have a serial-equipped Mac but plan to major in audio recording (again, with fewer than 16 MIDI channels).

a way through

Even if you own a USB Mac, you can still regain the choice of whether or not you use OMS or not by purchasing a serial-port PCI card. These typically cost less than £100, but you must also make sure that your MIDI interface is of the serial type, rather than USB.

setting up OMS

The first time you boot Cubase 5.0, you'll be asked if you wish to use OMS or not. If, at a later time, you decide that you want to use OMS after all (or not), go to the main menu and select Options>MIDI Setup>System. Then choose "In & Out" or "No OMS" from the OMS compatibility pull-down menu and reboot.

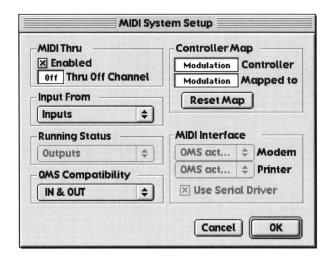

Now, from the same main menu, choose Options>MIDI Setup>OMS>OMS Studio Setup and use the resulting Opcode software to create a "master map" of your MIDI set-up. Once you've done this, all of your modules will be embedded in Cubase and can be selected from the Output column in the Track window.

extra hardware

Cubase is a very powerful program, but, like many other powerful programs, its use can be made much more enjoyable by investing in some extra hardware. Consider purchasing either the largest monitor you can afford (in fact, the larger the better) or, if you can afford it, a second display. When operating Cubase at full cry, you'll find yourself with a large number of palettes or windows – such as the Track Mixer, Channel Mixers etc – which can hide vital parts of the Arrange window while they're visible. By dragging these away to a second display, you can keep the Arrange window clear at all times and still have immediate access to them.

If you're doing lots of audio work, consider investing in a sound card. Audio also requires lots of hard-disk space – size matters, and so does speed – so, if the hard drive already inside your Mac is small by today's standards, consider purchasing an external one. This should be SCSI, if possible (which is faster than IDE), which means that, if you have one of the newer Macs, you may also need to purchase a SCSI card.

Many of Cubase's most potent features – built-in effects plus VST instruments – make massive demands on processor power, so it helps to have the fastest possible processor inside your Mac. Obviously, you can do little about this once you've purchased your computer – under no circumstances consider using a third-party accelerator card, since very often these prove to be incompatible with Cubase and often with later revisions of the Apple OS – so the only remaining option is to go gently with the built-in effects and VST instruments.

The perfect lyrics, a killer guitar riff or the ultimate breakbeat combination can leap from your imagination at any time, but merely getting notes on paper or a rough on tape isn't enough to capture today's sound or tomorrow's hit. To keep musicians happy, Apple has always made sure that your Mac is music-ready. It continues to be the choice of professional musicians for the recording, manipulation and playback of digital audio, due to its close integration of hardware and software. On top of all this, Apple's adoption of USB and FireWire technology means that Mac users can instantly connect digitisers, MIDI devices and DAT storage drives in order to capture high-quality, 44.1kHz audio tracks at ultra-fast speeds. The Mac OS, in all of its incarnations, includes a number of built-in technologies that make music computing significantly easier, and these powerful built-in technologies add critical support to many music applications. Also, and more importantly, they virtually eliminate the need for artists to become troubleshooters. With QuickTime 4, music producers also have the ability to stream digital content, and thus deliver MIDI, MP3 or Qdesign compressed audio over the Internet. This means that millions of people who have QuickTime software are ready to receive your audio files from CDs or over the worldwide Web. Let's face it, a lot of people regret getting a PC for music, but no one ever regrets getting a Mac.

chapter 3

getting started

"Music is art, Muzak the science."
  – Muzak Corporation slogan

With Cubase VST and a reasonable Power Mac, musicians have access to a fully integrated virtual recording studio that can be used to record, mix, edit and process MIDI and audio. Like all modern sequencers, Cubase uses a graphic interface, allowing blocks of sound or MIDI information to be copied, sliced and moved around. Also, audio and MIDI recordings are visible within the same window, thus making editing and tracking easier by showing you exactly where your audio sources are, in relation to your MIDI data. With the addition of VST (Virtual Studio Technology), Cubase – coupled with a few add-ons – can easily cater for nearly all of your recording and production needs. OK, if you're a fanatical audio purist or an anally retentive techie geek, you'll always be able to find something that's not absolutely perfect with various recordings, whether they're done on a Mac at home or in some famous commercial studio like Abbey Road – which, incidentally, also uses Macs and Cubase for a variety of projects. However, as the *I Ching* says, perseverance furthers, and if you know your music and know the sound you want, Cubase is more than capable of helping you achieve that special blend you're looking for. As I mentioned earlier, having the best-equipped studio, replete with obscenely expensive microphones, desks and effects would, like winning the lottery, be a wonderful solution in an ideal world, but most musicians don't live in an ideal world, and rarely win the lottery. And in the real world, even expensive, state-of-the-art studios still churn out a lot of well-produced, ear-numbing mediocrity like Steps, S Club 7 and the rest of the Britney/boy-band brigade, which simply proves again the old computer-industry acronym GIGO (Garbage In, Garbage Out). So don't allow yourself to be distracted by the savage rantings of self-styled, asinine audiophiles or ear-wax-impaired kit junkies. Just tap your foot to the strange rhythms in your head and listen to what you produce. Then decide what else, if anything, you might truly need.

VST is now the most common native audio plug-in, and was actually pioneered by Steinberg. VST plug-ins are available in both Mac and PC versions and provide help in handling all of the usual studio effects, such as compression, limiting, gating, reverb, echo, chorus and flanging. Nowadays, plug-ins are also available for pitch correction, creative or gratuitous distortion, vocoding, denoising, click suppression, spectral enhancement and other functions. As with a conventional mixer, effects such as reverb and echo can be used in an effects send-and-return loop on the virtual mixer, so that a single plug-in can be applied to as many channels as needed without soaking up additional processing power. However, other plug-ins, such as compressors or equalisers, still have to be used on a per-channel basis and must be patched in via virtual controls in much the same way as you would on a traditional desk.

Depending on the speed and efficiency of your Mac, Cubase VST can give you up to 64 audio tracks, each with four-band parametric EQ, eight real-time auxiliary effects slots and four real-time insert effects slots per channel. It's got an excellent plug-in architecture to accommodate a huge variety of third-party effects and processors, great mixdown facilities and clever time-stretching and "formant" pitch-shifting facilities. You can patch to a number of external processing devices, and features like Groove Analysis allow you to analyse the rhythmic structure of your audio recordings, which can then be applied to the structure and "feel" of your MIDI parts. Cubase incorporates the use of native audio processing, so you don't actually need any additional hardware to record and process audio. However, the more facilities you decide that you need from Cubase, the more processing power will be required, particularly when you start adding third-party plug-ins, or if you want to use a lot of audio tracks. The nice thing about Cubase is that it keeps up with your Mac and, as you increase your processing power, you actually unlock even more of its capacity.

main windows

When you get into a new car, it's always useful to sort out where the controls are for things like lights, heating, ignition, etc, before setting out on a road trip. The same thing applies to applications like Cubase – it's worth knowing where everything is and what everything does before you start trying to do any serious recording. Cubase has a number of main windows that provide access to various tools and key control elements of the program.

the Transport bar

The first window with which you need to be familiar is the Transport bar, which normally appears in the lower part of your screen, below the Arrange window. This panel works pretty much like the normal controls found on any standard tape player/recorder. You can play your recording, stop, wind forward or rewind, just as you can with any analogue system. However, in Cubase, the Transport bar has additional functionality, which allows you to set things like tempo and time signatures.

The Transport bar

At the left end of the Transport bar is the Record mode selector. This determines whether Cubase will add any existing sound when recording (Overdub mode) or overwrite what you've already recorded (Replace mode). The Record mode selector only affects MIDI data, and won't alter audio recordings. In Cubase, recording over an existing audio part won't rewrite or merge with existing audio but will instead create a new audio file for each new recording. This also means that only one single audio recording can be heard at any one time when the audio is on the same channel.

The Record mode selector

Immediately to the right of the Record mode selector is a panel that contains the left and right locators, the Cycle button, buttons for punching in and out of recordings and the AutoQuantize button. The left and right locators indicate the current positions of the locators and define where to start and end recording or what section to cycle. If you click on one of the locator labels (left or right) on the Transport bar, your song position is moved to the corresponding locator. The Cycle button is used for cycling between the left and right locator positions. Because Cubase can play back and record in a cycle (which is essentially nothing more than a loop), you can decide where the cycle starts and ends by setting the positions of the left and right locators. When the Cycle function is activated, you can listen to a section of an arrangement over and over again, recording more information each time. Playback with Cycle activated is also particularly convenient when editing or making adjustments in the Inspector, a new feature in version 5.0.

Top: left/right locator positions.
Bottom (l-r): AutoQuantize, Punch In, Cycle, Punch Out

If you've used a portastudio or a multitrack tape recorder, or you've done any recording in a traditional studio, you're probably familiar with a technique called punching in, as opposed to punching out. Punching (or dropping) in – as opposed to the technique used by the Gallagher brothers, known as punching out – is what happens when you start recording while your tape is rolling. This is particularly useful if you mess up a section of a lead or vocal line but the rest of the recording is fine. You simply drop in a replacement section over the flawed section and either punch out or carry on until the end. Contrary to notions popularised by the Gallagher brothers and other rock 'n' roll clichés, in recording parlance a punch out occurs when you stop recording without stopping the actual playback. In Cubase, you can either use an automatic or a manual punch in.

With the AutoQuantize button, you can choose to immediately quantize everything you record, according to whatever quantizing type you've selected. As with practically everything in Cubase, quantizing can be undone if the result isn't what you expected or intended. It's worth noting, however, that automatic quantizing only applies to MIDI recording and not to audio.

Moving, like William Hague, even further to the right, directly above the tape-style controls you'll find two timing display bars. The first of these shows the current song position in bars, beats and ticks (fractions of a beat). The second is essentially a time-code read-out, showing the current song position in hours, minutes, seconds and frames. Directly below both of these displays is the position slider. When the handle of this slider is dragged, its range will relate to the length of your arrangement. In other words, if you drag the slider all the way to the right, the song position will appear at the end of the last part. But we'll look at all this in more detail when we start laying down tracks.

Beat and time-code displays

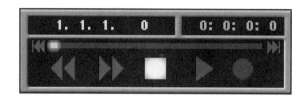

At the extreme far right, apart from George W Bush and his new Attorney General, you'll find controls for activating the metronome, tempo and time-signature readouts and indicators that show MIDI in (recording) and out (playback) activity. There is also a Sync button for synchronising the sequencer to external devices. Tempo determines the actual speed of your music and the number of beats per minute (usually quarter-notes). The time signature – 4/4, 3/4, etc – determines the overall "feel" of the beat.

Cubase offers two sources for choosing tempo. If, for example, you're recording a song with a steady beat throughout, you can turn off the Master button and set the desired tempo directly on the Transport bar. (You can still adjust the tempo at any time, even during playback.) However, if your song has a number of tempo changes, use the master track.

But don't worry too much about that just yet. We'll go into all of this stuff in more detail when we start playing with an actual recording session. One of the easiest ways of setting the tempo is to activate playback and adjust the tempo on the Transport bar while listening to the metronome pulse (triggered by the Click button) that's generated on each beat. Incidentally, if you start playback with the Click button pressed and still can't hear the metronome, you'll need to adjust the settings in the Metronome dialog box found in the Options menu. The narrow bar at the end allows you to resize the whole Transport bar.

Tempo and time-signature options and Click, Sync and Master buttons

the Arrange window

The heart of your digital desktop studio is probably the Arrange window, since this is the place where you actually record and assemble your songs. You'll want to make sure that you're particularly familiar and comfortable with this window and all of its functionality, since this is where you'll be spending most of your time in Cubase.

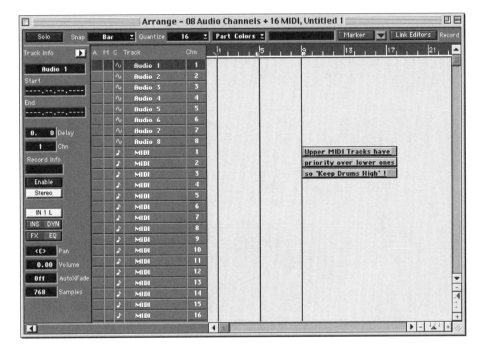

The Arrange window

The left side of the Arrange window is called the Track list, probably because it's divided into tracks, which you use to organise your recordings. As in a traditional multitrack studio, you might use a couple of tracks for drums, another for guitar, one for bass, several for vocals, etc, depending on the type of music you're recording and the sort of instrumentation and arrangement you're looking for. If you view this side as a sort of musical spreadsheet or Chinese menu, you've got:

- <u>Column A</u> – An activity column showing you whether or not anything is being played from that particular track in real time;

- <u>Column M</u> – A marker in this column indicates where tracks are muted or silenced. Single-click here to mute/reactivate a track. A bullet symbol indicates a mute;

- <u>Column C</u> – This is where tracks are classified as audio, MIDI, drum, mix, etc. You can choose these from a drop-down menu, but generally I've never used anything apart from "Audio" or "MIDI";

- <u>Column T</u> – Use this column to lock/unlock tracks (ie prevent them from further, unintended modification);

- <u>Tracks column</u> – This is where you name your tracks or designate instruments, etc, in the mix.

There is also a Channel column ("Chn"), which shows the channel number that each track is on. Behind the Part display, and usually hidden when you're actually working, is a column where you can choose MIDI output, and also an Instrument column, where you can name any combination of MIDI channels and output columns. (Incidentally, the Instrument column has no functionality for audio tracks.)

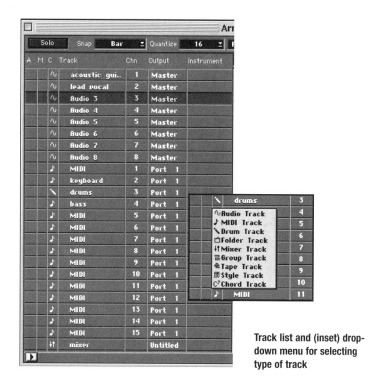

Track list and (inset) drop-down menu for selecting type of track

(Note that, with MIDI tracks, the output column lists the output port names of the ports or drivers you've installed with your audio card. If they're audio tracks, the column will contain the letters VST.)

The button at the bottom left of the Track list opens the Inspector, which gives you easy access to more detailed settings for active tracks in the same window.

Expanded Track list showing Inspector controls

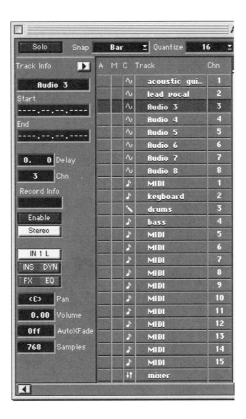

At the top of the Track list side is a red Solo button, which you can click to listen to only a selected track without any of the others playing back. Just remember that the Arrange window basically shows you time on a horizontal axis, in bars and beats and ticks, on the vertical axis or columns.

To the right of the Track list is the Part display. This is where all the real music goes, and it's also the place where you can edit and enhance the bits that you've recorded. Each audio or MIDI recording you make appears as a bar, and the width of that bar shows the length of the recording. The vertical position of each bar corresponds to the track that it's on in the Track list, and the horizontal position shows you exactly where the song part starts and finishes. Along the top of the Arrange window, near the Solo button you'll also find various pop-up windows and settings that will allow you to employ precision editing functions, such as moves and splits, and there's also a pop-up window for assigning different colours to different parts, which helps to differentiate sections when it comes to editing.

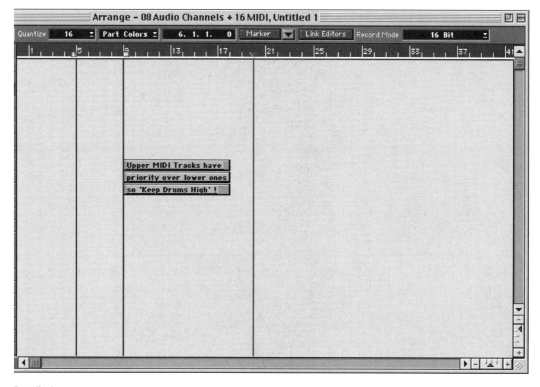

Part display area

In Cubase, because higher-numbered MIDI tracks have priority over lower-numbered ones, it's recommended that, when you're ordering your tracks, you put drums and percussion towards the top of the Track list.

the toolbox

In the latest version of Cubase, various tools used in various situations are gathered into toolboxes, and most windows in Cubase VST have their own particular toolbox with appropriate variations. The toolbox in Cubase is accessible from the Tools menu, and can be "torn off" and positioned anywhere on your screen for easy access and the manipulating and editing of musical parts in the Part display area. (If you're familiar with other Mac programs, you'll probably recognise some of these tools.) Some of the main functions accessible in the Arrange window include:

- Pointer – This is your main selection tool, and is used to move, copy and generally manipulate musical data anywhere on your screen;

- Pencil – Like most Mac drawing tools, the pencil is used to lengthen or shorten parts by grabbing start or end points and stretching or shrinking them. It can also be used to create new parts, by clicking and dragging in a blank space;

- Eraser – This does exactly what its name suggests, and is used for deleting parts by clicking on one or by dragging over several;

- Scissors – Used for splitting parts and slicing parts into smaller segments.

- Speaker – As you'd imagine, this is used to monitor the contents of an audio part;

- Glue – This is digital sticky-backed plastic used to join two or more parts together to make one long part, and is a lot neater than the old method of cutting and splicing audio tape;

- Match Q – Match Quantize is used to impose the timing characteristics of one musical part onto another by dragging from a source to a target;

- Mute – Another way of muting or silencing a particular part;

- Magnifying glass – Useful for closely monitoring the contents of MIDI or audio parts. Click once to zoom in or drag to zoom in on a particular area;

- Selection range – If you don't want to select a whole part, use this tool to make a selection independent of the parts;

- Volume – Use this to click on a part and adjust the volume by moving the slider that appears;

- Pan – Brings up a click-and-drag pop-up slider to change pan settings;

- Transpose – Brings up a pop-up keyboard for transposing the key of a part;

- <u>Logical</u> – Opens a pop-up menu of presets which apply a Spock-like logical preset to a designated part;

- <u>Groove</u> – Another pop-up menu of settings for applying a groove to a part;

- <u>Stretch</u> – Used to stretch or shrink a part and scale events accordingly. Audio parts are time stretched while MIDI parts are moved so that the relative distance between events is the same.

Toolbox for the Arrange window

You can open a toolbox temporarily by pressing the Control key and clicking the mouse on an applicable window. You can also choose between a horizontal and vertical toolbox by clicking on the zoom box on the window title.

There are also other important windows, such as the VST and MIDI mixer, Channel Settings, VST Instruments and Audio Pool windows. However, we'll look at those in more detail in context, when we start working through a proper recording session.

sequencers – short back and sides

Back in the old days, the original sequencers handled only MIDI data. Audio sequencers didn't arrive on the scene until some years later, when computers and hard drives got faster and cheaper. Modern digital sequencers are generally capable of providing an impressive number of audio and MIDI tracks, depending on the processing power of your Mac, the speed of your hard disk and the interface you use to get things in and out and connect external devices. In each of these departments – particularly when choosing a system for running Cubase – the two key things to remember are that speed is good and that size does matter. Like everything in the digital world, music software is improved and upgraded often, and even if you buy the most powerful Mac system that you can afford, you may still find yourself pressured at some point to upgrade to keep up with developments that you either want or think you'll need. It's at this point that you need to take a serious look at what kind of music you're making, what you require to continue making it and whether or not a slightly faster computer or marginally improved software application will really make a significant improvement to the way you work and the music you produce. It may be a cliché but, if it ain't broke, don't fix it, unless you win the lottery or have a good night on *Who Wants To Be A Millionaire*, in which case you can go out and blow the lot on high-end microphones, big mixing desks and loads of samplers, keyboards instruments, drugs – you know, the usual. And when you play live, demand a full-sized Steinway grand piano onstage with you, and then, instead of playing it, just put beer cans and ash trays on it.

As you've probably gathered by now, Cubase VST is a fully integrated, modern software sequencer suitable for recording, editing and processing both MIDI and audio data. And, as mentioned earlier, VST is the magic ingredient that turns it into a virtual recording studio inside your Mac. Cubase on the Mac provides a very intuitive and direct interface, featuring a comprehensive set of menus, keyboard short-cuts, pop-up menus, drag-and-drop editing procedures and a whole raft of features that will already be familiar to seasoned Mac users. Unfortunately, like any powerful application, it *does* take some getting used to, and to actually get the sort of sound and recording quality that you require may take a bit of practice, patience and an element of experimentation. The thing about the Mac is that it's made for experimentation, so don't be afraid to try things out. Generally, anything you do can be undone, and rarely will a healthy, heuristic approach to creativity result in anything disastrous. Just as the best music often comes out of improvised jams, often the best recordings happen when you bend the rules or ignore them completely and just work on creative intuition. Getting your head around how a sequencer like Cubase works isn't really much more difficult than figuring out how to use a four- or eight-track portastudio, and you'll definitely find that you have a lot more freedom, control and functionality with a digital studio than you would with even some of the best analogue equipment. For example, things like overall room acoustics and background noise become less of an issue when you're recording, because in a digital environment you can edit and clean up all of your input and add effects to simulate any kind of room or ambience you desire.

Cubase is one of those applications that can by stretched as far as you want to stretch it. As I said in the introduction, this book is designed for musicians and Mac users who simply want to have a go at creating music with a digital studio. Sure, hardcore tech-heads, or even sound engineers and technicians with loads of traditional studio experience, will be able to use Cubase and explain everything you never wanted to know about decibels, waveforms, impedance, ohms and room acoustics, and it's cool and extremely impressive that an application like Cubase can offer so much to so many different users; but don't be over-awed by all the science, and above all don't let it get in the way of the music. Provided that you've got a reasonably good microphone, a basic MIDI kit and, perhaps, some sort of sampling capability, you can easily produce music that will sound as good as – if not better than – most of the stuff currently being produced commercially. If you want to know all the science and techie bits, there are plenty of books out there to choose from; but if you just want to play, compose and record interesting music, then learn how to do what you need to do for what you want to produce, even if you don't fully comprehend all the jargon and technical explanations behind it. However, science or no science, before you get down to some serious recording, you must have some idea of how to get an audio signal into your Mac, how to record and manipulate MIDI data and how you're then going to produce it in a form that you can then feed back into the real world.

what is digital audio?

Audio is just plain sound, and you can use any sound source that you can connect to the sound input of your Mac. With the right equipment, you can use a microphone, keyboard, electric guitar or essentially anything with a plug. Raw audio input becomes digital audio when your Mac converts the signal into numbers, which Cubase captures and then stores on your hard drive. Once it's in the box, you can creatively start to manipulate and process your recordings. In Cubase, audio files are created each time you record on an audio track. The important thing to remember here is that audio files can be exceedingly large, and they're written to your hard disk during the actual recording process. This is why size is important, when it comes to storage, and also why you should always defragment your drive before starting a recording session.

The quality of your digital audio depends entirely on the performance of the converters found in your Mac or audio card, particularly sampling rate and bit resolution. When people talk about sampling rate, all they mean is the number of times an analogue signal is measured each second. Bit resolution (usually eight, 16, 20 and 24 bit) is a measure of the accuracy of a system. The higher the number of bits, the more levels of resolution are available to measure the analogue signal. For example, Cubase VST has a default sampling rate of 44.1kHz, with 16-bit resolution. This is the same as a normal audio CD.

Cubase 5.0 now handles up to 32 bits of audio data at once, as opposed to the 24 bits handled by earlier versions. Considering that CDs only handle 16 bits, this may seem like overkill, but in fact the situation is analogous to graphics scanning. Images are typically scanned at very high resolutions, up to 2,400 dots per square inch, even though no printing device on Earth can cope with such dense grids of ink. Colour images are normally printed at a maximum of 200dpi, while greyscale ones seldom exceed 300dpi. The reason for this is that the graphics expert gets far better results by scanning an image at these enormously high resolutions and then, when the image is ready for printing, dithering down to a grid more acceptable to image setters and high-resolution laser printers. All of the data is still in the original file and can be reprocessed, if necessary.

It's exactly the same with audio data. Although, in the end, all CD-based audio must be reduced to 16 bits, far greater initial accuracy can be obtained by "scanning" (in this case, recording) at these very high resolutions and then mastering at 16 bits.

However, since the Macintosh's built-in sound (mic/headphone) ports are limited to a resolution of 16 bits, if you want to use Cubase VST/32 5.0 to its full capacity, you'll need a sound card. These live in a PCI slot, and typically cost between £200 and £500. If you plan to use lots of audio with Cubase and you want to make this as professional-sounding as possible, you'll definitely need a sound card, or you'll be restricted to 16 bits. Even so, this is still enough to produce excellent results, and also – an important point – creates much smaller (although still large) data files. However, running at a full 32 bits with a card produces gigantic documents for each audio track, which in turn imposes burdens on your hard disk, in terms of both size and operating speed. Therefore, if you want to use a sound card, you'll need the largest possible hard disk, with plenty of free space, and if this is a SCSI rather than an IDE type, so much the better.

Each audio bit that you record into Cubase also includes a number of useful properties which give you control over how you process and use them. Cubase can play any chosen part of an audio file for any chosen length of time, because it saves properties within audio events and segments. For example, an event contains a reference to a segment, has a start point relative to the part where it resides and includes a Q point for quantizing. Each segment contains a reference to the actual audio file on your hard disk, start and end pointers determining which part of the file is to be played, a file name and controllable volume and pan curves. Audio events can be viewed and manipulated in the Audio Editor, changing only the references to the audio file on your hard disk without actually changing the file itself. For example, if the start reference for an audio event is dragged to a new position, your original audio file on your hard disk stays the same but the playback begins from a new position.

If you've worked with portastudios or other analogue multitrack recorders, you should understand that there are some aspects of digital audio that require a different approach. In traditional studios, it's not unusual to push certain sound signals so that VU meters occasionally peak into the red. In an analogue environment, this sort of technique can add a natural kind of warmth to the mix, and although there is mild, graduated distortion, it tends to be rounded off in the recording and is hardly ever offensive to the ear. With digital audio, however, you can't have levels going into the red without getting a truly nasty distortion. This means that, with Cubase, you must ensure that no such clipping occurs, and you may find that you need to record at lower average levels than those you're used to using with analogue sources.

However, as I suggested earlier, you'll find that the advantages offered by digital audio generally outweigh the occasional disadvantages. Apart from the convenience of being able to store it on your hard disk, digital audio also tends to have less background noise and hiss, provides a better dynamic range and can be copied with no loss of quality. Also, with Cubase and an assortment of VST plug-ins, you can easily apply a whole range of signal-processing effects.

what is MIDI?

MIDI is another one of those annoying acronyms, and stands for Musical Instrument Digital Interface. It's essentially a form of computer code that was developed as a means by which synths and other devices could talk to and interact with one another. For any techies that may have tuned in, MIDI is an asynchronous, serial interface which is transmitted at the rate of 31.25 kilobaud (or 31,250 bits) per second. For the rest of us, a MIDI synthesiser or similar device works a bit like a musical printer. Your Mac sends information to it that specifies the notes, sound, instrument type, etc, that you want to play, and it gets on with creating the actual audio. This means that you can take a recording made on, say, a piano and play it back on a guitar sound just by changing the settings on your synth.

General MIDI – or GM, as it is usually referred to – was an attempt to create a standard system for MIDI parameters, whereby songs created on one

GM-compatible synth could be played back on any other GM synth and sound like the original. In other words, if the original composition specified particular sounds to be played, then any other GM synth, when handed the GM MIDI file to play, would reproduce the correct sounds assigned by the original composer. In practice, for particularly mundane applications – such as playing and singing along to a sequenced backing of 'Wild Rover' down the pub – this sort of system works fine. Landlord buys a GM MIDI file of 'Wild Rover', punter loads it up in a drunken stupor, hits Play, and all the sounds that should be heard will play back and everyone will sing badly and bang the table at the appropriate time, spilling puddles of beer all over the floor.

However, GM does have restrictions. One of these is that you're tied to a fairly standard, unadventurous palette of sounds. So, if you've created some wicked tune featuring a clever little sound that you've programmed on some non-GM device, this sound won't be recognised by GM and could come out sounding like a duck.

Another restriction is the use of controllers. Since GM specifies fixed controller numbers for certain functions, basic parameters – such as pan, volume, sustain, etc – are represented, but unfortunately more advanced functions – such as filter resonance and cut-off – are not.

GM was agreed as a standard in 1991 by the Japanese MIDI Standards Committee (JMSC) and the American MIDI Manufacturers' Association (MMA). General MIDI system level one specifies 24-note polyphony, 16-part multitimbral operation. All of the drum sounds are defined by a note number, and the 128 sound patches for the other instruments are also defined.

There are also extensions of the GM standard, called GS and XG. GS is Roland's extended version of GM, which adds some extras on top of the GM settings. It does this by utilising the GM Bank Change command. For all parameters, MIDI has a fixed range from 0 to 127, so original GM allows only 128 sound patches, all stored in one bank, while the GS Bank Change command allows further banks to be accessed, each with a further 128 patches. Also added are extra Non-Registered Parameter Numbers (NRPNs), which add extra controller numbers to allow you to twiddle things like filter control, envelope control and extra effects parameters. In practice, GS files will play back on a GM synth, but none of the extras will be recognised, except by another GS-compatible device. As with Roland's GS format, Yamaha's XG system also offers extra sounds and control parameters, although these aren't recognisable by General MIDI or Roland GS devices, and vice versa.

OK, maybe that sounds a little too much like Muzak, but while MIDI can seem a bit confusing and downright cantankerous to wire up properly, it's extremely useful when it comes to digital recording, so you'll be pleased to know that Cubase supports General MIDI and both extensions from Roland and Yamaha.

chapter 4

audio and MIDI set-up

"We are robots. We have become robots through our experience of working and living. We are musical workers."
– Florian Schneider-Esleben, Kraftwerk

The way in which you choose to configure your own system for Cubase will ultimately depend on what kind of music you want to make, which kinds of external devices you require and how elaborate you want to make your personal recording environment. Obviously, for making even the simplest MIDI-based recordings you'll need some sort of input device, such as a synth, MIDI keyboard or, perhaps, a sampler. For audio recordings, the minimum is probably a microphone that will plug into the audio input of your Mac or sound card, or perhaps an electric guitar or bass. You may want to start with a small-scale system that provides the minimum set-up necessary to record and play MIDI and audio in Cubase and perhaps work up to a larger set-up, or you may want to customise your own personalised environment to look like something in between the kinds of digital studio lay-outs suggested here.

setting up audio

Since this book is aimed at musicians and curious Mac users with an ear for music, I'm guessing that you could be using an audio card with analogue stereo inputs and outputs or that you might even simply be using the audio hardware built into your Mac. As it happens, the built-in audio input on most Macs only accepts line-level signals, which means that the input gain probably won't be enough if you want to record the output of a decent microphone, an electric guitar or some other low-output source. However, you can get around this with a separate microphone pre-amp or mixer. If

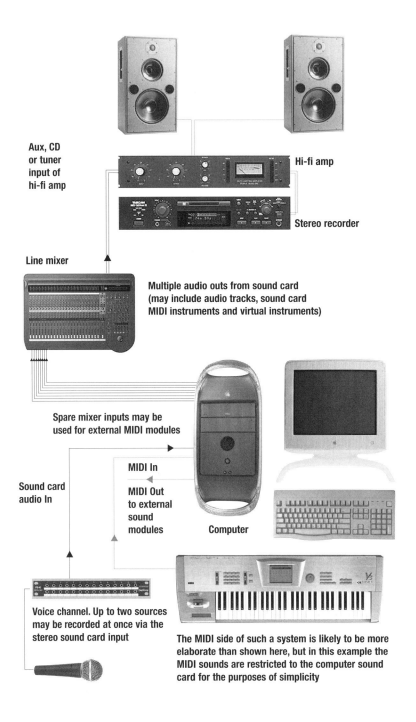

Aux, CD
or tuner
input of
hi-fi amp

Hi-fi amp

Stereo recorder

Line mixer

Multiple audio outs from sound card
(may include audio tracks, sound card
MIDI instruments and virtual instruments)

Spare mixer inputs may be
used for external MIDI modules

MIDI In

Sound card
audio In

MIDI Out
to external
sound
modules

Computer

Voice channel. Up to two sources
may be recorded at once via the
stereo sound card input

The MIDI side of such a system is likely to be more
elaborate than shown here, but in this example the
MIDI sounds are restricted to the computer sound
card for the purposes of simplicity

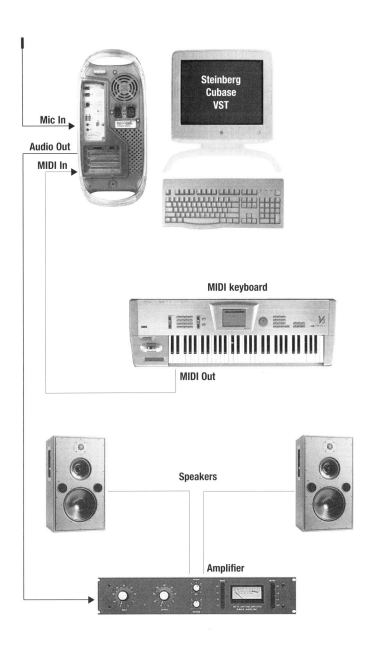

Mic In

Audio Out

MIDI In

Steinberg
Cubase
VST

MIDI keyboard

MIDI Out

Speakers

Amplifier

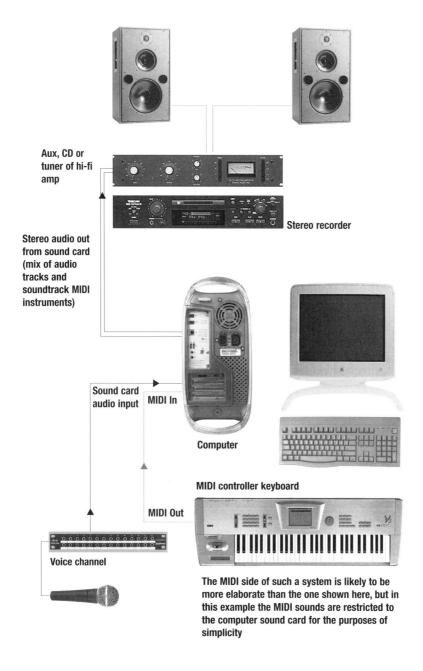

Aux, CD or
tuner of hi-fi
amp

Stereo recorder

Stereo audio out
from sound card
(mix of audio
tracks and
soundtrack MIDI
instruments)

Sound card
audio input MIDI In

Computer

MIDI controller keyboard

MIDI Out

Voice channel

The MIDI side of such a system is likely to be
more elaborate than the one shown here, but in
this example the MIDI sounds are restricted to
the computer sound card for the purposes of
simplicity

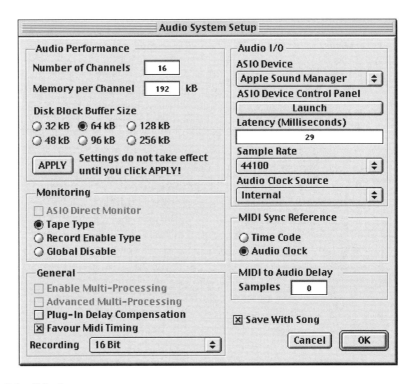

Audio System Setup dialog box

you decide to use a mixer, however, you should ensure that you use the mixer's input gain controls to match the levels of the different sources. You'll also have to check to make sure that the mixer's output signal being sent to your Mac isn't too loud or too weak. (As mentioned earlier, digital audio is much more sensitive to distortion and noise than traditional analogue recordings.) Line-level instruments connected directly to your Mac's audio input will need similar monitoring. While Cubase can lend a hand by indicating input levels, remember that there are no actual input-level settings within the program itself, and so, if you're simply using the built-in audio hardware in your Mac, you'll have to adjust input levels with the audio hardware you're using, or from the ASIO control panel accessed via Cubase's Audio System Setup dialog box. ASIO is yet another acronym, this time for something called Audio Stream Input/Output, a technology developed by Steinberg which acts as a connector between an audio application, such as Cubase, and the audio hardware. This means that, despite the problems described earlier, you usually have to select the proper ASIO driver to record and play back in Cubase.

To get your initial set-up out of the way, open the Audio System Setup dialog box from the Options menu and select a device from the ASIO menu. If you're not using an audio card, choose "Apple DAV" for a PCI Mac or "Apple Sound Manager" for all other Macs. If you're using an audio card with a special ASIO driver, be sure to select this from the menu, too. One of the advantages of using additional audio hardware is that dedicated ASIO drivers generally give much lower latency and can provide a number of hardware-specific features.

Audio cards supplied with ASIO multimedia drivers tend to suffer from significant latency when you're monitoring via Cubase. Latency is essentially the amount of time it takes for an audio signal to pass through the entire audio system, which includes entering via inputs, passing through the card into your Mac and finally making its way to the outputs. Latency can also cause similar delays between fader/control movements in the Master window and the Channel Mixer window, etc. Specific ASIO drivers that come with quite a few audio cards can reduce the latency to more acceptable levels, so always choose a card supplied with its own dedicated ASIO driver. Usually, audio playback and recording timing won't be affected by latency, because VST takes latency into account and adjusts timing accordingly. That's also why, when you play back MIDI parts routed to VST instruments, playback will be sample-accurate, regardless the level of latency.

You might want to adjust the number of channels in the Audio Performance section while you're in the Audio System Setup dialog box. This determines how many audio recordings you can play back at the same time. Remember, stereo recordings use two audio channels.

You can disable audio input and output in situations where, say, you only want to record and play back MIDI and don't want to waste power on the audio engine. Again, in the Options menu, choose Audio Setup and then Disable Audio. You can also use this option if you're running an older or minimal-spec Mac that may not be powerful enough to run Cubase with the VST engine enabled. It's also possible to disable audio on start-up simply by holding down the Shift key when you launch Cubase.

setting up MIDI

While there are certain recommended conventions to follow, the precise way in which you'll need to set up your Mac and Cubase for MIDI recording and playback will depend on what sort of MIDI devices you have and how you want them to operate. The Cubase manual describes four examples of possible ways to configure a MIDI system, based on some typical permutations. Your chosen MIDI devices will also come with appropriate documentation for how they should be connected and configured. So, essentially, what you need to know is that, if you want to be able to play MIDI tracks, you need to have an external MIDI device, such as a synth, connected to a suitable MIDI interface box, or you can use VST instruments.

In a typical basic MIDI system, the way in which the instruments are linked means that they all receive the same MIDI information. In order to allow the master instrument to communicate with the slaves on a more selective basis, the MIDI channel system was devised. There are 16 MIDI channels available, numbered from one to 16, and they work in a very similar way to TV channels. Most people in the UK receive five TV channels (forget Sky just for now), and yet all five channels arrive at the same aerial and reach the set down the same piece of wire. The one that we actually watch depends on the TV channel selected on the set.

With MIDI, the information sent down the MIDI cable can be transmitted on any one of 16 channels selected on the master keyboard. Similarly, the sound modules may be set to receive on any of the 16 channels. If, for example, you set the master keyboard to transmit on MIDI channel 1 and connect up three different MIDI modules set to receive on channels 1, 2 and 3, only the first module, set to channel 1, will respond. The others still receive the information, but the MIDI data tells them that the information isn't on their channel, and so they ignore it. (Of course, you can set all of your modules to the same MIDI channel and have them all playing at once, if you really want to.) So, by switching channels at the master keyboard, up to 16 different modules – set to the 16 different MIDI channels – can be addressed/played individually, even though they're all wired into the same system.

Most MIDI instruments have three MIDI sockets, labelled In, Out and Thru, although some older models may not have all three. The master instrument always sends information from its MIDI Out socket, which must be connected to the MIDI In socket of one of the slaves. The MIDI Thru of the slave is then connected to the MIDI In of the next slave and its Thru is connected to the MIDI In of the next one, and so on. What you end up with is a daisy chain which, in theory, can be of an infinite length. This isn't the case in practice, however, because the MIDI signal deteriorates slightly as it passes through each successive instrument. After passing through three or four instruments, the MIDI messages may start to become unreliable, resulting in notes which stick or refuse to play at all.

A better way to interconnect multiple instruments in anything other than the smallest MIDI system is to use a so-called MIDI Thru box. This takes the Out from the master keyboard and splits it into several Thru connections, which then feed the individual modules directly. (In practice, many people use a combination of MIDI Thru boxes and short daisy chains of instruments.) Although the MIDI Outs of the slave units aren't normally used during performance, they're useful when you want to hook up your keyboard to a MIDI sound editor or a librarian program running on a MIDI-equipped Mac.

In Cubase, you have to verify that the appropriate MIDI output port appears in the Output column for each MIDI track used in the Arrange window. (If you can't see the Output column, drag the split point at the left edge of the Part display, click in the Output column name of a MIDI track and a pop-up menu will appear displaying the output ports available for you to choose as appropriate.) Check that Cubase is both receiving and transmitting MIDI data by selecting a MIDI track and monitoring the MIDI in/out activity indicators as you play a MIDI device connected to your system. Also, make sure that you have MIDI Thru activated in the System dialog box in the MIDI Setup sub-menu in the Options menu.

As mentioned in Chapter 2, one of the first choices you'll need to make before you start recording is whether or not to use OMS, which allows you to see what instruments/modules you've got plugged into your system. If you're not running OMS, all channels say "Printer Port" (USB) instead of the connected device. MIDI only allows 16 channels per port, so without OMS you're reduced to a total of 16 channels for all modules, even though all MIDI modules are capable of 16 channels each. OMS allows you 16 channels per module, not per port, which is an advantage if you're running a basic four-in/four-out interface or better.

However, be aware there are problems with OMS. It's not particularly stable, and has always been a bit flaky. This is a particular problem for new Macs, since OMS is still in 64K code, rather than PowerPC (PPC). Since there's a good chance that OMS won't ever be rewritten for PPC code, it will continue to make life with new Macs rather unpleasant.

As I mentioned earlier, older Macs used a modem or printer serial port for MIDI interfaces, while the newer Macs use USB. If you're running a newer G3, G4, iMac or PowerBook, you may experience some difficulties with USB MIDI interfaces, depending on which brands you choose and how you configure your system. Some critics have even suggested that a combination of USB and OMS is problematic because you can't always control which other signals, over and above what your MIDI stream is generating, could be floating about on the USB bus. To minimise these problems, try to ensure that:

- you don't overload your USB interface with extraneous signals when working with data-intensive areas of MIDI;

- if you have two USB connectors, you try to keep the MIDI interface on one and put any other USB devices on the other;

- if performance deteriorates, you re-install OMS and keep an eye on your MIDI supplier's Web site for driver updates;

- if the manufacturer of your sequencing software also produces a MIDI interface or strongly recommends a particular brand, you use it.

The problem with USB MIDI interfaces is that all too often a device will work fine on one particular Mac configuration but inexplicably won't work on a similar configuration. This is another reason to use a slim-line extension set and to watch out for programs that could misbehave and cause conflicts. I've had experienced users tell me that the ideal Mac for use with music is an original beige G3, because it has two serial ports and an internal floppy drive. There's a lot to be said for opting for the path of least resistance, and until there's more choice for music add-ons with USB support this is worth keeping in mind. However, the real trick is to simply get your system – whatever it might be – running smoothly, whether you know why things work or not.

working practices

In both playback and recording, I've always been an advocate of the heuristic approach. Once you understand the basics of how Cubase works, the best way to master it is to get in there and start experimenting. Trial and error is an excellent teacher, and finding things out for yourself is always more valuable then being spoon-fed someone else's opinions every step of the way. After all, that's the only way you'll ever develop your own unique approach and creative method. However, before we look at some actual studio and recording tips, let's look at some of the other peripheral equipment you'll need to really get the best results out of Cubase and your own performance.

Once your Mac, your MIDI set-up and Cubase are sorted out, there are a few additional priorities that you really can't afford to neglect, if you're interested in making serious recordings. First, if your budget is tight and you have to cut corners, whatever you do, don't skimp on your microphones. This is one bit of advice that cannot be over-emphasised. I mean, think about it. The final sound that you produce will never sound better than the original source signal. If your budget is limited, buy one or two high-quality mics, rather than several lower-quality ones. As a matter of fact, to begin with, buy only one exceptionally good mic, if money is tight. You can do more with one good mic than with several cheaper models, even though in some instances it might seem like the latter option would make sessions more convenient. However, if you can have only one mic, try to have something like an AKG C-414. There's practically no sound that these mics don't do at least a good job with, and they usually cost slightly under £500, although you might find them cheaper if you shop around. If that's still out of your price range, the AKG C-3000 or the Audio Technica 4033 are both pretty decent mics which retail for under £300. There are also a number of other modestly priced condenser mics coming onto the market that would be worth a look. If you're really on a budget, the Shure SM-57/SM-58 is a good performing workhorse that can also be used for reasonable recording. If you can't come up with that, well, how serious are you?

Second, you don't need a 20-space rack full of signal processors (reverbs, delays, etc) to make a pro-quality recording, particularly with the range of VST plug-ins available. That sort of stuff always looks impressive but, when you come right down to it, it's not essential. One or two good reverbs and a couple of good-quality compressors could be useful, if you can stretch to this, and there are several decent, low-priced reverbs available, including the Alesis Quadraverb, the Lexicon LXP-1 and the Yamaha REV-500. You can also find acceptable low-priced compressors – such as the DBX 160A and the RNC – at reasonable prices, and it's always worth trying to pick up second-hand units. While there are advantages to some of these hardware processors, as I mentioned earlier, you should definitely check out the range of VST plug-ins that offer the digital equivalent of all of these sorts of effects processors. OK, none of the hardware units I've mentioned is going to startle the world or give you a Top-Ten hit, but if used correctly and creatively they can yield surprisingly professional results without you having to rush off to the bank for a second mortgage.

Since you're recording directly onto your hard drive, you don't have to worry too much about things like ADATs or multitrack tape. However, a DAT recorder or MiniDisc can be useful when dubbing down your master mix or when mastering and pressing CDs. While the MiniDisc format is a good and cheap digital medium, keep in mind that it does some very funky data compression, which can occasionally wreck all of the harmonics and overtones of your material, depending on how you use it.

If you're at all serious about production, at some point you're going to need an external mixing desk. A good one to start with is the 16-channel Mackie, or something like a Spirit twelve-channel Folio, although some people seem to really like Tascam mixers as well. Like everything else, it's worth shopping around and checking out second-hand sources. If you can afford it, it can also be a good idea to pick up a good-quality microphone pre-amp. This isn't to say that the pre-amps in all mixers are particularly bad – the ones in the Mackie, for example, are pretty good – but even many mid- to upper-mid-level mixing desks can have mediocre mic pre-amps. The only reason for this that I can think of is that most pro engineers have their own outboard mic pre-amps that they like to work with and probably won't use the ones in the console, anyway, and so manufacturers ask themselves why they should jack up the pre-amps and the price when nobody is going to care. Low-priced pre-amps to look for are the Symetrix and DBX units, although they may not be a great improvement. Really good mic pre-amps cost at least as much as top-notch mics, and if you've got the cash (or the credit) then spring for an Avalon or Focusrite model. However, be warned: once you use one, you'll never be happy with anything less.

Monitor speakers will also have a great impact on the finished sound of your mixes, so don't use those three-ways that came with your JVC stereo system. In the affordable range, you could consider models like the JBL and the industry-standard Yamaha NS-10 models, which don't sound all that incredible but seem to mix very well, once you're used to them. The problem with just plugging into your home stereo is that consumer speakers have built-in EQ curves and other parameters to sweeten their sound. What you want to hear when mixing, however, is the absolute sonic truth. Pro audio monitors don't lie – well, not nearly as much, at least – and it's also worth keeping a pair of really cheap Sony boombox speakers or the equivalent around just to gauge a reference once in a while. After a few hours spent mixing, your ears tend to go woolly, and you'd be surprised how a mix can sound like the voice of God over good speakers and later like muddy trash over your friend's Audiovox car system, so have at least two sets of monitors – a set of good ones and a set of garbage ones.

If you want a reasonably serious studio system, you can put together an adequate home/project studio for around £4,000, if you shop around.

Anything less and you're probably better off just going out and paying somebody who has some gear to do your recording for you. However, even with all the power and functionality of Cubase, it's worth remembering that you don't have to have 64 tracks to make a damned fine recording. As the old cliché goes, The Beatles' *Sgt Pepper's* album was cut to eight tracks (well, actually, two four-track machines synchronised together). Cubase and your Mac have already given you a much bigger edge than this, so to create a truly great album you just need to be sure that the peripheral gear you have is top notch and, most importantly, you need a good understanding of how to maximise its potential. Of course, great performances from the musicians wouldn't hurt, either.

session planning

Without going into a lot of detail about how to plan your recording session, it's worth mentioning a few basic practices with which some of you are perhaps already familiar. The way in which you actually structure your recording session will, of course, depend on the generic style of your music and the instrumentation and arrangements involved. However, in most instances, it's best to start by laying down rhythm and bass tracks, either to a click track, a guide vocal or perhaps a main MIDI track. Once you've got the rhythm, bass and chord parts down, you've effectively established the structure and shape of the song, and you can build, layer and arrange from there. Cubase makes it easy for you to adjust the mix as you record new parts so that, by the time you've got everything recorded, you've got a mix that will be pretty close to your desired final sound.

While this may be stating the obvious, it's absolutely imperative that you tune all of your instruments with a tuner before you start any recording session. Despite what a lot of musicians may claim, most of us don't have perfect pitch, or even relative pitch, and properly tuning an instrument is one of the first key steps to getting a good recording. It also avoids problems cropping up later, when you start laying down a track with a new instrument only to discover that, somewhere in the previous mix of tracks, something is out of tune. Incidentally, most MIDI instruments are tuneable as well, so if you make sure that all of your instruments are at least in tune with each other, it'll make your life a lot easier.

Once you get into recording sessions, you'll discover that there are several different ways of doing the same job, and most people will simply choose the one they like best and use that one most of the time. As mentioned earlier, the way in which you organise your sessions depends entirely on the type of music you're playing, your line-up of instruments and the generic sound you're trying to achieve, so let's hunker down and see what we can achieve.

chapter 5

studio session part one

"I just don't hear anyone else making the music I'm making in my head, so I'll have to do it myself."
  – Bob Dylan

laying down tracks

For most real musicians, the music is the message, and getting the best sound and performance, either by playing live or in a studio, is really what it's all about. Creating and playing music should also be fun, so there's no reason why recording it shouldn't be fun as well. As you've probably gathered by now, your Mac and Cubase VST provide the equivalent of a hugely powerful studio system at a fraction of the cost of a traditional tape-based recording set-up, and as an added bonus you can even set it up and record in the comfort of your own home. So, unlike so many other things in life, Cubase VST and your Mac offer a wonderful and convenient opportunity to be creative, make music and have fun, all at the same time.

While Cubase VST running on a suitable Mac fitted with MIDI and audio interfaces will allow you to perform most of the tasks you'd be able to perform in a traditional recording studio, don't forget those important extras mentioned in the previous chapter, such as a reasonable monitoring system, reasonable-quality microphones and, perhaps, mic pre-amps and external recording facilities, such as DAT, MiniDisc and CD burners. It's also worth mentioning a few simple tips on studio lay-out, which might help to make the whole recording process run a bit smoother.

Unless you only want to use MIDI sound sources that can be generated within your Mac, you'll definitely need an external mixer and some external sound modules. The mixing desk has always been the centre of a traditional recording studio, so you'll want to keep your mixer close to your Mac system so that you can operate both without moving from your ideal monitoring position. MIDI keyboards and samplers can be positioned to either side or even underneath your keyboard position, and you can experiment with racked or tiered arrangements. (Just remember that nothing should be placed or racked higher than the bottom of your monitor speakers or placed anywhere between the monitors and your head.) Also, make sure that your cables are kept out of harm's way, and avoid running mains leads alongside signal cables. Don't ever remove any earth leads from any equipment, and if you use multi-plug extension blocks, once you've plugged everything in, leave it plugged in, as plugging and unplugging mains plugs will weaken contacts and you could end up with dodgy connections or annoying pops and crackles.

If you tend to work alone, try to get hold of a combined mic, pre-amp and compressor for your audio recording, as these work reasonably well for voice or instrument recording. Make sure that you've got a reasonably long mic lead as well, since you'll want to get your mic as far away from your computer and peripherals as possible in order to avoid picking up hum and fan noise. I've got a lay-out with a computer-style desk housing my G3, monitor, CD-burner, Jaz drive and a MIDIman Omni I/O integrated desktop audio station connected to a MIDIman Delta 66 audio card. A shelf above the monitor holds a Spirit Folio mixer, and the bottom shelf is occupied by a Yamaha A5000 sampler. On shelves to the right and immediately behind me, I've got a Roland SoundCanvas keyboard, a mixer, a DAT recorder and additional tape players. Small monitors are positioned on a shelf above the unit, just above ear level, and for vocal and other mic recordings I run the mic out into the kitchen or into a small cupboard, where I can shut the door and block out the majority of extraneous noises.

While real voices and miked instruments are affected by the acoustic environment in which they're recorded, you can do quite a lot with Cubase to enhance, process and fix that sound, so don't panic if you don't have total isolation facilities or you get a bit of bleed-through or background noise. One of the disadvantages of the digital revolution in music has been a sort of compulsive obsession with perfectly pure audio hygiene. Personally, I think a completely clean sound is over-rated, rather sterile and generally – unless you're an anally retentive audio geek – totally inoffensive to the average ear. The natural world is full of interference and unintended reverberation, and rarely do we hear music played in the acoustic equivalent of an hermetically sealed environment, particularly in live performance. Let's face it, some genres of music actually benefit from a lo-fi approach and, despite what you might hear from the cultural prudes, a bit of audio dirt can in many instances add an important element of warmth and soul.

When you record, always record "dry" (ie with no effect). Effects such as reverb and VST plug-ins are extremely demanding on processing power, and it's always advisable to add them after you've laid down your tracks. A general tip for both music production and for Cubase in general is to always remember that less is more. Just because you have the functionality doesn't mean that you need to use it. And when it comes to arrangements and mixes, don't use six violins if you can use two. Use only what you need when you need it.

Cubase VST is designed to be easy to use before you even read the manual, so you can make a recording simply by pressing the Record button on the Transport bar and easily end up with something. However, if you want to get the best out of the system, it pays to dip into the manual and plan your recording session, or you might be disappointed with the results, which would defeat the whole purpose of trying to make a recording in the first place. Remember, depending on the style of music you're playing and the way that you want your final recording to sound, there may be whole sections of Cubase VST that you'll never need to use, which isn't a problem. If you can produce a recording that accurately reflects the sound you want to hear, you're probably using everything you need.

recording MIDI

In many respects, recording MIDI tracks with Cubase could be considered easier than recording audio tracks. With, say, a MIDI keyboard, you can essentially record all of the different parts of your musical score, one at a time, and then play them together in perfect synchronisation. Even after recording, sounds can be changed, tempo altered, and it's extremely easy to experiment with the musical arrangement by, say, copying verses or drum breaks to new locations or looping sections.

To get the best out of MIDI, ensure that your keyboard is velocity-sensitive. This means that it responds like a real instrument in that, the harder you hit the keys, the louder the notes will be. This is important to the overall dynamic of your song, and will allow your various MIDI parts to sound more natural and expressive.

Before you begin your MIDI recording session, double-check the following:

• Is your MIDI interface connected and working properly?

• Have you connected a MIDI keyboard or other controller and a MIDI sound source?

• Is your sound source compatible with General MIDI, GS or XG? (If you don't have a GM-compatible sound source, you won't be able to select sounds from the pop-up menus in Cubase VST.)

Make sure that your MIDI keyboard is connected to the MIDI In of your particular MIDI interface. You can make sure this is working by checking the MIDI In activity indicator on the Transport bar while you play a few notes on the keyboard. Also, make sure that the MIDI Out of the interface is connected to the MIDI In of the keyboard, and make sure that MIDI Thru is enabled by selecting the System option from the MIDI Setup sub-menu in the Options menu.

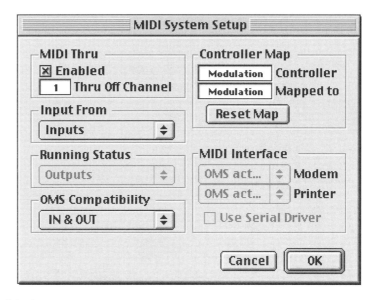

MIDI System Setup dialog box

Let's start with a simple MIDI recording in the Arrange window, which is Cubase VST's usual location for MIDI recording. To keep it simple, I'll assume that you're using one MIDI interface only, connected to the modem port or USB socket, and that you have no problems with the MIDI Thru settings. Start with the Autoload song displayed on the screen, shown in the illustration below. The song has an Arrange window called "Untitled 1", which has 16 tracks set to MIDI channels 1-16 and is loaded when you start Cubase, if it's in the same folder as the program itself. I'll also assume that you have one or more MIDI instruments, each set to one MIDI channel, or that you have one or more multitimbral instruments with each sound set to one MIDI channel.

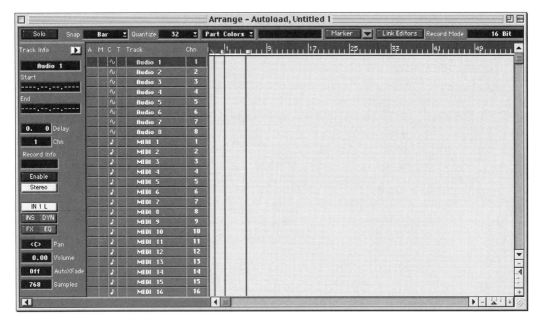

Default Autoload screen, with 16 MIDI and 8 audio channels

about Autoload

The Track list appears on the left-hand side of the screen, now displaying 16 tracks set to send on MIDI channel 1-16. In the column marked "CHN" (channel), click on the MIDI channel value for the first track. If you click once with the pointer, a menu appears which allows you to re-allocate the channel number of the track. If you double-click on the value, a small box opens up, where you can change the value by entering a new one via your keyboard. Use any of these techniques to set the first track to the right MIDI channel.

Channel Allocation menu

tracks and channels

Once you've got the settings right, you can play sounds into Cubase from a keyboard or, if you have a GM-compatible device, you can select instrument types in a pull-down menu in the Instrument column on the left-hand side of the screen. If you're using a sound from a keyboard, you can either enter that name in the Instrument column for your chosen track or you can change the track name to reflect the instrument you're recording. To do this, simply double-click on the first track in the Instrument column and a small box will open up where you can enter a name for the sound or instrument you want to use. (You can do the same in the Track column.) Type in whatever sound you'll be playing into that track and press Return when you've finished.

Pop-up box for naming instruments in either the Track or Instrument columns, plus the Instrument menu (I), for selecting GM instruments

OK. Now, as they say on *Blue Peter* and similarly interminable children's TV programmes, here's one I made earlier. I'm running a G3 system with a MIDIsport 2x2 interface hooked up to a Yamaha A5000 sampler running through a Roland SoundCanvas SK-88Pro. For this example, I've loaded in a number of sampled instruments, including a mandolin, a twelve-string guitar, a violin, ensemble strings, an acoustic bass and a harmonica, and I've knocked out a little set of imitation Irish tunes. I've actually loaded each instrument twice to make it easier to play different parts on the same instrument just to add a bit of variety to the finished sound.

Since everyone will have a different MIDI instrument set, I won't go into great detail concerning the wiring and settings – this is one instance where you should read the manuals, both the Cubase manual and, particularly, the ones that come with your various MIDI devices. MIDI can be temperamental, so be prepared to experiment with plugs, cables and settings. Generally, no matter what your configuration, you should remember to make MIDI Thru active. In Cubase, you'll find this in the MIDI System Setup dialog box, under the Options menu. When this option is ticked, it ensures that any MIDI data received at the MIDI In socket is echoed or put through to the MIDI Out.

And here's one I made earlier...

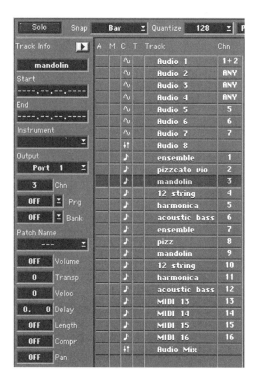

Make sure that you set the Metronome (in the Options menu) for an appropriate pre-count and click track. If you tick the Precount, Prerecord and MIDI check boxes, Cubase sets a pre-count of two bars. You can set the MIDI click channel and output to a drum or percussive sound, if one is available, and MIDI channel 10 is the standard channel for drums and percussion sounds. The default C#1 as the note for a MIDI click is the standard setting for a rimshot sound, and if you want to use this then make sure that the audio click is deactivated.

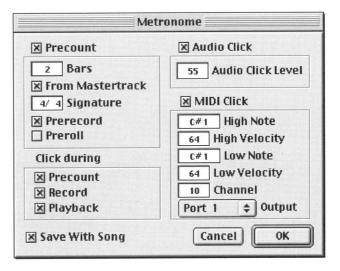

Setting the click track and pre-count intro

Set your key signature and tempo to the settings that you want for your song on the Transport bar. Before you start recording, however, make sure the Click button is activated so the guide click track will play through your speakers or MIDI instrument. For now, leave all other settings on the Transport bar in their default positions.

Set the desired tempo and key signature and ensure that the Click button is activated. Note that the In/Out read-out will light up to indicate whether or not your MIDI instrument is playing through

You can check the click and tempo before you start recording by selecting the Play button on the Transport bar or by using the Enter key on your numeric keypad.

Set the left and right locators to the track length you need, or use a setting somewhere around 1.1.0 and 5.1.0 by clicking in the position bar above the arrangement area. If you want to record with a count-in pre-count starting from some point other than the beginning, hold down Option and click in the bar display (above the Parts display) at that position. This changes the settings of the left locator, and the new setting is shown numerically in another box on the Transport bar. By holding down the Command (Apple) key and clicking in the bar display, you can set the right locator. Also, make sure that the Cycle Record mode is set to Mix, so that you can add to the recording on each lap of the cycle. When you're ready, click the red Record button on the Transport bar, or the asterisk key on the numeric keypad, and start playing after the two-bar count-in for as long as you wish.

Click the red Record button to lay down your first track

When you've finished, click on the Stop button or press 0 on the numeric keypad. A black rectangle should be displayed on the first track. This is a selected part, and it shows your recording on a track. A part can be dragged around on the screen with the pointer, and if you hold down the Option key while dragging you make copies of the track, duplicating it. The first track I've recorded here is a mandolin track. Using that as a guide I'll add a number of additional parts, which I can then mix into a finished song.

First mandolin track recorded on channel 3

Press the yellow Stop button (0 on the numeric keypad) twice to get back to the beginning of the song, and click on Play or press Enter to play it back.

After playing back the track, return to the beginning of the song and sort out what you want to play next. As before, select a new track by clicking on it and set it to the MIDI channel for the next sound you want to record and enter an instrument name for that as well, and then record on the second track just as you did with the first. You can listen to your first track while you're doing this and, if you make a mistake somewhere, you can erase what you've done by selecting Undo from the Edit menu.

Once you've recorded a track, you can quantize it to sort out any timing discrepancies in your playing. To do this, you first have to set the right quantize value. There's a box at the top of the screen labelled "Quantize", and if you press the mouse button inside that box a pull-down menu appears in which you can select the quantize value you need for your music. This quantize value will now remain valid until you change it. Now select a part by clicking on it and then pull down the Functions menu and select Over Quantize.

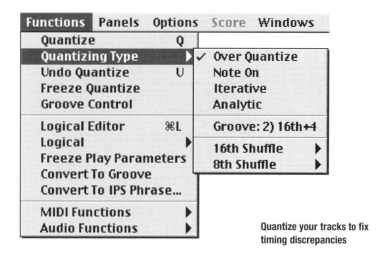

Quantize your tracks to fix timing discrepancies

Continue to record as many more tracks as you like. If you want to use an instrument or a sound that has already been used, press the mouse button with the pointer in the Instrument column and select that instrument or sound from the pull-down menu that appears. The track is then automatically set to the right MIDI channel. If you want to make a track send out on another MIDI channel, just change the number in the Channel column for that track. Once you've laid down all of the tracks of the various instruments that you need for your song, you'll end up with something that looks a bit like this.

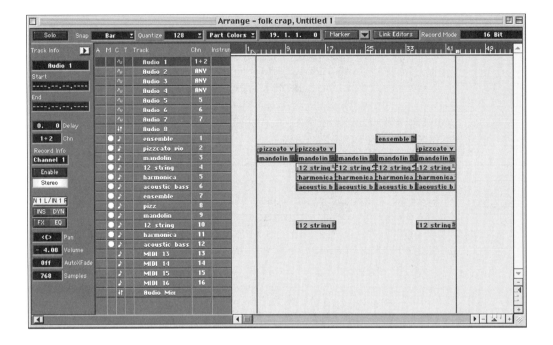

OK, maybe this is a subjective, artistic call, but a lot of musicians recommend using at least one acoustic instrument, even in a MIDI mix, as it tends to give a "warmer" sound.

All of the parts that are created can be moved freely between tracks and duplicated, if required. They can also be split, joined, lengthened, shortened, grouped, and much more besides, even while the music is being played. If you pull down the Tools menu, a toolbox appears, and you might want to experiment with this. (Refer back to Chapter 3 if you've forgotten what all the tools are for.)

A typical Cubase toolbox

If you want to delete one or more parts, select them and press Backspace. When you're happy with your piece, pull down the File menu and select Save As, then enter a name and save the file to disk, just as you would in any other Macintosh program.

This should give you a reasonable feel for how simple Cubase is to use when it comes to recording MIDI. Now let's have a go at recording an audio track.

recording audio

In Cubase, audio tracks are recorded in much the same way as MIDI tracks. It's all managed in the Arrange window, and you can input audio directly into your Mac's mic input or through an audio card. To begin with, let's assume that you're using a basic audio card with two in/two out or the built-in audio on your Mac. For now, let's assume that you're using a microphone with the signal fed into a standard stereo-in/stereo-out audio card. If you're using a mono source, connect the cable to the left input socket, if you've got them available separately. If you're not using a mixer, you'll have to make sure that Sound In is enabled on your Mac. To do this, choose Audio Setup>System from the Options menu in Cubase.

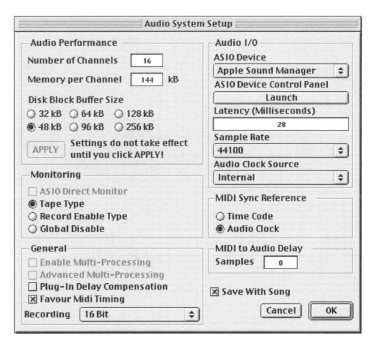

For now, stick to the default settings and choose Launch

From this menu, choose Launch. Hold down the mouse button on the Source box and choose Sound In. Also, make sure that the Play Thru box is ticked if you want to hear what you've recorded when you want to lay down another track.

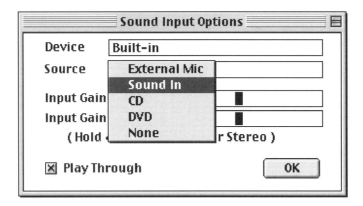

To ensure that your inputs are activated, select VST Inputs from the Panels menu and you should see a list of available input ports in the left-hand column. Choose the one you want to use and make sure that the indicator in the middle column is lit, which signifies that the input is active. (It's always a good idea to switch the light on and off just to make sure that your devices are awake.)

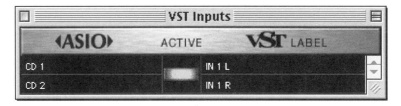

Default available inputs. These will vary, depending on your audio card and its configuration

Before you start recording audio, you also have to set the sample rate. This setting determines the quality of your audio recordings, and the higher the value, the better the quality. As I said earlier, it's a bit like scanning – you should always scan or sample at a higher resolution than you require for your final illustration. However, you should remember that, as with graphic files, higher-quality sampling uses more disk space and processing power. The usual sample rate for CD-quality audio is 44.1kHz, and you might also find that some audio hardware will support only a limited number of rates. For now, leave the Record mode on the Status bar in the Arrange window at the default 16-bit setting. We'll look at the ramifications of 24-bit and 32-bit recording later on.

mono and stereo recordings

It's important to know that each audio channel in Cubase can play back one mono audio recording at a time, while stereo recordings play back on two audio channels, as you might expect, with one for each stereo side. In the Channel column, you'll note that stereo-channel pairs always consist of an odd channel and the next even one (in the illustration here, the channels shown are 1 and 2), so for stereo work you should always select an odd-numbered channel to set up your track. To set up an audio track, simply click on one or create one from the pull-down menu in the C column. Set the track's channel in the pull-down menu in the Channel column, as before, and name this track just as you did with your MIDI tracks.

If you're recording in stereo, click the Stereo button in the Inspector to activate it.

To select a folder for your audio files, click the Enable button, which is located just above the Stereo button. The first time you do this, Cubase will open a dialog box asking you to select a folder in which to store your files. (If you can afford it, it's a good idea to store your audio files on a separate, fast hard disk, to optimise performance.) Once you've done this, you can still change the folder for your audio files during a recording session by pulling down the Options menu and selecting Audio Files Folder from the Audio Setup sub-menu.

You can monitor (ie listen to) the signal you're recording in three different ways: if you're using an external mixer and audio card, you can listen to your connected equipment or sound source directly from the mixer, over either speakers or headphones; if you're using a very basic configuration, you can manually activate the Through or Monitor feature of the audio card, either through the card's ASIO control panel, accessed via Cubase's Audio System Setup dialog box, via the Sound control panel in the Apple menu in the Finder, or via a mixer application that comes with your card; or you can monitor directly via Cubase, with audio passing from the input into Cubase and back to the output, so that you can control the monitoring with settings within Cubase. If you choose to monitor via Cubase, this option is automatically activated when you Record Enable a track. An advantage of monitoring through an external mixer is that it avoids the problems with latency and timing associated with laying tracks and overdubbing.

As mentioned in previous chapters, when it comes to recording levels, digital recording isn't nearly as forgiving as analogue recording, when it comes to banging the needle into the red. While it's common practice to have peaks in traditional analogue recordings, where you've got plenty of audio headroom, in Cubase this sort of behaviour will result in some extremely unpleasant distortion and hard clipping. You also have to be careful not to record your input signals too low, or you won't have enough gain to work with. You can get around both of these problems in Cubase by accurately using the input meter on the Channel Mixer window to check your levels and adjust your input. (We'll look at these internal mixers in greater detail in the next chapter.)

Once you've done all that, set your locator bars in position, in the same way that you do when recording MIDI, and also set your metronome, tempo and time signature. Make sure that the Sync, Master and Loop buttons are inactive on the Transport bar, and then start your recording just as you did for your MIDI tracks. When you've finished, click the Stop button. You should now have a track that looks something like this.

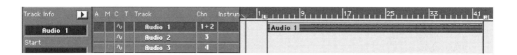

If you don't like what you've recorded, don't panic – you can always undo or delete the track and start again. However, you should be aware that, unlike MIDI parts, when you delete an audio part, the segment and audio file aren't really deleted. Sure, they disappear from the Arrange window, but the audio file is still hanging around on your hard disk and the segment is having a great time swimming around the Audio Pool. This is no great problem; it just means that you've got to delete all of these unused segments and files later.

Recording digital audio can be a bit like trying to perform an ancient magick spell from a modern translation of some dusty grimoire. All of the symbols are probably there, the ingredients are readily available, but the phrasing and procedural order for completing the great work may have got a bit muddled along the way. If you find yourself confronted by an entourage of unexpected or unwanted demons, draw a circle around your Mac and ask yourself the following riddles:

• Are my cables and connections faulty, or is it the input signal itself? The source is switched on and active…or is it?

• Have I tested my audio card to make sure that it's installed correctly? Is there some sort of impedance mismatch between my source audio signal and the card? Is the card switched on in the Input and Output Port lists in the ASIO Setup panel?

• Have I confused the left and right inputs on the card, and have I chosen the correct input on the selected audio track?

• Are the inputs for the audio card active, with the green light on?

As I've already mentioned, audio files are huge, compared to Cubase VST song files, MIDI files or other Mac files, such as word processor documents. Just to give you an example, for each minute of recording at 44.1kHz mono, you'll burn through 5MB of hard-disk space for each mono audio channel. You don't have to be a Carol Vorderman to figure out that this means that, in order to record continuously on four channels for three minutes, you'll need a massive 60MB of free hard-disk space. Keep that in mind when you start thinking about using real instruments of live vocals.

OK, that's your first recording session completed. You should have managed to lay down a number of tracks. If you've experienced any additional problems so far – particularly with recording audio – and you've tried the tips mentioned above, they're probably due to the savage, inexplicable intervention of gremlins in the range of parameters related to the audio hardware you're using. However, don't despair. As I said earlier, the best way to get the sounds you want is to continue to experiment and try out functions as you feel you need them. And if you really have to, get all the manuals that come with your various add-ons, put them in the loo and read them at your leisure.

chapter 6

studio session part two

"Romantic realism. In our music, we make the machines sing."
  – Ralf Hütter, Kraftwerk

According to Frank Zappa, cigarettes and coffee are food. So, while we stop for a little food break, let's think about where we are. If you've adopted a suitably heuristic approach, you should be reasonably confident about getting some basic MIDI and audio tracks into Cubase. However, like working in a traditional recording studio, the whole creative process doesn't stop there. Now you need to think about layering instruments, cutting up sections, sorting out timing and adding various effects, which will ultimately allow you to create the perfect finished mix. Cubase VST provides you with an impressive assortment of virtual mixing consoles and effects racks, which include sophisticated EQ controls, adjustable reverb, delay, chorus and other fun toys which will allow you to achieve just the sound and feel you're looking for. While you're on a food break, it's also a good time to reflect on the fact that the whole concept of multitrack mixing can't really be separated from the rest of the recording process, and in the digital studio the neatly packaged tasks common to traditional studios become blurred so that, in a sense, you're building your mix and final sound in a much more fluid and flexible manner, which allows for more artistic control at each step in the process. Best of all, of course, you're not paying for studio time by the hour.

That being said, however, even Cubase can't work miracles. If you make a recording with crap sound input, don't kid yourself into thinking that you can fix it in the mix. Sure, you can always improve on what you've got, but you should always make sure that what you've got is the best that you can get, and keep the words "silk purse" and "sow's ear" in mind at all times. Even clever features like quantizing won't fix a totally spastic rhythm, and no amount of effects or processing will turn a tuneless dirge into a rock anthem.

Although we'll look at the musical aesthetics of mixing in more detail later in the book, it's now probably a good time to check out the essentials of the built-in mixing functions found in Cubase VST.

mixing MIDI

As you might expect, the easiest way to mix and change levels, pans and other settings is to use the MIDI Track Mixer. To mix MIDI tracks, your MIDI instruments have to respond to Volume and Pan messages, and if they happen to support Roland's GS extension of General MIDI, or Yamaha's XG, you'll be able to control a whole range of other parameters, such as effects, filters and envelopes. You can access the MIDI Track Mixer from the Panels menu, and it looks like this.

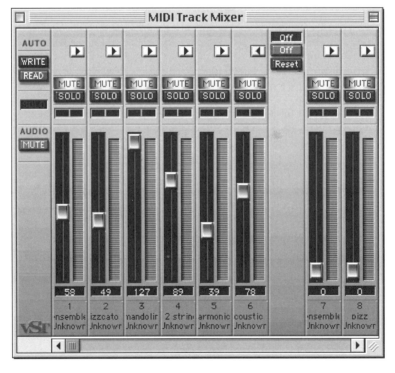

Each channel also includes a level/velocity meter to the right of the fader.
The buttons beneath the Mute/Solo buttons control pan

This mixer works by sending out MIDI Controller messages to your various MIDI devices and instruments, and you might notice that a number of these mixer settings are also available in the Inspector section of the Arrange window. Inspector settings made for a track will be reflected in the MIDI Track Mixer, and adjustments made to the mixer's settings will affect the Inspector settings for the track. Individual parts aren't affected, however, and Inspector settings made for single parts won't reflect in the mixer. Any mixer automation created with the Write/Read buttons won't reflect in the Inspector, either.

The Track Mixer works exactly the same way as any real-world analogue mixer, except in a virtual environment: you slide the faders to increase or decrease volume, and each channel has a Mute (which silences the output of the selected track) and Solo button (which silences the output of all other tracks shown in the mixer). You can, of course, have several MIDI tracks set to the same MIDI channel, but it will mean that mixing one of these tracks will affect all of the other tracks set to the same MIDI channel. At the bottom of each fader, you'll notice that there's a little window that displays a value for the MIDI Volume message that's sent out on the corresponding MIDI channel. (I'll explain how you can automate these level settings by using the Write/Read buttons a bit later.) At the top of each channel is an arrow button which, when clicked, extends the channel strip to display a variety of other settings for effects and synths, etc.

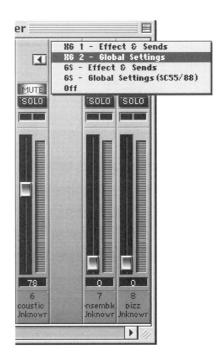

Extended channel strip. Click the top Off button (shown in the previous example) to display the additional settings

When you first install Cubase VST, the following modes are available (you can also add custom-made modes yourself, if you like):

- XG 1 – Effect And Sends (effect sends and various sound-control parameters for use with instruments compatible with the Yamaha XG standard);

- XG 2 – Global Settings (global settings for instruments compatible with the Yamaha XG standard);

- GS – Effect And Sends (effect sends and various sound-control parameters for use with instruments compatible with the Roland GS standard);

- GS – Global Settings (global settings for instruments compatible with the Roland GS standard);

- Off (no control parameters available).

If you want to work with just your MIDI tracks, you can switch off all audio tracks in a song by clicking the Audio Mute button on the MIDI Track Mixer. (Incidentally, the flashing level meters next to each fader pictured in the previous illustrations show the velocity values of the MIDI information being played back. This means that the faders themselves don't affect the meters but simply adjust the volume of the instrument.) In case you haven't noticed, the MIDI Track Mixer allows you to perform real-time mixing and automation in the same way that you'd carry out audio mixing.

Another clever thing about the MIDI Track Mixer is that it automatically expands or contracts if you add or delete a channel, and you can expand up to 128 tracks, although if you ever need that many it's probably worth investing in a second monitor. I've seen studios set up like this, and since the Mac is so easy to use with two monitors, the Arrange window can be on a large screen and the Transport bar and various tools and plug-ins can be on another, smaller one.

OK, that's a quick overview of the MIDI Track Mixer. Now let's look at how you can use a similar virtual mixer for audio.

the VST Channel Mixer

For mixing your audio tracks, Cubase provides two VST Channel Mixers, which are accessed – like the MIDI Track Mixer – from the Panels menu. Again, the familiar fader metaphor is used, and each channel will be labelled with the value that you've already set in the Channel ("Chn") column for that particular track. At the top of each fader, above a cluster of buttons, you'll find a button displaying the name of the input you've selected for that channel. If you've selected "Stereo", you'll need to select different inputs for the two channels, as described in Chapter 4. In the following illustration, you'll note that channels 1 and 2 are set up as a stereo-channel pair. Like the MIDI Track Mixer, this one also has Mute and Solo buttons and pan controls for the setting of the stereo position of each audio channel. Depending on how you want your final mix to sound and where you want instruments positioned, you can play with the pan controls or simply set a more or less traditional pan, with the left channel panned hard left and the right channel panned hard right.

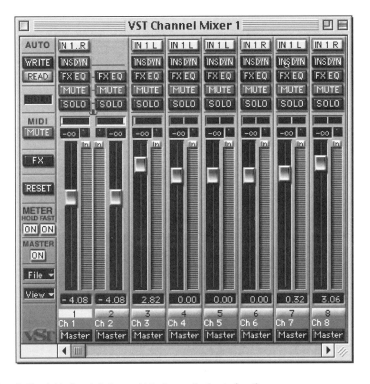

Channel Mixer window. To the right of each fader – which change the level of audio output – is a channel level meter, which registers the level of the audio input or output signal. At the top of this meter is a small input-metering switch, which shows the level of the input signal when activated and of the channel output when deactivated. Sitting on top of this is a box that registers peak level and clip indicators. If it lights up, you've overloaded the signal and you'll have to reset the indicators by clicking on them and then lower the fader and try again until there is no clipping

If you click the Mono switch in the Master Mixer, it won't matter how you've set your pan settings, as they'll have no effect whatsoever. More on the Master Mixer later...

The cluster of buttons at the top of each channel fader gives you access to a range of VST settings for adjusting EQ (four bands, parametric), dynamics, effects, etc. You can click on each of these and individually set parameters for each channel.

Parametric EQ module

On the left-hand side of the module is a duplicate of the selected VST channel fader, an insert effects section, two rows of effect-send knobs and four EQ control modules linked to an EQ curve display. If you happen to be using a stereo-channel pair, as in the above illustration, when you make equaliser settings for the left channel, these same settings will be applied to the right channel in the pair. Clicking the On buttons below the EQ curve display lights up the box and activates the modules, and the EQ can be adjusted by twiddling the knobs. Whenever you switch on a module, a point is automatically added to the curve display. When you've set the EQ for the sound you want, close the Channel Settings window. You'll now be able to turn the set EQ on and off from the VST Channel Mixer window.

Above the EQ button in the Mixer window is the Dyn button, which gives you access to something called a *dynamics processor*, which you can use to alter the dynamic range or level of your audio tracks. The module itself contains five separate processors, including AutoGate, AutoLevel, Compress, SoftClip and Limit, and it works pretty much the same as the EQ module. (We'll look at its functionality and the application of effects in more detail in Chapter 9.) Like the EQ module, once you've made your settings, you can turn them on and off in the VST Channel Mixer window.

VST Dynamics module

the Master Mixer

Once you've got your individual MIDI and audio tracks balanced the way you want them, you'll need to open the Master Mixer and set the levels for your final mix. To do this, simply repeat the procedure you followed when opening the VST Channel Mixer. At the bottom-left-hand side of the mixer, you'll see a Master button. When this is activated, the VST Channel Mixer is magically transformed into a VST Master Mixer.

VST Master Mixer window

Check to see if your mixer has opened with the In buttons and the Read and Write buttons switched off. The Read and Write buttons are used in the automating of mixer movements, but for now let's do things the old-fashioned way and mix by hand. Your VST Channel Mixer channels are routed by default to the master faders on the right-hand side of the panel. You can re-route to other output buses by using the output routing system, but the master faders provide a kind of normal output through which you can send your final stereo mix.

OK, just like in a traditional studio, you'll need to activate playback and use the faders on the mixer to set the desired volumes for your audio channels. For any stereo-channel pairs in your mix, both faders will be linked and will move together. If you need to change one of the pairs and not the other, you can do this by holding down the Option key and dragging the fader to its desired position. When you're doing this, though, watch the clipping indicators in the Master Mixer and don't let them light up. Remember what I said earlier about the horrors of digital distortion?

Although overdriving your digital audio signal is generally to be discouraged, some dance and experimental musicians and groups actually do this on purpose to create textured distortion effects. So, just because someone says you shouldn't do something, this doesn't always mean that you shouldn't do it. Often – particularly in more adventurous music – serendipity, or even a major mistake, can add an unexpected and positively creative element that makes a recording really special.

Set your pan controls to the desired levels of separation. (When you're changing a channel's pan setting, the value is shown numerically in the level display under the fader. If you click the Mono switch in the Master Mixer, all of your audio playback will be in mono and the pan settings won't have any effect.) After this, play around with the various effects and apply them here in your final mix. If you like what you hear, stop and play back your song. Have a really good listen and try to think of ways to improve it, although don't be tempted to add more effects just because you can. If you're satisfied, you can even burn your song onto a CD.

To record onto CD, DAT, MiniDisc, etc, go back to the Arrange window, make another audio track and save it under a new name. Play your newly mixed tracks so that the output goes into your Mac and is recorded onto an audio track. If you're using an external mixing desk, take the output from your desk that goes into your Mac, or wherever your MIDI output goes, and plug it into the Mac's sound channel. Play your track and see if it shows up in Cubase VST's Audio Mixer and check your levels. If your signal isn't loud enough, you can boost it in Cubase or some other editing/mastering application, such as Peak. After this, you can normalise the song in the Wave window. You can start with the default setting, but again you basically need to experiment until you get the right result. Play it by ear, as they say.

click, time and tempo

You've got two editors which you can use to adjust your song's tempo in Cubase: the Graphical Mastertrack and the List Mastertrack. The Graphical Mastertrack allows you to "draw" tempo changes in a very intuitive Mac-like manner and provides a useful visual indication of any tempo changes, while the List Mastertrack is better for fine-tuning tempo settings and allows for more precise and detailed adjustments. When the Mastertrack button appears in the Transport bar, your tempo is controlled by the tempo events in the mastertrack. When it's off, the song's tempo is controlled only by the setting in the Transport bar. Generally, it's easier to switch off the mastertrack when you're recording and use it later to adjust your tempo, if necessary.

The Graphical Mastertrack is opened from the Edit menu, and you can either edit or add tempo changes with the Pencil tool by holding down the Option key as you drag or reshape the tempo or make quick changes by clicking and dragging with the Line tool.

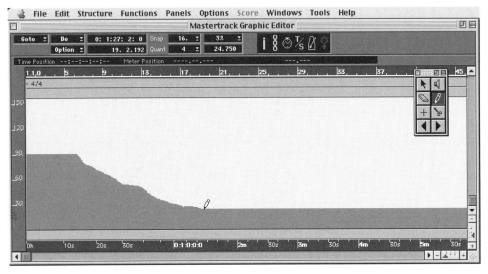

Editing with the Graphical Mastertrack

To change an existing tempo setting, just drag it up or down using the Pencil tool in the Graphical Mastertrack and watch the tempo indicator box. To delete any events or changes, use the Eraser tool. Time signatures can be inserted by clicking in the Time-Signature bar with the Pencil tool, and you can edit the values of these in the Information bar. You can also insert "hit points" to mark important movements in the time scales or metre of your song. In MIDI, adding hit points can be a good way of marking passages of audio material in order to create a tempo map. You can add them in Cubase in normal Play mode, as long as the Graphical Mastertrack is open. Essentially, if you need to have tempo changes within your song, you need to use the mastertrack. (It's always in Replace mode, so any tempo changes you record will replace existing data.) You can record tempo changes in real time by ticking the Record Tempo/Mutes option in the Options menu, and when Cubase is in Record mode you'll be able to record any tempo changes made – they'll automatically be put in the mastertrack. If the changes you've made or drawn sound too abrupt, use the Smooth feature in the mastertrack Do menu to…you've guessed it…smooth them out.

(Incidentally, these functions work best with MIDI tracks. Although Cubase provides functions for changing the tempo of audio parts, you don't really want to go there unless it's absolutely unavoidable. If you're going to change the tempo after you've made a recording, make sure that you leave any audio recording until after the changes have been finalised. If you happen to be working with loops, put down basic tracks with loops first and then add MIDI parts later.)

You can use these features to change the tempo within your song, and you can also transfer tempo events from one arrangement to another. Since the mastertrack works like all of the other Cubase editors, you can copy and paste things like tempo events and time signatures between arrangements, or you can use the Export and Import commands to transfer an entire mastertrack to another arrangement.

You can change the majority of tempo settings by adjusting the integers in the Transport bar. The value shown is in bpm (beats per minute) and, as shown earlier, you can adjust both speed and time signature. The easiest way to set the tempo is to play back your song and adjust the tempo on the Transport bar while you listen to the metronome click generated on each beat. (Remember that, in order to hear the metronome, you'll need to ensure that the Click button on the Transport bar is activated.)

In more complex recordings, you may decide that you want to record a piece out of time but still be able to view it in an editor with all of its notes positioned on their relevant beats. The solution in Cubase is to use *time-locked tracks*, which are essentially fixed in time so that, if you change the tempo anywhere, the events on your track still stay in their same positions. You can time-lock a track by clicking in the T column in the Arrange window, which will then display a padlock icon. If a track is time-locked, any ghost parts will automatically become real parts. Oh, yeah – ghost parts are a bit like Mac aliases, since they're simply copies of existing parts which borrow and reflect the data of the original. For example, if you have a sequence or break which repeats, you can record it once and then use ghost parts anywhere else in the song where you need that riff or sequence. Then, if you make a change in one part, that change happens in all of the ghost parts. To create a ghost part, hold down the Command key and drag the part you want to copy to a new point in your song. Ghost parts are easily recognisable, as their names appear in italics.

As you've probably gathered, this is just a brief glimpse at some of the things that you can do to manage and manipulate tempo and time-signature events. The Graphical Mastertrack and, particularly, the List Mastertrack are jam-packed with advanced features which are simply too techie for this sort of book. If you want to get your head around all of their functionality, don't be afraid to experiment. Just don't experiment on anything that's really important.

chapter 7

editing and manipulating tracks

"They're just songs, songs that are transparent so you can see every bit through them."
– Bob Dylan

ew musicians can go into a studio and lay down a perfect track first time, every time. Sure, there are exceptions, and probably a lot more who just think they're exceptions, but for most of the rest of us, it's nice to know that, if we don't get something right the first time, we can either do it all over again or, if we're using Cubase, get right down inside the song and try to fix it or modify it. As Dylan might have put it, Cubase effectively makes your song so transparent that you can see every bit of it in exceptional detail. This means that, in many instances, you can effectively edit your song and its overall sound visually. So far, we've looked at some of the main techniques involved in getting your tracks recorded at the arrangement level. Once you've recorded all of your parts, however, you can then begin to use Cubase VST's powerful tools to carry out a wide range of editing functions that will help you to manipulate your tracks and arrangement until your song sounds exactly the way you want it to.

As mentioned in Chapter 5, all of the parts that you create in the Arrange window can be moved freely between tracks and duplicated, if you wish. They can also be split, joined, lengthened, shortened, grouped and much more, even while the music is being played. Cubase also provides a number of specific editors that allow you to look at and work with the contents of each part in more detail. You can also resize your Arrange window using the buttons in the lower-right-hand corner to enlarge even the most complicated arrangement or individual part.

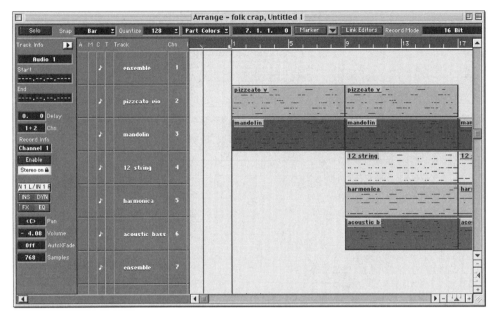

A song viewed in the Arrange window

With Cubase, it's easy to edit and manipulate parts in the Arrange window, and most of the techniques involved with simple tasks such as changing the order of, moving, duplicating, splitting, joining, changing the length of, deleting and creating tracks apply to both MIDI and audio parts.

- Changing the track order – Click on the track you want to move and simply drag it to the desired position with the mouse button pressed. When it's where you want it, release the mouse button. The track is now in its new position and all parts on the track are moved with it.

Selecting and dragging a track to a new position

- Duplicating tracks – Click on the track name in the Track list while holding down the Option key and drag the track to a new position. When you release the mouse button, a duplicate is created complete with parts.

This also works for simply changing or duplicating parts. Just click on the part instead of the track name.

- Selecting parts – To work with a part in Cubase, you first have to select it. Use the Arrow tool to select or deselect parts. As in other Mac applications, if you hold down the Shift key you can select multiple parts, or you can hold down the mouse button and drag a marquee rectangle outline around a number of parts to select them.

- Moving parts – Click, hold and drag. When you do this, the pointer changes to a hand.

- Changing part length – Select the part or parts you want to lengthen or shorten and then use the Pencil tool to click the outlined end of the part and drag it to a new length. (Incidentally, if you make a MIDI part shorter, all events in the missing section will be erased.)

- Splitting parts – Select the Scissors tool and click where you want to cut a part. New parts have the same name as the originals.

Using the Scissors tool to split a part

- Joining parts – Select the Glue tool and click on the first part and it will be joined, or "glued", to the next part on the track. If you hold down the Option key and click on a part while the Glue tool is selected, all consecutive parts on the track will be joined together to form a single track.

- Deleting parts – Click on a part to select it and press Backspace, as you would in any other Mac application. Alternatively, you could use the Eraser tool. However, be aware that, with audio parts, the eraser doesn't delete the actual audio file or segment from the audio pool. To delete an audio part and erase its corresponding file from your hard disk, select the part and hold down Command and press Backspace.

- Creating parts – While parts are usually created automatically when you record something, you can add an empty part and fill it with an event in an editor by drawing it in with the Pencil tool.

editors

While working with your song parts in the Arrange window, you can look at and manipulate parts in finer detail by using a number of editors within Cubase VST. These include the Key Editor, the List Editor and the Drum Editor. While the Key Editor and the List Editor are essentially designed for working primarily with MIDI data, the List Editor is also designed to display audio events.

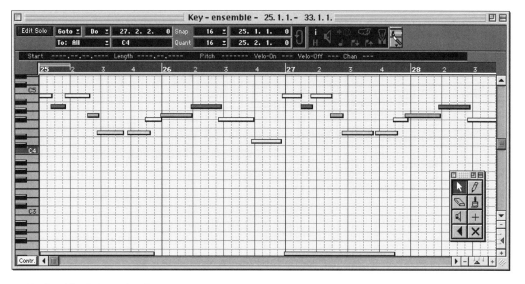

The Key Edit window and toolbox

If you double-click on one of the MIDI parts in the Arrange window, you'll open the Key Edit window. This gives you a more detailed visual representation of the particular part, and I suppose that, musically, it resembles an old-fashioned music-box cylinder, or an old player-piano spool. Notes are displayed as graphic strips or bars, and when you click on them their characteristics are displayed in the Information bar. The keyboard on the left shows the notes being played, and you can use the Pencil tool to add, remove, lengthen and shorten notes, etc. The Key Edit window also allows you to view your data as it's being quantized, so you can actually see how the notes are being shifted in time. You can also move notes manually to tighten timing to grid lines, although inserted notes will be shifted onto the nearest fraction of a beat, according to the Snap value. The length of any inserted notes will also be governed by the Quantize box value.

This is a great place to edit a guitar part, for example, where some of the notes are just that bit too long or overlap. You can also edit out the odd duff notes, edit timing values where a few bars are out, get rid of velocity errors or produce crescendi or fades, graphically, with the ease of using the Pencil tool. This window is particularly good for musicians who don't like working with notation but prefer instead a more visual feel to editing and even composition. You can also make sampled and synthesised instruments sound more realistic by adjusting the phrasing so that they sound more like they're being played by actual musicians. This includes things like easing off when say a wind player would have to take a breath or adding fret squeaks to make guitars sound more live and realistic.

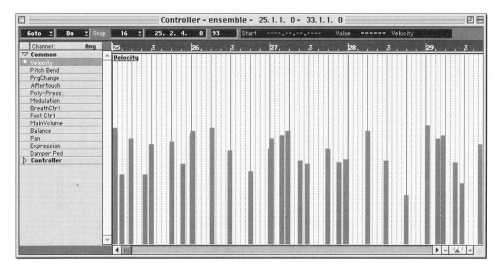

Use the Controller window to do things like create fades and adjust velocity and pitch bend

The Controller window is accessible either by clicking the Controller button in the lower-left-hand corner of the Key Edit window or by selecting Controller from the Edit menu. With the Pencil or Line tool, you can write new events in the Controller window for any of the menu options.

The List Edit window allows you to view and edit most of the various types of event in all of Cubase VST's different track classes. The columns in the list represent different values, depending on their track class and event type. You can insert any type of event, including notes, and you can set the length of the note manually while you're entering it, just as you would in the Key Edit window.

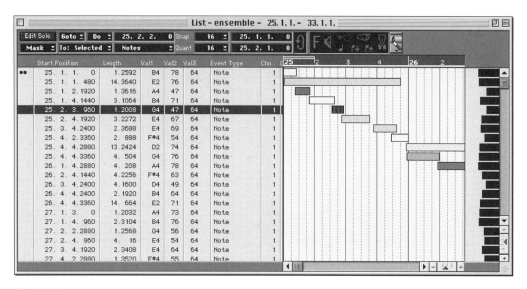

The List Edit window

Personally, I find the List Edit window rather daunting, and in truth you may never even need to use it, unless you're involved in recording massive arrangements which require an extreme level of detail for editing MIDI events. While the Key Edit window is more accessible, with its graphic approach, the List Edit window is probably the province of aspiring sound engineers interested in editing non-note events and system-exclusive (sysex) data. However, unlike the Key Edit window, in the List Edit window you can edit only one track or selected part at a time, although you can edit audio events, as well as MIDI events, in fine detail. It's up to you whether or not you ever use it, and if you're using an external sampler then you'll already be doing a lot of these kinds of tasks with that.

From a musician's point of view, however, the Drum Edit and Drum Map windows are both interesting and useful, and here, in particular, you might find that the more detailed parameters found in the List Edit window make more sense. In MIDI instruments, drum sounds are usually differentiated by being placed on separate keys and assigned to different MIDI note numbers. This means that, when you use a keyboard to record a drum part in a sequencer, you usually use one key for the bass drum, one for the snare, and so on. On many instruments used to play back drum sounds – such as drum machines, samplers and some synths – you can rearrange the order in which the sounds of the single instruments are assigned to the keys. Unfortunately, there's little consistency in the industry, and most manufacturers of MIDI instruments place their drum sounds on different keys and in different orders. This can be a real pig if you've made a drum pattern using one instrument and you want to try it on another. When you switch, it's very likely that your snare drum will become a ride cymbal or your hi-hat will turn into a tom.

To solve this problem, and ostensibly to simplify several aspects of MIDI drum kits, Cubase VST uses a track class called *drum tracks*, and parts on drum tracks are referred to as *drum parts*. The thing that separates drum tracks from MIDI tracks is that everything played back from or routed through a drum track is "filtered" through a drum map. Among other things, this drum map determines exactly which MIDI note number is sent out for each sound in your drum pattern, and thereby which drum sound is played on the receiving instrument. So, from a musician's point of view, it would seem to make sense to make up drum maps for all of your instruments. In this way, when you wanted to try your drum pattern on another instrument, you'd simply switch to the corresponding drum map as well, and your snare sound would remain a snare sound.

In Cubase, a drum map consists of settings for 128 drum sounds, which can be named and set to represent particular drum sounds on your synth, sampler or drum machine. You can have up to 64 drum maps in your song at once, so you can create several different drum tracks, each with its own drum map. (Keep in mind the fact that each drum track only uses one drum map at a time.) When you've defined a sound, all of the notes already recorded with that sound appear as diamonds on their particular line in the note display. One of the drum maps that comes with Cubase is called the *default drum map*, and it displays the following general properties:

• There is always a default drum map present in a song;

• When you create a new drum track, it's automatically set to use the default drum map;

• When you edit MIDI tracks in the Drum Edit window, the default drum map is used.

Not all parameters are available when you edit MIDI tracks in the Drum Edit window, but when you load a drum map from disk you can choose whether or not you want it to be the default drum map.

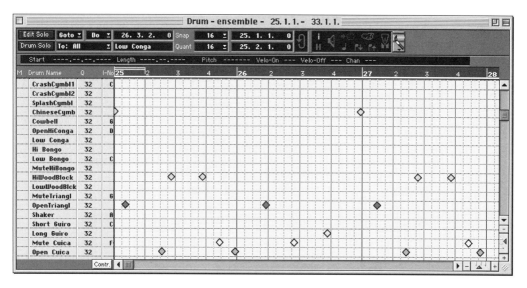

Default GM drum map

For each of your drum sounds, you can define what might seem to be a lot of complex parameters. However, for most musicians, only two are really important for understanding drum maps: the I-note and O-note values. The I-note is a certain key or MIDI note number used to play a sound. Setting the I-note value will allow you to choose a key on your MIDI instrument, drum pad or whatever to play the sound. (Keep in mind that two sounds can't share the same I-note.)

The O-note, meanwhile, is the MIDI note number that the sound actually outputs when played by you or played back by the program. Let's say that you have a rack synth with some drum sounds in it but they're spread over the range of the keyboard in a way that's inconvenient for your playing style. You can get around this by first setting the O-notes in the drum map so that they match the actual notes that play back the sounds on your instrument. If the instrument plays back the bass drum on the C2 key, set the O-note for the bass drum sound to just that, C2, so that the sound of a bass drum is produced. Now you can rearrange the whole "drum kit" so that the fingering suits you just by setting the right I-notes.

While each of the 128 sounds each have a note number, this is neither the I-note nor the O-note value but simply a note number used to sort and keep track of the sounds. This may seem like more than you want to know, but only this "real" note number is recorded. As soon as you open a drum part in another editor, the "real" note numbers are revealed. If you open a drum track in the List Edit window, or open a folder track containing drum tracks in the Key Edit window, the notes are shown with their "real" note numbers, which could make things rather confusing. Therefore, it's always a good idea to edit drum tracks in the Drum Edit window only. Like Key Edit, Drum Edit also has a Controller display, but it only shows data for the sound that's currently selected.

While the Drum Editor makes it relatively easy to create, edit and generally muck about with percussion patterns and even create your parts from scratch with the Drumstick or Brush tool, using a keyboard in real time will usually give you a more natural and realistic feel. Try recording whole sections rather than just a few bars and looping by copying and pasting. Recording a couple of drum tracks at a time can also give a more natural sound than recording each one separately. Of course, this isn't a hard-and-fast rule, and if you're programming some complex breakbeat or some other dance stuff then you may decide to program things differently. Also, when you're creating a new drum map, it's often a good idea to start with a map which is similar to the sort you want, if available, and simply edit this. After all, re-inventing the wheel is never the most productive use of your creative endeavours.

Here's a brief description of the parameters in the Drum column:

- Drum name – The name of the sound;

- I-note – When this MIDI note is sent into Cubase VST (ie you play it), the particular sound is "triggered", or played;

- O-note – When the sound is triggered, either by you playing it or by the program playing back a drum part, this is the MIDI note number that is sent out;

- Chn – The MIDI channel on which the sound will be output;

- Output – The MIDI output used by the sound.

- Instrument – A way of naming the combination of MIDI channel and output, just as in the Track column;

- Q – Quantize value, used when editing;

- Len – A length value, used when inputting notes. Since most drum sounds are one-shot sounds, length is normally irrelevant;

- "Diamond values" – These are four different velocity values, used when notes are created in the Drum Edit window;

- Delay – This column shifts the timing of sounds forwards or backwards, and is used to compensate for timing variations or glitches with sounds from different instruments in the same drum map or for special rhythmic effects.

Hi Bongo	32	C3	64	
Low Bongo	32	C#3	64	◆ ◆ ◆
MuteHiBongo	32	D3	64	
HiWoodBlock	32	E4	64	◇

Diamond values playing sounds can be entered with the Drumstick tool

If you do read and write music, Cubase VST has an extremely sophisticated Score editor, which can be used for editing or composing parts for your song. The design and features provided will depend on which version of Cubase VST you own, since Cubase VST Score and Cubase VST/32 now include larger Score editors for professional-level lay-out and printing. If you're more comfortable with real notation, there are a number of settings that can be made here to clean up the score and various performance inaccuracies without having to change the actual MIDI data.

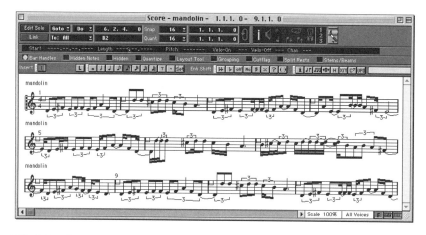

In the Score Edit window, if you're editing parts on several tracks at the same time, a striped double bar line at the beginning of the score indicates the active track

Cubase's transparent nature and it's ability to let you edit your music at almost any level and degree makes it an exceptionally powerful tool and ally. Essentially, anything that you can do in the Arrange window relating to playback or recording can also be done in the various editors. As well as going from the Arrange window to any editor, you can just as easily go from one editor to another or have several editors open at the same time. Editing happens in real time, so you can edit while music is playing or even while you're recording. If you don't want to record in real time, you can use step recording to input drum tracks or other instrument tracks one note at a time. For convenience, you can also select Follow Song from the Options menu, which will cause the window to scroll automatically during playback so that your current song position is always in view. And if you activate Cycle, you can fine-tune your recording and instantly hear the result without having to rewind to the right section.

the Audio Editor

Like the various MIDI editors, the Audio Editor offers a way of looking at, editing and manipulating your audio data in a more detailed way than is possible exclusively in the Arrange window. Audio parts contain elements which are available for editing known as *audio events*, which in many ways are comparable to MIDI events. As mentioned briefly in Chapter 3, an audio event is rather like a box which contains a segment plus some additional settings, so your audio part is like a box that contains one of several audio events, rather like the way in which MIDI parts contain notes or other MIDI events. When you edit an audio part in the Audio Editor, you don't change the actual recording or the audio file; instead, you alter the properties of the segments in the audio events in the part. This means that no audio data is lost, and you can always change your settings back to the way they were before you started editing.

Audio events appear as boxes with waveforms in them, and you can have a virtually unlimited number of events in the Audio Editor at one time, as they don't consume any more memory than MIDI events. They can also be arranged in any way – with gaps between them, overlapping each other, etc. To open the Audio Edit window, click on the audio part or parts that you want to edit. While this window is similar to the MIDI Edit windows, and should look familiar by now, you'll notice that it's divided into horizontal sections, called *lanes*. Each lane is labelled at the left end of the window with the audio channel of the part currently being edited. When you edit audio which is on a single channel, all of the lanes will be labelled with the same channel number. Conversely, when you edit several audio parts on different channels, each lane will be labelled with different channel numbers. You can move or copy events between lanes, but the results depend on the audio channel setting of the track you're editing. When you move an event between lanes with different channel numbers, you change the audio channel on which the event is played back.

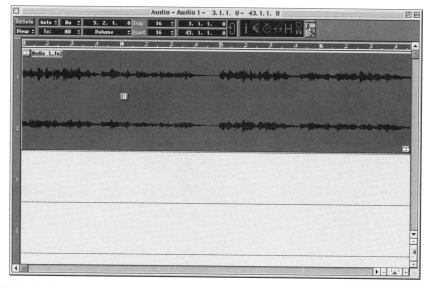

The Audio Edit window. If you click at any point on the position bar, the song pointer jumps to that position

You can move the events between the lanes as you like and add new events on any lane, and playback isn't affected by the lane on which an event is set. The only reason why you'd use more than one lane when editing a single-channel track is because you'll probably find that it gives you a better overview of what's going on. Remember that, in a single-channel track, all events will "compete" for one single, monophonic audio channel, so if they overlap, time-wise, they'll cut each other off during playback, even if they're on different lanes. Stereo recordings occupy two lanes, and these two lanes use one audio channel each, one for each side in the stereo pair.

Apart from this, editing stereo tracks isn't much different from editing mono tracks. As you experiment, you'll discover that the lanes that appear in the Audio Editor can be used as a means of moving events between audio channels and even between tracks. Lanes are also particularly useful for manipulating multiple takes on the same audio channel.

Recording from within the Audio Editor is no different from recording in the Arrange window, and if you're editing several parts at once you'll be recording into the active track, and the active part is always indicated by the window title. To activate another part, simply click in the Lane Info field for that part. Each audio event has a Q-point, which is marked, as you might expect, with a "Q" flag on a vertical line, and this can be dragged to any point within the event. Once you've positioned this where you want it to be, it's used by the Snap value to position the event whenever it's moved or quantized. Q-points are used to mark musically significant points in a song, and in an audio track this could be a downbeat or the start of a breakdown or fill.

As within the MIDI editors, you can move, duplicate, repeat, delete, mute and loop audio events, and the procedures are essentially the same. Double arrows in the top-left-hand and lower-right-hand corners of each event mark the start and end insets, specifying where the audio file starts and ends. These insets are generally used to trim audio events to specific sections of the audio file for things like isolating a particular instrument or, perhaps, cutting out unwanted sections of noise or silence. You can also split audio events with the Scissors tool.

In case there's one recording that doesn't play back as intended, the Audio Editor is the one you'll want to use to find out if several events are competing for an audio channel. If two audio events try to play back on the same audio channel at the same time, only one of them will be heard. To trace potential problems, try the following:

• Select all of the parts that you think might be competing for audio channels. (This may very well mean selecting parts on several tracks);

• Open the Audio Editor, displaying the selected parts;

• By selecting "By Output" from the View pop-up menu in the Audio Editor, all events that play back on the same audio channel are put on the same lane, regardless of whether they're on different tracks or the same track;

• Check for overlapping events along the lanes, as some audio will be cut off at these points.

There are times, of course, whey you may intentionally want to have overlapping events, such as when you've had to punch in on a track to correct a mistake in a vocal part. The punch-in recording overlaps and therefore hides the original faulty recording. There's always a chance that you'll accidentally get overlapping parts, and this feature will help you find them.

As I mentioned earlier, you record in the Audio Edit window in exactly the same way as you do in the Arrange window. In studio sessions, it can be more convenient, in some instances, to work on recordings in the Audio Editor, rather than in the Arrange window. For example, if you're recording a live vocal and the singer is having a problem with a particular passage. You can record in Cycle mode, and in the Arrange window the track will be recorded as one long audio file. However, when you look at the track in the Audio Edit window, it will be divided up into convenient segments and stacked in separate lanes, each representing the length of a lap of the cycle. This method means that you're less likely to lose the "magical" performance of an unrecorded practice take, but it also means that a cycle of lengthy takes will play havoc with your hard-disk space. It can still be worth doing, but you should keep an eye on the demands that it makes on your processor storage space.

You can also import audio data by selecting the Pencil tool and clicking in a lane. A file dialog box will then open, allowing you to locate and select the audio file you want to import. This new segment will then be added to the display and also to the list of files in your Audio Pool. An audio file will be created at the point at which you clicked. You can also drag and drop segments from the audio pool or even drag in audio files directly from the desktop.

Always create a new folder to save your audio and give it the name of the project on which you're working. Also, use sub-folders of the part type – ie, "Vocal" – so that you have more room in the file names to refer to the quality of the take. The easiest way of doing this is to create the folders outside Cubase.

Make sure that all of your audio files are in one place, so that you don't accidentally erase a default file name. Also, use the Prepare Master function in the File Pool option under the File menu – it'll copy only the used segments to a new folder. You'll now have to save a new song version with these new streamlined files, ideally with a new name in the same folder, and you'll need the same amount of disk space, as it copies the files. Delete the originals once you're happy. It's a kind of combination of the Purge Segments, Erase Unused and Prepare Archive functions.

the Audio Pool

If you're used to the way in which the Finder manages your files and folders on your Mac, you'll understand how to use the Audio Pool to manage your audio segments and files. You can open the Audio Pool from the Panels menu, and the window lists all of the audio files used in a song. In other words, it shows the files for all Arrange windows that belong to the song.

Each file is represented by a line in bold text preceded by a triangle. There is information and a number of settings for each file, plus a waveform image on the right-hand side. Each of the files that appear in the Audio Pool represent an audio file on one of your hard disks that is being used, or has been used, in the song. Files themselves are never used directly in the song, but rather segments are played back from the tracks. For each file, there are one or more of these segments, which are specifications for a section of a file. Segments are mainly created when you record audio and when you edit in the Audio Edit window.

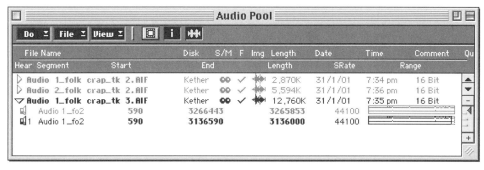

The Audio Pool window

To listen to a segment from the beginning, click the speaker icon to the left of the segment and hold down the mouse button. The entire segment will then be played, or it will play until you release the mouse button. If you don't want to audition the segment from the beginning, you can click anywhere in the waveform image on the right-hand side of the window. The segment will then play from the point at which you clicked and for as long as you hold down the mouse button.

As I mentioned earlier, you can also drag and drop segments into the Arrange window and import other audio files into the Audio Pool itself. Just choose Import Audio from the pop-up File menu in the Audio Pool and follow the dialog box. To be allowed into the Audio Pool, a file must:

• be AIFF, WAV, SDII or MP3 format;

• be an uncompressed 16-bit or 24-bit file;

- have a sample rate that is the same as the one used in your song;

- be mono or stereo.

AIFF files are most common on the Mac, while WAV files are more common on PCs, and of course you can also import audio files directly into the Arrange window by using the Import Audio File command in the File menu. If you want to work with MP3 files, keep in mind that these are compressed and can't be played back directly by Cubase VST. When you import an MP3 file, Cubase creates a copy of the file, converts it into WAV format and places the converted file into the folder selected for your song. While the original MP3 may be quite small, the converted WAV file will definitely be a lot bigger.

Cubase provides another set of functions for the quick, efficient manipulation of large numbers called *global functions*, which are accessed from the Structure menu. All of these functions work in the same way – the area being worked on is defined by the locators, and any muted tracks remain unaffected. Global Cut removes the area between the locators and moves all of the following parts back to create a seamless join, while Global Insert moves all of the parts that appear after the left locator to the right locator, thus creating a break in your song. Global Split, meanwhile, works in the same way as the Scissors tool, except across all tracks. When selected, parts are split at the locator points. If you only want to create one split, either set both locators to the same position or move the right locator to an empty area in the Arrange window. Finally, Copy Range copies all events that fall between the two locators and inserts them at the current song position.

OK, I know I said I wasn't going to go into a lot of weird-science geeky tech stuff, and I know it's about as dull as the sharp end of a dull thing, but even if you're a practising musician, and not an aspiring sound engineer, a basic understanding of a lot of these features in Cubase is important, even if this does little more than allow you to decide not to use some of them. In the world of desktop digital recording, even experienced musicians may be seduced into becoming overly preoccupied with the technical details of their MIDI system and start to forget that the object of the exercise is to create some music. We've all witnessed the sad scene in the recording studio when the musicians wait for hours on end while the newly converted programmer grapples with all kinds of arcane and obscure parameters in the digitally misguided quest for musical perfection. If you're a real musician, you know deep inside that musical perfection simply doesn't exist. That's why we always strive to do better. And even if this mythical musical perfection did exist, a MIDI sequencer isn't what you should use in some kind of grail quest to find it. As you've noticed, some level of technical involvement is inevitable, but believe me, the true secret is to know the essentials of the software and to have a clear idea of the style, feel and sound of the music that you want to record. Remember, the great thing about Cubase is that, for the most part, you can choose how deeply you wish to go and how much comprehension of the program's functionality you require for your own individual needs. As I mentioned earlier, just because you can do it doesn't mean that you have to.

chapter 8

VST instruments and effects

"You can synthesise your existence. We created ourselves synthetically. I suppose you might call it 'ersatz', but the real meaning of the word synthetic is 'putting together', which is all we are doing."
 – Ralf Hütter, Kraftwerk

Maybe we can't synthesise our existence just yet, but Steinberg's VST provides us with a lot of cool tools for improving and augmenting the music we put together in our digital studio. Cubase VST comes with an impressive array of VST plug-in effects and virtual instruments, and you can buy and download scores more direct from Steinberg, from various other sites on the Web or from other manufacturers and music outlets. Essentially, there are two kinds of VST plug-ins: instruments and effects. You'll probably find that VST instruments are being heavily promoted as convenient, cheap alternatives for the usual range of expensive hardware synths and samplers, and in many respects they are. However, while you can think of these plug-ins as the musical equivalent of QuarkXPress extensions or Adobe Photoshop filters, you must remember that they take up a huge amount of memory and will ravenously eat into your processor power.

Another disadvantage of VST instruments is that, generally, there's too much latency. I touched on this problem briefly earlier, but – depending on your audio hardware and its ASIO driver – this latency may make it difficult to play these VST instruments with the kind of precision timing you'd expect from a real instrument. However, in most cases, you can work around this problem by playing and recording your parts with another MIDI sound source selected and then switching to the desired VST instrument when you play back. All VST instruments are played internally via MIDI, and their audio outputs appear on separate channels in the VST Channel Mixer.

VST instruments

You can access the VST instruments that are bundled with Cubase VST by selecting VST Instruments from the Panel menu. What you'll get initially is a window with no instruments selected.

When you click on this menu, a pop-up menu will appear listing all of the VST instruments currently installed on your system.

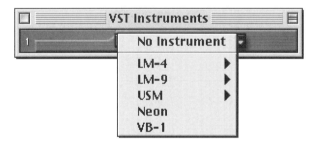

Each time you choose an instrument, it's added to your bank, which looks a bit like this.

When the red button on the left is switched on, the instruments are ready to use. Cubase VST normally comes complete with LM-9, a simple drum machine; USM (Universal Sound Module), a General-MIDI-compatible sound module; Neon, a simple software synth; and VB-1, a virtual bass guitar. I've also added LM-4 (a more sophisticated drum machine) to my own system, and with each of these instruments I can also select a number of patches and settings, providing direct access to the instrument's controls.

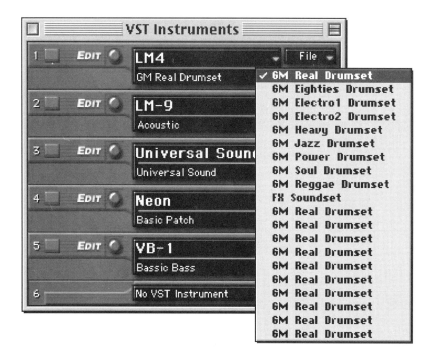

LM-4

LM-4 gives you access to a selection of General MIDI drum kits with a variety of sound styles. Once you've selected your preferred kit, you can click on the Edit button and have access to the control panel for this device. The plug-in looks like and operates in a similar fashion to various hardware drum machines – you can adjust volume, velocity and other parameters for each of the elements of the kit you've chosen. The buttons in the lower-left-hand corner allow you to either choose another drum-kit set from the menu or to toggle through the list which appears in the long window.

You play and record your VST instruments in the Arrange window by selecting a MIDI track and activating the chosen device via the pop-up Output menu for that track. Any instrument that you're using is automatically added to the MIDI Output list, which will help you to keep track of what you've got active. When you play your MIDI keyboard, the incoming MIDI is sent to your selected instrument.

LM-9

LM-9 is a simple polyphonic drum machine that has up to nine voices. It receives MIDI in Omni mode (ie on all MIDI channels. You don't need to select a MIDI channel to direct MIDI to LM-9 – it responds to the MIDI Note On/Off message, and its volume is governed by velocity. It comes with two sets of drum sounds, "acoustic" (featuring samples of an acoustic drum kit) and "beat box" (features classic analogue drum-machine sounds), and the mapping is GM-compatible. You use the Program button to switch between the two supplied drum sets, just as you'd switch between effect programs. The Velocity command sets the global velocity sensitivity, and the higher the value, the more sensitive LM-9 will be to incoming velocity data. If this is set to zero, the sounds will play back with a fixed velocity value. The volume sliders are used to adjust the volume for each individual drum sound, while the pads are used to audition the individual drum sounds and to select a sound for adjusting pan. Panorama is used to position an individual sound in the stereo image, and this setting will apply to the currently selected sound, which is indicated by a glowing yellow LED over the Pad button.

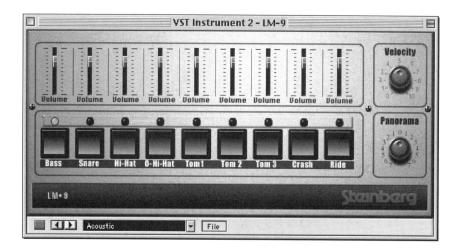

LM-9 DRUM SOUND	NOTE VALUE
Bass	C1
Snare	D1
Hi-hat	F#1
O-hi-hat	A#1
Tom 1	D2
Tom 2	B1
Tom3	A1
Crash	C#2
Ride	D#2

USM

The Universal Sound Module is a General-MIDI-compatible sound module. As I mentioned in earlier chapters, General MIDI defines a standardised group of sounds and the minimum requirements for General-MIDI-compatible synthesisers or sound modules, so that a specially prepared sequence or MIDI file that is sent to the instrument via MIDI will play back on the correct types of sounds, regardless of the make and model of the instrument on which it's played.

MIDI identifies sounds by their Program Change numbers, and before the General MIDI standard was introduced the same MIDI Program Change number often addressed totally different types of sound in any two synthesisers or sound modules from different manufacturers – ie a flute sound in one instrument could be a piano sound in the other. However, this has changed with the introduction of GM-compatible instruments, because these instruments now have to use the same Program Change numbers for the same types of instruments. So, if you want a melody to be played by a "piano", you can use a certain Program Change command embedded in the sequence to automatically select a piano sound in any GM-compatible sound module. Even so, the GM standard doesn't specify in any great detail how that piano should sound; it's simply assumed that the manufacturer has reproduced a representation of an acoustic piano that sounds more or less like an acoustic piano. A consequence of this is that, depending on the GM module used, a song can sound very different on another instrument, even though the sounds were mapped correctly. USM solves this problem, however, and with Cubase you can make sure that any music you've created using the USM will sound exactly the same when played back on another computer, simply because the sound reproduction is no longer hardware-based.

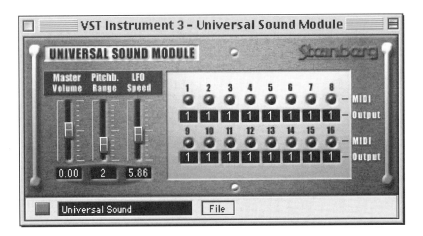

The USM features over 70MB of sampled waveforms and four stereo outputs. It's also polyphonic, with up to 96 voices, and it receives MIDI in 16-channel Multi mode (ie simultaneous multitimbral playback on 16 MIDI channels). In other words, one USM unit can play up to 16 MIDI tracks, each with a different sound. (Keep in mind that, according to the General

MIDI standard, MIDI channel 10 is reserved for drums, and that this cannot be changed.) It also features 128 different sound patches, and program selections are carried out by sending Program Change messages, either numerically, using the Prg Value field in the Inspector, or by selecting from the Patchfield pop-up menu. The USM features four stereo outputs, allowing for flexible routing of sounds to different effects processors, etc, and all MIDI channels are routed to USM stereo output 1 by default. To select an alternative output, simply click the Output field below the Channel Activity indicator for the MIDI channel that you want to direct to another output. This opens a pop-up menu that allows you to select one of the four stereo outputs.

The Master Volume control sets the master output volume, while Pitch Bend Range sets the range for incoming MIDI Pitch Bend messages, which can be selected between one and twelve semitones. LFO Speed governs the speed of the vibrato, and the depth of the vibrato is controlled via MIDI Modulation messages. MIDI channel-activity indicators 1-16 indicate activity on the corresponding MIDI channels, and if you click on the Output 1-16 field a pop-up menu opens, allowing you to direct the corresponding USM MIDI channel to one of the four available stereo outputs.

Neon

Neon is a simple polyphonic software synthesiser with up to 16 voices. However, since each added voice consumes a considerable amount of processor power, the maximum polyphony may be limited by the speed of your Mac. The Neon receives MIDI in Omni mode, and you don't need to select a MIDI channel to direct MIDI to the Neon. The synth also responds to MIDI Note On and Note Off messages, and the volume is governed by velocity.

When using a software synth, try to remember to pan the two instrument channels hard left and hard right, if you want to use MIDI Pan messages. When controlling the synth, Range selects an octave range for the oscillators – 16, eight or four feet – and the basic waveform for the oscillators is either triangle, sawtooth or square. LFO Speed governs the speed of the vibrato, and the vibrato depth is controlled via MIDI Modulation messages. Osc 2 Detune allows you to detune the second oscillator up or down seven semitones, although by setting this to a value close to "twelve o'clock" you'll get fine-detuning, for a warmer, fatter sound. VCF Cut-Off is the cut-off frequency for the filter, which governs the amount of high frequencies that are incorporated in the sound.

On Neon, the Cut-off control also serves as a depth control for the filter envelope, so that, the lower the setting of the Cut-off parameter, the more the filter is affected by the filter envelope. VCF Resonance is a control for the filter which can be raised to produce a more hollow, pronounced filter effect, while the Filter Envelope parameters – VCF Attack, Decay, Sustain and Release – determine how the filter should open and close with time when a note is played The Amplitude Envelope parameters determine how the amplitude, or volume, should change with time whenever a note is played.

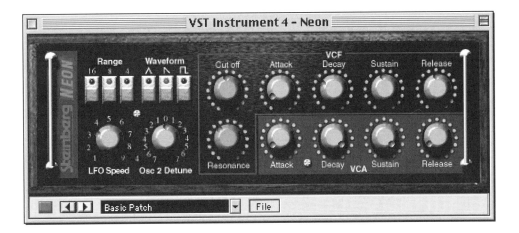

VB-1

Although it's not a 1962 pre-CBS Fender Jazz Bass, VB-1 looks like a fairly funky virtual bass built on real-time physical-modelling principles. However, with this one, it's a case of "nice interface, pity about the sound". VB-1 is polyphonic, with up to four voices, and it receives MIDI in Omni mode (ie on all MIDI channels). Like a "proper" electric bass, the Volume control regulates the VB-1 volume and the Damper switch controls the length of time that the string vibrates after being plucked. You can also adjust the position of the pick-up, and by dragging the "mic" left or right you can change the tone, while positioning it towards the bridge produces a hollow sound that emphasises the upper harmonics of the plucked string and placing it towards the neck produces a fuller, warmer tone. The Pick Position parameter determines where along the length of the string the initial pluck is made, and this controls the roundness of the tone, just as it does on a real guitar. The Wave Morph parameter selects the basic waveform used to drive the plucked string model. However, be aware that this parameter can drastically change the character of the sound. The control smoothly morphs through the waves, so if you're not careful, it's possible to create sounds that have no relation to a bass guitar, although of course there might be times when you'd want to do this.

All things considered, the VB-1's bass sounds aren't all that wonderful, and you'd probably be better off using bass sounds from something like the Neon.

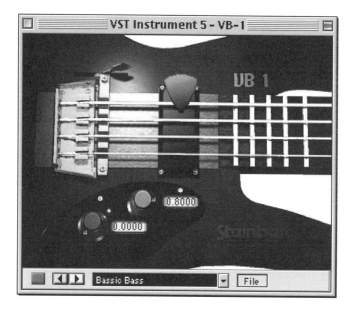

With each VST instrument that's activated, an extra channel strip will automatically appear on your VST Channel Mixer providing you with control over criteria such as volume, pan, additional effects and EQ. VST instruments can be a convenient and economical way of adding high-quality sounds to your recordings, provided that you've at least got an external keyboard connected to your Mac to trigger them. If you're planning to use VST instruments with any regularity, make sure that the audio card you're using produces minimal latency. Although I said earlier that VST instruments are real processor hogs, these instrument tracks can be easily converted to audio tracks, which put a little less strain on your system, so if speed and memory become a problem, you can convert them by using the Export Audio command in the File menu or in the Master Mixer window.

VST effects

VST effects are essentially digital simulations of the effects that musicians have traditionally had access to via pedal or rack systems. Many of these effects are used for live performances as well as for recording and, like VST instruments, the plug-ins bundled with Cubase VST can save you a lot of money and hassle. Steinberg have improved the whole standard with their introduction of VST version 2.0, which allows plug-in parameters to be controlled via MIDI information in more or less the same way that hardware effect boxes can be controlled via MIDI. Version 2.0 allows effect plug-ins to receive MIDI from Cubase VST, which makes it possible to include things like tempo-based delays, MIDI-controlled pitch-shifters and harmonisers. MIDI timing information is also automatically provided for VST 2.0 plug-ins that "request" it.

Cubase VST 5.0 comes with a completely new set of effect plug-ins, although, to ensure backwards compatibility for those with songs created using previous versions of Cubase, the previous standard set of VST plug-ins is included as well, located in the sub-folder cleverly named "Earlier VST Plug-Ins" in your effect menus. If you accumulate a lot of VST plug-ins from different sources, it's always a good idea to move all of your plug-ins to a single folder and then direct Cubase to use this folder when it asks you for the location of your plug-ins.

Several of the new VST plug-in effects can be synchronised to the song tempo in Cubase VST, and several of the VST plug-in effects affect the stereo image, particularly with panning, stereo enhancement or stereo ambience. However, for this to be audible, the output of the effect must be routed to a stereo channel or bus, or the output will be mixed to mono, as you'd probably expect. For this reason, stereo-image effects won't be heard if the effect is used as an insert effect for a mono audio channel. If you want to apply an effect such as auto-panning to a mono audio channel, either use a send effect or route the mono audio channel to a group channel and apply the effect as an insert effect for the group channel. If you decide on the first option, you'll probably want to activate the Pre-Fader Send switch and turn down the volume fader for the audio channel.

I'm not going to go into great technical detail about these bundled plug-in effects, because the best way to find out what they can do is to have a play around with them. To decide what effects (if any) will enhance your particular recording, you need to hear how an effect alters your recording rather than read about what the effect is supposed to do. In addition to these fairly common effects, you can also get VST plug-ins for pitch correction, noise removal, creative distortion, spectral enhancement, vocoding, etc. However, as a quick reference, here's a brief run-down of the main new effects included in Cubase VST 5.0.

Chorus

The Chorus plug-in adds a short delay to the signal and modulates the pitch of the delayed signal to produce a kind of doubling effect. Chorus is often a nice effect for acoustic instruments, particularly guitars and strings, or for rounding out pad sounds. If you don't overdo it, chorus can create an illusion of movement and help you build a front-to-back perspective in the mix. However, it does detune your sound a bit, and can get a bit samey if the effect is too strong. It can also push sounds further back in the mix.

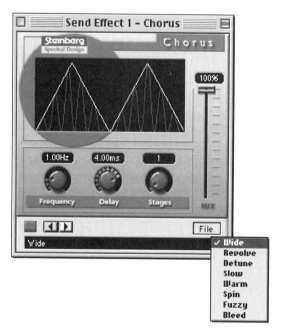

DoubleDelay

Delay is effectively an echo control, and this effect provides two separate tempo-based delays, while Cubase automatically provides it with the current song tempo. Along with judicious use of reverb, delay can be one of the most useful effects in your production process, although it's perhaps more important with this effect than with any other that it's applied in the mix, rather than during the actual recording. However, it can be used effectively on guitars, vocals and most other instruments, apart from heavy bass sounds.

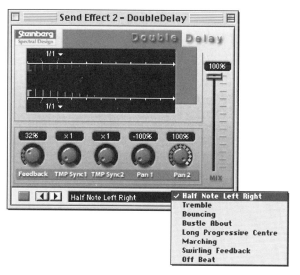

ModDelay

This is another kind of delay which modulates repeats. It can either be tempo-based or it can use freely-specified delay-time settings. This works particularly well on things like vocals, guitars and pad sounds.

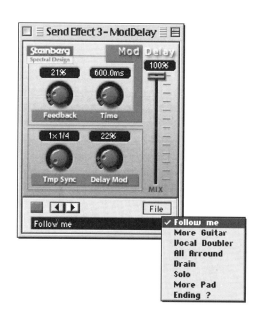

WildFlanger

WildFlanger is a classic flanger effect with stereo enhancement. Flanging is similar to the chorus effect but gives a more sweeping sound, with some elements of the phaser. While flangers can be reminiscent of '80s MOR, this is a really cool effect, and can be useful for thickening or sweetening your mix and producing some funky effects with beats. It works well with a whole range of instruments, including bass and strings, and this is one effect that actually works well when combined with other effects.

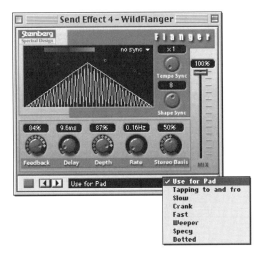

Symphonic

The Symphonic plug-in combines a stereo enhancer, an auto-panner synced to tempo and a chorus-type effect. This is another effect that is very good at fattening up a sound and creating a warmer effect. It's good for strings and acoustic instruments, and for best results try applying it to stereo signals. It's also great for pad sounds.

Phaser

Unlike the classic *Star Trek* weapon that can be set to stun or kill, the Phaser plug-in produces the classic swooshing sound immortalised in stunning, iconic rock tracks such as 'Itchycoo Park' and Status Quo's nearly credible 'Pictures Of Matchstick Men'. (Just kidding about the "stunning" and "iconic" references, by the way.) Of course this effect has been used in loads of different ways by loads of different artists, and it works by shifting the phase of the signal and then adding it back to the original signal, which causes

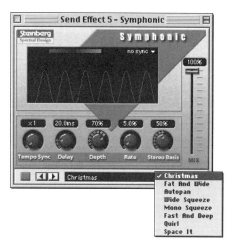

partial cancellation of the frequency spectrum. It's very good when used with pads, but if it's used too much, it can muddy the mix. It can also be used effectively in combination with other effects.

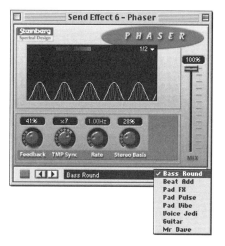

Distortion

The Distortion effect plug-in is capable of producing anything from a soft crunch to all-out distortion. There's a selection of factory presets available, and these presets are different basic distortion algorithms rather than stored parameter settings. The basic characters of the distortion preset "models" are indicated by their names, and while it may not make you sound like Hendrix you can get a lot of the classic rock/grunge guitar sounds with this.

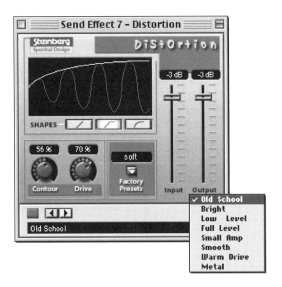

Overdrive

Overdrive is a distortion-type effect that emulates the sound of a guitar amplifier. There's a selection of factory styles available, and none of these are stored parameter settings, either, but different basic overdrive algorithms. Like Distortion, the characteristics of these are indicated by the style names. This effect could be helpful if you want to sound like Jerry Garcia.

Chopper2

With no resemblance whatsoever to a Harley Davidson, Chopper2 is a combined tremolo and autopan effect. It can use different waveforms to modulate tremolo level or pan position, using either the Tempo Sync control or manual modulation speed settings. It can also produce autopan effects when set to stereo and liven up synth sounds, and it also works well with a flanger.

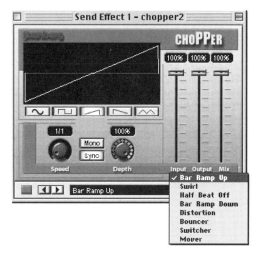

Reverb

Reverb is used to add ambience and space to recordings, and it's one of the most important and most commonly used effects in popular music. It works well on instruments and vocals but, like all effects, should be used sparingly.

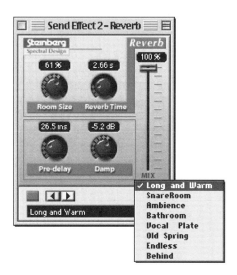

Reverb 32 (VST/32 only)

Reverb 32 is a reverb plug-in which provides smooth, dense reverb effects. Even better than normal reverb, this actually gives you dimensional sound, and you can control the size and depth of the "room".

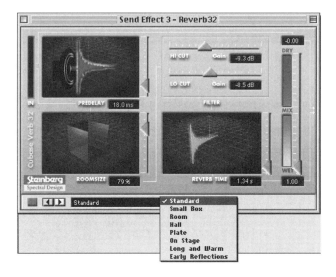

Metalizer2

The Metalizer2 feeds the audio signal through a variable-frequency filter, with tempo sync or time modulation and feedback control. This is great if you're looking for that Aerosmith or Black Sabbath sound.

Tranceformer2

Tranceformer2 is a ring-modulator effect in which the incoming audio is ring modulated by an internal, variable-frequency oscillator, producing new harmonics. A second oscillator can be used to modulate the frequency of the first oscillator, synchronised to the song tempo.

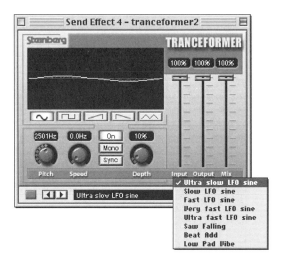

Karlette

This is a four-channel delay that emulates a "tape-loop" echo, like that produced by units like the CopyCat in the late '60s. The four "tape heads" can be set to a certain note value or a certain time, depending on whether

Tempo Sync is activated or not. For each of the four "tape heads", you can set a variety of parameters, and it's a great program for making early-Brian Eno effects. The sync feature is ideal for automatically adjusting delay times to the tempo of your song, and it's a good general effect for lead or solo instruments.

Grungelizer

The Grungelizer adds noise and static to your recordings and produces sounds which are kind of like those produced by a poorly tuned radio or a worn and scratched vinyl record. It's great for use with beats and samples, for remixes or for artificially ageing a sound, and it can also be used with other effects to create an absolutely filthy guitar sound.

Cubase dynamics

You can radically alter the dynamic range or level of audio material in Cubase by using the built-in Dynamic processor. Each audio channel has its own VST Dynamics section, which is opened by clicking on the FX button of the chosen channel strip in the Channel Mixer or by clicking the FX button in the Inspector.

This panel gives you access to AutoGate, AutoLevel, Compress, SoftClip and Limit processors, and when you click on one or more of the processor label buttons the dynamic is inserted after any regular insert effects and before the EQ section and channel fader. As soon as any of these processors is activated, its label lights up, as does the Dyn button in the channel strip. When you've enabled the desired processors and made your settings, you can turn dynamics on and off for particular channels via the VST Channel Mixer window by holding down the Command key and clicking the Dyn button for the channel.

So, what do these weird processor names actually do?

- <u>AutoGate</u> – This is a noise gate similar to that produced by hardware devices found in traditional studios, and is used for cutting out unwanted signals such as noise and interference which may be present between sections of the stuff you want.

- <u>AutoLevel</u> – This is an automatic level control designed to even out signal differences in audio material and to boost low-level or attenuate high-level signals.

- <u>Compress</u> – Like standard audio compressors used in traditional studios, this converts loud parts into quieter parts and quiet parts into louder parts.

- SoftClip – This is like an automatic gain control which you can't really adjust. It's designed to keep sounds within certain decibel parameters and to create a warmer, valve-amp-style sound.

- Limit – This is generally used to stop an output signal from passing above a set threshold, no matter how loud the input becomes.

These VST dynamics are only available for regular audio channels and won't work with groups, ReWire or instrument channels.

applying effects

Effects in Cubase are applied essentially in three ways:

- Insert effects – These are applied separately to each channel using the channel insert in the VST Channel Mixer and are used when you want all sound from a particular channel to be processed. You can use the same effect a number of times in different insert racks, since each audio channel has its own set of independent insert effects;

- Send effects – These are applied separately to each channel by using the effect sends in the VST Channel Mixer and are used when you want to mix the effect with a signal you've recorded "dry". You usually use these with reverb, chorus, delay, etc. Send effects are usually mono-in/stereo-out devices;

- Master effects – These accept stereo input and are inserted into the master mix when you want to process the final stereo mix. This is where to use things like noise-reduction devices, compressors, limiters or anything that will change the overall characteristics of your final stereo sound.

The Bypass buttons on the various effects mentioned above deactivate the effect or EQ so that you can hear your original sound. To reduce the load imposed on your processor, switch off any effects that you aren't using at the time.

Another tip is not to be tempted to bash the send and return levels of the send effects full on and leave them there. Instead, set the level to around 75-80% and adjust accordingly while keeping an eye on the clip indicator, which is just above the On button in Cubase's send effects rack. Remember what I said about distortion, and don't let it clip.

Before you use any effect anywhere in your music, stop and ask yourself, "Why?" Or perhaps, more specifically, "Is this really necessary?" Because they're so easy to use, effects generally suffer from over-use. Obviously, different generic types of music require – or, at least, lend themselves to – particular effects which would otherwise be about as inappropriate as spats at an Idaho picnic. Remember, effects are there to create an illusion, so don't let them become delusions.

chapter 9

studio session
part three

"The ability to use digital audio editing tools on Macs gives more power to musicians. It allows a guitar-based band like ours to do our own sampling and producing."
  – Jeff Robbins, guitarist with Orbit

B y now, you've begun to discover that, when it comes to organising a recording session and laying down tracks in Cubase VST, there are a number of ways of doing the same job. Because Cubase VST is so packed with features and functionality, it's easy to become overwhelmed by the sheer potential of what's on offer. However, as I've said before, and will probably say again, think about the style of music you're trying to record and the overall sound you're trying to achieve. Then think about how you like to work. Do you like to adjust every possible parameter manually, or are you happy to automate certain tasks and features? Do you want to play every real instrument yourself, or are you happy to use samples or MIDI instruments? Are you recording set songs with arranged parts, or do you want to use Cubase as part of the creative process of composing and arranging "on the fly"? How complicated are your arrangements and instrumentation? What are the limitations of your overall system – Mac, sound card, external mixer, microphones, etc? Cubase VST is like Photoshop, QuarkXPress or any other powerful Mac application: everyone uses it differently. As Karl Marx suggested, it's a case of to each according to his or her ability, to each according to his or her need. And you should need no extra encouragement from Apple or anyone else to "think different".

As we've seen, it's reasonably straightforward to select an audio or MIDI track, press the Record button and end up with a track to work with; but the more you use Cubase, the more you may find that you want a bit more visual feedback to help you get a fuller picture of what's going on with your song at each stage in the recording and polishing processes. Depending on the size of your monitor, you'll probably want to keep the Arrange window and the Inspector open during recording, and you'll always want access to the Transport bar. You may also want to keep the VST Channel Mixer open and monitor the level of your input signal during recording. When you start recording seriously, you'll find that it's always better to save all files related to a song in the same folder. It makes life easier later on, and you don't have to go searching all over your hard disk.

OK, so now you know the basics of audio and MIDI recording and can record tracks into Cubase. You know what tools to use for basic editing, and you know how to access VST effects and instruments. You also know about the internal mixers and how you might begin to mix and process the tracks you've recorded. So now let's get back into the virtual studio and look at some of these features in more detail and check out some other techniques and functionality that might improve your creative working practice and help you polish that final mix.

more of the same

When you record on an audio track, you can always go back and record more onto the same track simply by moving the left locator to the position where you want to start recording. This might be a free area or a particular point where something has already been recorded and where you want to overdub another version or a new part. When you position the left locator and record as normal, a new file is automatically created. However, MIDI tracks behave slightly differently when it comes to overdubbing parts, in that, when you record over a part, what you end up with is determined by the setting of the Overdub/Replace switch on the Transport bar. In Overdub mode, your new recording is added to whatever was already on the track, and when you play back you hear both recordings. (You can edit out the bits you don't want later.) However, when Replace is selected, whatever you record replaces what was previously there. So, you can use Overdub when you want to experiment with a number of different variations and then decide what to keep later, while you can use Replace if you've just made a mistake and you want to correct it by laying down a new version.

MIDI Overdub and Replace

pleased as punch

One of the most useful tricks in any multitrack recording is the ability to punch in sections of a song. While we'd all like to be one-take wonders, the reality of studio recording is that, more often then not, you simply don't get an absolutely perfect take. For example, you might get a wonderful vocal performance that has a few glitches in the chorus, or maybe half of that guitar solo was brilliant but the last bit was complete pants. Rather than risk a whole retake and, quite possibly, an inferior performance, you can punch in a new section at the point where the mistakes occur and keep the rest of the performance intact. When you punch in, you activate Record mode while the track is playing and replace the section you've chosen. To do this smoothly, mark the section you want to replace or note the timing, get the singer or the guitar player to start at the beginning of the section, or at least several bars before the glitch, and then simply click the Punch-In button on the Transport bar and click the Punch-Out button when you've finished. (Remember, if you're punching in a MIDI track, click the Replace button on the Transport bar before recording the punch-in point.)

Punch-In button activated on the Transport bar

You can automate the punch-in and -out points by positioning the left or right locator at the point where you want the new bit to be punched in and clicking the Punch-In button. Then, when your song plays and reaches the left locator, Record mode will be activated. You can then either punch out by clicking the Punch-Out button manually, or you can set the right locator to the point at which you want recording to stop and then click on the Punch-Out button. Then, when the song reaches that point, recording will stop. You can also punch in while recording in Cycle mode, so that the track or section plays back in a continuous loop until you get the part right.

leaving a mark

To make it easier to determine which bit of a track you want to punch in or make other alterations to, you can define an area with a marker track. Marker tracks give you more visual information and make it easier to move locators and the song position in the Arrange window. To create a marker track, click the Marker button at the top of the Arrange window.

Using the Pencil tool, draw a part in the ruler. When you've finished, a box will appear and you can name the part.

Then type in a name for the part or leave the default name for the track. Now you've got an additional visual marker to help with your arrangement.

You can use the Arrow, Pencil, Eraser, Scissors, Glue and Selection-Range tools to edit your marker tracks, and generally these tracks are handled just like regular parts. However, marker tracks cannot overlap. Also, it's not possible to select an entire marker track, and neither can you click and drag to select several marker parts. If you want to select several parts on a marker track, you have to hold down the Shift key and click on the parts one at a time, or you can hold down the Shift key and double-click one part to select all consecutive parts. Clicking on a marker part with the Selection-Range tool selects everything in the Arrange window between the start and end points of the marker part. You can use this tool as a quick way of copying and moving sections of an arrangement or dragging the marker part to a new position.

folder tracks

A wonderful feature introduced with Cubase 5.0 is the *folder track*. This is a way of reducing the clutter associated with a large number of tracks in the Arrange window, and also of simplifying use of the Track Mixer window.

Folder tracks can be used in many helpful ways, but a good way of grasping their potential is by considering how your arrangement breaks down, in terms of sections. For example, if you're composing an orchestral piece, you may decide that all of the various string sounds you're using (violins, violas, cellos etc) can be regarded as a section – that is, as a single, mixable entity. If you create a folder track called, say, "Strings", and place all of the associated channels inside that folder, then not only can you temporarily hide them within the Arrange window but you can also reduce the number of (temporarily) visible channels in the Track Mixer merely by closing the folder. If you're using a lot of instruments – and under OMS it might be several hundred! – then the Track Mixer can be wider than even two 21" monitors can display at once. However, it also means that, provided that you've mixed the components of the folder relative to one another, you can then close the folder and use only the "Strings" fader within the Track Mixer to control them all at once. This is the same as using the Group mixer with audio tracks, and it offers the same convenience.

There are times when it's useful to group instrument tracks into a single folder. For example, when you lay down all of your drum and percussion tracks, you could put all of those tracks into a single folder. Or, if you want to experiment with a number of different takes, you could group these together into a single folder, too. This is also a good way of soloing and muting several tracks easily, as well as editing and mixing several tracks as one entity. Consistent with all Mac applications, Cubase folder tracks can contain any type of track, including other folder tracks.

Folder tracks are created just like any other track. Simply select Create Track from the Structure menu, pull down the pop-up menu in the C column for the newly created track and select Folder Track. You'll see a folder appear in the C column, indicating that the track is a folder track, and you can name it just like you can any other track. You can move any type of track into a folder by dragging and dropping or by using the Structure menu. Just click on a track that you want to move in the track list and drag it into a folder track. Tracks inside a folder can be edited as one entity by selecting a folder track and opening an editor. However, the events which are shown in the editor will depend on the classes of the tracks within the folder. With instruments grouped in folders, you can also pre-mix each of them and then only have to "master mix" the folder in the Track Mixer.

Option-Command-clicking on a single folder within the Arrange window will open or close them all at once. Here, the folders are open

Folders closed

quantizing

In music perhaps more than anything else, timing is everything. Without it, your whole composition and performance will fall apart. This is why one of the most often-used features in Cubase – no matter what style or genre of music is being played – is the Quantize function. Although we've looked at this function briefly in earlier sessions, it's definitely worth getting to know it on a more intimate basis. Cubase offers a number of different types of quantize functionality, but in principle quantizing essentially shifts notes onto or close to the division of the bar that is set in the Quantize box.

When working with MIDI, the "Quantizing Type" is selected from the Function menu, and when you access this you'll note that there are five basic quantizing types.

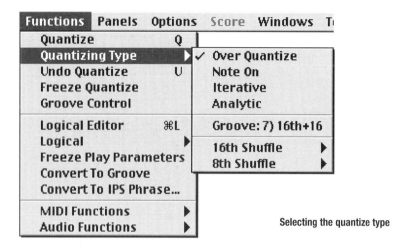

Selecting the quantize type

- Over Quantize – This is the one you'll probably use the most, since it's the Cubase equivalent of a spell-check or auto-correct. What it does is move your notes to the closest quantize value without changing the actual lengths of the notes themselves. It also detects if your playing is consistently behind or ahead of the beat and will quantize your chords in a reasonably intelligent manner.

- Note On Quantize – This is probably the least musical method, since it uses the Note On element of notes to shift them to the nearest quantize value without giving much thought to context. It's supposed to leave your original note lengths unchanged, and essentially it quantizes the start positions of the notes just like Over Quantize but, since it doesn't move the end positions, in effect the note lengths are adjusted slightly.

- Iterative Quantize – This is a good choice if you want to clean up your timing but you don't want an overly rigid or precise feel to the music. Instead of moving a note to the closest quantize value, this option moves it only part of the way, and you get to specify how far the notes should be moved towards the selected quantize value with the Iterative Q: Strength Percentage parameter in the MIDI Quantize dialog box in the Preferences. Here, you can also choose Don't Iterative Q Notes Closer Than, which is a value in 16th notes and ticks which tells Cubase how far to shift notes that aren't close enough to the quantize value. Since only notes further away than the specified value get moved, you can allow for a certain amount of "loose" timing while still being able to tighten up those really dodgy notes.

- Analytic Quantize – This corrects timing glitches according to an intelligent analysis of your music based on the quantize value and the music's actual characteristics. You'll want to use this with complex rhythms and solos.

- Groove Quantize – As the name implies, this is used to create a rhythmic "feel" or "groove", rather than to simply correct errors. It compares your music with a groove pattern and moves notes so that their timing matches that groove. You can create your own rhythmic templates, or groove maps, or you can use the selection of grooves included in Cubase VST.

- Match Quantize – This is a special function in the Arrange window toolbox that is designed to impose timing and an overall "feel" of a particular part. It also works when you drag an audio part onto a MIDI part.

The three quantizing types you'll probably use most in Cubase are Over, Iterative and Groove Quantize. With MIDI parts, quantize affects only the notes and leaves other kinds of MIDI messages unchanged. With the exception of Iterative Quantize, your original notes will always be used for calculating any subsequent quantizing, since none of your MIDI data is changed permanently.

To quantize audio, you're better off working in the Audio Editor rather than trying to do it in the Arrange window. Also, you can only use Over Quantize and Groove Quantize for most audio work, although Match Quantize can be used to push the timing of audio material onto MIDI data and vice versa.

quantize value

You can decide how accurately or roughly to quantize you tracks by setting a value in the pop-up menu in the Status bar of the Arrange window.

Quantize Value menu

If you select Off, obviously no quantizing will take place. The number in the column below the Off option selects basic note values, ranging from 1 (a whole note) to 128 (a 128th note). To put it as simply as possible, the larger the number you choose, the more accurately Cubase will quantize your notes and the grid that it will quantize to will be that much finer. The larger the number you choose, the larger the grid to which Cubase will quantize and the less precise the match. If you also drag the mouse to one of the columns on the right, you can add a "T", which will result in a tuplet; or if you select a ".", the result is dotted.

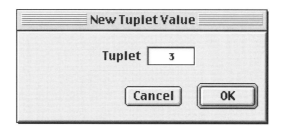

Choosing a tuplet value

Generally, you'll want to set the tuplet value to 3 so that you can use triplets for quantize values. OK, that's great if you understand music theory and notation, but if you don't then just think of the value menu as a graduated control and experiment with the sounds produced by different settings.

So, how do you know if you've used the right quantize option? Well, listen to the result. Is it the sound you wanted? If it is, you've made the right choice. If not, it's easy enough to go back and try some of the other options.

multitrack recording

Among all of the cool features of Cubase, there's a function called Multirecord, which can seem like a bit of a mystery to dedicated non-readers of manuals. Although I've been told that this is a popular subject in Steinberg Technical Support, you can get your head around this in a few easy steps, and there are probably occasions when using Multirecord will make your recording life a lot easier.

So, what exactly can you do with multitrack recording? Well, to begin with, multitrack recording allows you to record a band – or at least a number of players – all at the same time and still have their performances appear on one track each. This can be particularly useful if the audio channels that you're about to record aren't directly related but you still want to record them at the same time. If you have a keyboard or some other MIDI controller that can transmit on several MIDI channels, multitrack recording allows you to record different MIDI channels onto different tracks. Multitrack recording also allows you to "layer" several MIDI sounds and record them on one track each.

To set up multitrack recording, go to the Options menu and select Audio Setup and then System, which will launch the Audio System Setup window. Make sure that you have the correct card and driver selected before you continue.

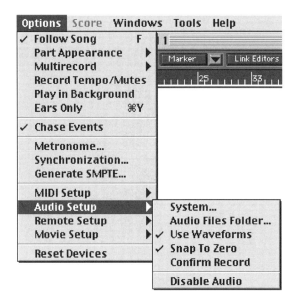

Selecting options for
multitrack recording

Go to the pull-down Panel menu and select VST Inputs. At this point, you'll see a list of the inputs that your audio card is capable of activating. The only thing that might throw you off here is that everything is listed in stereo pairs. For example, channel 1 = IN 1 L, and channel 2 = IN 1 R. This can get extremely confusing, so what you can do to make things simpler is rename the inputs as simply Input 1, Input 2 and so on. Now, to set up Multirecord, go to the Options pull-down menu and select Multirecord. Basically, what you want to do in this case is make sure that Multirecord is set to Active and also Merge. This will ensure that not only will you be able to multirecord but also that everything that's recorded will be recorded to its own track.

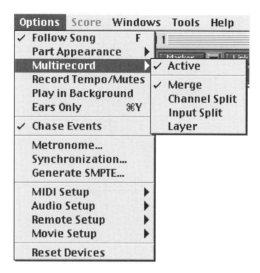

Setting Multirecord mode to Active and Merge

Routing the audio is the next step. You'll notice that, when the Audio 1 track is selected, the input that's selected on the far left is Input 1, while Audio 2 will be Input 2. When you get to Audio 3 or further, you'll notice that the input selected for this audio track is Input 1 again. This obviously won't do, so all you need to do is select a new input for Audio 3, which you can do by holding down the Command key and selecting a new input. For example, Audio 3 should be set to Input 3 and Audio 4 should be set to Input 4. You'll want to repeat this until all eight of your audio tracks have their own selected audio input.

Your set-up is now complete. In order to start multirecording your audio, just Enable the audio tracks that you want to record onto and you're good to go. As you can see, multirecording is easy to accomplish with just a few quick set-up steps.

samplers

Ever since the Musicians' Union complained to the BBC about the use of synthetic orchestras when the Mellotron first came into use, in the mid '60s, the use of virtual orchestration has been gaining in popularity and realism.

When the Fairlight CMI brought digital sampling to the musical world in the early '80s, it brought with it unprecedented capabilities, which are now commonplace. While an increasing amount of contemporary music relies heavily on sampling, producers and audiophiles seem to delight in maintaining a barrier of mystique around a process which – conceptually, at least – is really very simple.

A sampler is essentially a synthesiser into which you can record your own sounds to use as raw material, rather than relying on a set of factory samples or waveforms. Unlike the permanent ROM-based sounds found in synths, samplers store everything in RAM so that, when you turn off your machine, all of your sounds are lost. Obviously, some form of larger, permanent sound storage facility is essential, like a hard drive or a removable drive, such as a Zip or Jaz drive. Otherwise, you'd have to sample a new sound every time you switched on, which would be extremely frustrating and tedious. Most samplers come with an built-in floppy drive, but you can be sure that this will be far too small for most serious sampling work. Unfortunately, the most common samplers also have their own floppy-disk formats, so you can't duplicate these floppies in your Mac's floppy drive (if you still have one) or transfer your samples directly to your computer's hard drive.

When semi-affordable samplers first came onto the scene, in the late '80s, everyone went around smashing bottles, hitting pans, recording the dog and doing all sorts of other wacky things to come up with new musical sounds. With a sampler, even the most mundane sound can be transformed into something musically useable simply by shifting it out of its usual pitch range. To make these sounds play back as chords, the sampler needs to work polyphonically, in the same way as a synthesiser; and, just as on any synth, there's a limit to the polyphony at your disposal.

After the novelty of sampling the dog barking or cousin Cletus burping, most serious musicians figured out that, if they could sample individual notes from instruments, they could also – given enough RAM memory – sample entire musical phrases or whole bars of drum rhythms. That's partly why sampling whole chunks of music is the cornerstone of modern dance music, which is generally built up from a series of drum loops. The term *loop* here simply refers to a sampled section that can be repeated to form a continuous piece of music. However, you wouldn't normally loop this in the sampler; you'd trigger it once every bar.

Using samples with Cubase can really enhance your music. However, as with so many things to do with digital recording, be aware that working with samples always requires more memory than you'd imagine, and more often than not you'll always need more memory than you have. Keep in mind that a one-minute-long mono sample will require about 5MB of RAM at the CD sample rate of 44.1kHz. A minute may seem like a long time, but recording stereo samples will halve the available time. What's more, if you use the sampler multitimbrally, the memory will have to hold several sounds at the same time, which further reduces the lengths of individual sounds. As if that wasn't bad enough, some instruments have to be sampled every few semitones in order to create a set of samples that sounds convincing over the entire keyboard range, and again this takes memory. The good news is that RAM is now quite cheap, and most modern samplers let you add regular computer RAM, rather than expensive proprietary memory boards. So, even if you're working on a tight budget, it's worth filling your sampler to capacity as soon as possible.

The process of sampling isn't difficult, but it can be incredibly time-consuming, especially where multisampling or looping is required. Loads of high-quality instrument sounds are available from sample libraries provided by companies like Time & Space. Although sample CDs and CD-ROMs can be expensive, they relieve you of an enormous amount of work. And when it comes to orchestral sounds, for example, few struggling musicians would have the resources to create these for themselves, let alone hire in an orchestra. CD-ROMs do all the looping and key-grouping work for you, while CDs contain audio samples alone, which you still have to loop and organise into key groups, so I'd strongly recommend that anyone without a CD-ROM drive gets one as soon as possible. Most library CD-ROMs are supplied in a format suitable for Akai samplers, but current Roland and Emu models will usually read each other's formats without too much trouble.

If you get into using a sampler, you'll discover that most sounds can become quite unnatural when transposed too far from their original pitch. Although this can sometimes be a creative advantage, in most instances you'll probably want instruments to sound as realistic as possible, especially pianos and orchestral instruments. The only way to maintain a natural sound is to take several samples of the instrument at different pitches and then use each sample over only a limited part of the keyboard. Ideally, you'd take a fresh sample every semitone, but that gobbles up a load of memory and takes forever. In practice, using the same sample over a range of three or four semitones is generally accurate enough even for the most critical instruments, and often you can get away with far fewer samples. Pianos are very critical, but things like bowed strings and wind instruments are more forgiving. To get the most natural sound possible, even though you're playing from a keyboard, try to play instruments with the same style and intonation with which they're played in real life – ie don't play chords on instruments like flutes or other instruments that aren't naturally used for chords.

Sample CDs come in a number of different formats, and it's important to know which format will be best suited to your budget and your studio set-up before you buy. This most basic and, therefore, cheapest way of presenting sounds is on a sample audio CD, like the ones you play on a normal audio CD player. Nearly all releases support this format, which allows quick access to all tracks and is an excellent way of auditioning sounds before you fire them into your sampler. On the downside, you do have to do all of the sampling, editing, looping and programming of the sounds yourself, and if you're sampling the Mormon Tabernacle Choir or string multisamples from the New York Philharmonic, this can be a real pig to get right and often requires an in-depth knowledge of your chosen sampler platform that borders on the geeky and the patience of a particularly patient saint. Some sample CDs consist of longer drum loops or instrument grooves, and these are often easier to deal with in audio format than, say, a CD's worth of complex orchestral or piano samples.

The best and most efficient way of presenting sampled sounds is the CD-ROM. The main advantage of this format is that all of the sounds are stored on the CD-ROM – as well as programmed data, loop points, crossfades and preset names – as good old digital information, which can be fed directly to your sampler via SCSI. Once your CD-ROM is in your sampler's SCSI chain, it can be treated like any another independent (read-only) hard drive. Loading up a preset or group of presets from a CD-ROM is an extremely quick and easy procedure and, of course, gives you all of the sounds you need to use already edited, named, assigned to the appropriate keys and ready to play straight away. The main disadvantage of CD-ROM samples, however, is their relatively high price. You'll find that it's not unusual for sample ROMs to retail at around the £150 mark, as opposed to their audio equivalents, which sell for around £60. But then again, where else could you get a full symphony orchestra to perform on your track for less than half the price of a basic effect unit?

The other main format – which is becoming increasingly popular, particularly in the budget section of the market – is the "mixed-mode" CD-ROM. As its name implies, this format contains both conventional audio recordings and sample data, which is stored so that it can be accessed via SCSI. These days, a common mixture of the two can be found, for instance in the *Creative Essentials* library from Time & Space, where, as well as audio files that can be auditioned and sampled from any CD player, the raw sample blocks are presented as both WAV and AIFF files, so that they can be accessed directly by a PC or a Mac.

In practice, as a musician, just try to remember that an open-minded approach works best for any sample-CD sound source. Don't instantly assume that the sounds you'll end up using in your track will be anything like the CDs from which you sample, and keep in mind the vast number of effects options available with even the humblest sampler. Try to use sample CDs less as a preset-bashing exercise and more as a platform for creative experimentation. For example, instead of loading up an entire program of string or choir multisamples, why not just look at a single sample? What might it sound like an octave higher, or lower, and what happens when you play around with its ADSR (Attack, Decay, Sustain, Release) envelope? Could that single cello sound with the sharp attack work nicely as a grindy techno bass noise? Or could you drop it by a few octaves, add a long release time and use it as an underscore for the next series of *Roswell High*?

If your sampler allows you to play with any resonant filters, think about what effect these might have on the overall sound. This is a particularly common effect used on dance drum loops, where the same sample is assigned to a number of different keys, each with a slightly more open filter setting than the last, restricting the top end of the sound. The effect is that of a drum loop starting as a sort of distant, lo-fi grinding noise, and each time it cycles around it becomes louder and more defined, until the sample plays back at full bandwidth in all its glory. This is a neat trick, and it requires little programming.

Everyone gets stuck in creative ruts, and one of the most enlightening experiences is to watch someone else work with the same sounds and approach things from a completely different point of view. This also applies to Cubase in general and it's always enlightening to see how other musicians and producers work. Although sequencers and samplers don't normally allow more than one person to work on them at once, musical collaboration is perhaps more relevant now than it ever was, so don't be shy about inviting like-minded individuals around for an afternoon of playing with your sample CDs to see which sounds they find most interesting. With experimentation in mind, don't be afraid to get really stuck in with external effects processing or even maybe even resampling the same sounds and applying additional effects. You'll need an additional hard drive or removable drives to store your new versions of sounds, but you'd be surprised at just how much life you can breathe into even the dullest drum loop or bass groove if you beef up the EQ, add some compression and chorus and even perhaps a touch of distortion, mix it to DAT and re-record it as a new sample.

While software packages such as Steinberg's ReCycle can be a big help in re-grooving old samples, fairly simple cut-and-paste editing within your sampler can give you the constituent beats of a loop which you can then re-program with a completely new feel, tempo or groove. Once you're happy with the loops, drop them down to DAT (or similar), with a suitable effect if need be, and resample them as single one- or two-bar loops. And don't be afraid to mix and match your samples; releases that offer you groove tracks complete with drums, bass and keyboards are often more flexible than you might think. Don't assume that the sax solo from track 2, for instance, won't sound great over the drum and bass line from track 24.

There's no doubt that, as sampling becomes a bigger and more influential part of our musical lives, we will see more and more sounds released in the sample-CD format. Some manufacturers even provide downloadable sounds from their Web pages. However, the most creative implements in your toolbox are the ones stuck on the sides of your head. If it sounds right, it is right. You might even find that the most useful samples come from your own recordings, since these samples will generally display the right style and the right kind of character to fit the music. It may not be a sample-manipulation technique as such, but you should get used to listening out for those golden moments in your own material. Sampling extracts from your own music and running them through EQ and effects could send you off on an unexpected journey, if not a completely weird and twisted trip.

chapter 10

studio session part four

"There's a lot of stuff in there that I never use. I go through the menus, and there's just a lot of things I have never even gone into."
 – Moby on using Cubase

In the weird world of audio recording, it's generally agreed that the word "mixing" means two different things. It's the process of adjusting the fader levels, balance, equalisation, etc, so that the live sound is properly recorded in the first place, but it's also the art of turning the live, recorded sound into a finished, polished masterpiece that's ready to listen to. OK, so you might argue that I'm splitting hairs here, since the second step involves much of the same kind of adjusting, balancing and EQing as the first, and particularly with programs like Cubase VST – where these boundaries and processes are conveniently blurred – it might be difficult to see where the boundaries are. I suppose you could say that the techniques and skills involved in recording are more prosaic, while mixing tends to border on the poetic. Mixing down from multiple tracks to stereo is the second step of the overall process of making a finished song. With Cubase, you'll basically be flipping a few virtual switches on your mixers, turning your machine from a recording console into a mixing console. As in cooking, you'll be adding seasoning – such as effects and EQ – to taste.

While most people focus on recording, most of the creativity and personal satisfaction of the entire proccss can often come in the mixing session, for much the same reason that some people would rather be film editors than cinematographers, I suppose. Mixing is where all the hard decisions are made, and can make the difference between either arriving at a workmanlike recording and achieving a masterpiece of sound with the same given source material.

When your mix is finished, you'll need to think about mastering it to a medium such as DAT or CD. This also takes some special skill, but it's also something that you pick up with experience.

Before the modern era of multitrack tape and the eventual evolution of desktop digital studios, recording and mixing were essentially part of the same process. You had to get a good balance between the voices and instruments and the best possible sound right there during the recording session, because there was no way of making adjustments later. In these kinds of situations, the final recording needed to sound as close to the original as possible.

Today, although this still might be your own personal goal, with your Mac and Cubase you now have a lot more flexibility over how you lay down your tracks and ultimately mix them together to create your own sound. During the recording process, basic monitoring facilities can provide you with a reasonable "ear" to help you adjust a range of parameters, such as level, pan and auxiliary sends; and since, with Cubase, you can hear exactly what's on your tracks as you progress through the recording, if your monitor mix sounds good then your final mix will probably sound great. You should regard everything you do as being part of the finished product and make it as perfect as possible.

Ideally, you'll probably want to start the mixing process as soon as your project gets off the ground. You should have a pretty clear idea of the sound you're aiming for, allowing for a certain amount of scope for creativity and synchronicity, although of course this will depend on the nature and style of your song. For instance, if it's a dance record, you'll need to understand the style well enough to know the elements of the music demanded by your audience, and you should always look to include new and different sounds and textures to add to those elements to push your particular style that little bit further.

One of the great advantages of recording with Cubase on your Mac is that you're in control. You're the one who knows how every step of the preparation and recording process is going to contribute to the final mix. This means that, theoretically, without the interference of an extraneous engineer or producer, the mixing stage should be straightforward and painless. In practice, however, what this really means is that it's up to you to get the arrangement right, select the right sounds, make sure that the musicians play in time and in tune and obtain a good performance from the singer by whatever means necessary. If there's a problem with any of these areas, you can only turn a deaf ear to it for so long, and that's about as long as it takes you to get to the mix. Any problems present in your tracks at the mixing stage will have to be disguised, covered up or fixed…if possible. However, because of the power and functionality of Cubase, you should be thinking about fixing things as you go along. If there's a problem with a performance, or with the way in which a particular track is recorded, those problems should be corrected as soon as they occur. Remember, this is your studio, and you're the one who has to play producer and engineer, as well as perhaps writer, performer and arranger.

As more tracks are added during the recording stage, you can be actively working with a mix that may bear a passing resemblance to your finished product. The monitor mix is what you listen to during the recording process, and with Cubase it's usually good enough to allow you to get a proper feel for the music and to give you a reasonable idea of how the recording is shaping up. In Cubase VST, monitoring simply means listening to the signal while it's being recorded, and the exact monitor mix you end up with will depend a lot on how you've configured your own personal system. As I mentioned in Chapter 5, you've got three choices when it comes to monitoring in Cubase: via an external mixer and sound card; via Cubase VST, where the audio passes from the input into Cubase and back to the output, allowing you to control monitoring via Cubase; or directly via your audio hardware, where your Mac's audio input is connected directly to its output. This can be done either manually – by activating the Through or Monitor features on your sound card, using the card's ASIO control panel, accessed via the Audio System Setup dialog box through the Sound control panel in the Apple menu in the Finder – or in a mixer application that might be bundled with your card. Alternatively, if you have ASIO-compatible hardware, you can monitor via ASIO Direct Monitor.

Obviously, monitoring via Cubase direct has an advantage in that any effect or other setting you may make while recording will also be "accessible" on the monitored signal on both the recordings you've already made and the playback, while this won't be possible if you monitor directly via your audio hardware. The main disadvantage of using this method, however, is that there will be a certain amount of latency, although the level of this will depend on your sound card and its drivers, and cards with separate ASIO drivers may have a low enough latency to give you a signal accurate enough for monitoring purposes. When you decide to look for a sound card, make sure that you ask your dealer about problems with latency, and make sure that he understands what you're talking about. Although most cards now are pretty good, dealers still tend to skirt around the whole latency issue and respond to questions about as directly as politicians playing dodgems with Jeremy Paxman.

If you decide to use Cubase monitoring, always make sure that there's no Monitor or Through function activated in your audio hardware's mixer applications. With some audio hardware – including your Mac's built-in audio – you can change settings at any time by using the ASIO control panel in Cubase VST's Audio System Setup dialog box.

A fairly traditional style of album recording involves putting down all of the basic tracks, overdubbing other instruments and vocals and then taking a break for a few days before starting to mix the whole lot. If you work on a song at a time, all the way from getting basic tracks to mixing, your ears will go woolly and you can easily lose perspective and artistic judgment. If you over-familiarise yourself with the song and the recording, you might not be able to judge it in the same way that a punter would. Taking a break between recording and mixing means that you can come back to the song with fresh ears, and you should be able to hear very clearly which bits need to be brought out and which elements play an important but perhaps subordinate role.

The mechanics of mixing are fairly straightforward. However, what makes a good mix is a bit trickier. Since you're not a sound engineer, using Cubase as a musician means that you don't need to know all of the details about how to mix, but as a musician you *do* need to be able to recognise when something is right and to be able to understand what's missing when it isn't. You need to keep in mind the purpose of your mix – is it a dancefloor mix that should sound great on a club PA, or is it going to be listened to on a CD at home? Depending on your style and approach, you may even want to create a radio mix, emphasising some sort of "buy me" factor (whatever you think that this might be) which will attract particular listeners to your particular release.

As a general housekeeping rule, always sit in the optimum listening position (directly between the speakers) while mixing. Once you think you've got the sound you want, you'll probably want to wander around the room and listen to the mix in less-than-perfect conditions, which is exactly the way that the record buyer will probably be hearing it. Different people listen to music in different ways – in a club with the bass turned up to stomach-pounding levels; on an average, home hi-fi; or on a car radio in heavy traffic with a hole in the exhaust. Ideally, your mix has to sell the song in each of these situations, so you'll need to be listening out for the overall impact. If the mix sounds good from any listening position in your studio, it's probably OK. Proper monitor speakers will give you a true-ish representation of your sound, but you should also have a cassette copy made so that you can check the mix on a cheap stereo, on a Walkman or in the car. The more ways that you can listen to your mix the better.

Once you've completed your mix, you'll want to transfer it to DAT or burn it onto a CD. Recording geeks still whinge that DAT isn't always entirely satisfactory, because it's only 16 bit, which means that its sound quality isn't any better than the CDs people listen to at home. Personally, I tend not to worry about things that I can't hear. Most of the work that I've done in traditional studios has still been dumped to DAT, and the CD masters produced from them haven't been noticeably inferior in any way, shape or form. And despite the warnings about MiniDiscs earlier, in a lot of cases these will work just fine.

Just keep in mind that the mix is an evolutionary thing. On virtually every song you record in Cubase, you work through to the mix. The great thing about Cubase is that you never have to get to a stage where everything is finished before you start mixing; it simply evolves as you work.

OK, even though you can't really separate mixing from the rest of your recording process, it is of course the one magical point where all of your previous efforts come together and, whether we like it or not, a mix can make or break a finished song. Chapter 6 looked briefly at the various mixing desks included in Cubase and their basic functionality, so now let's see how you can use them a bit more efficiently in the final mixing process.

the VST Channel Mixer

When it comes to mixing, if your Mac was the *USS Enterprise*, Cubase's Channel or Monitor mixer would be the bridge. Like the huge hardware consoles in expensive commercial studios, this is where the real work of mixing gets done in your virtual studio.

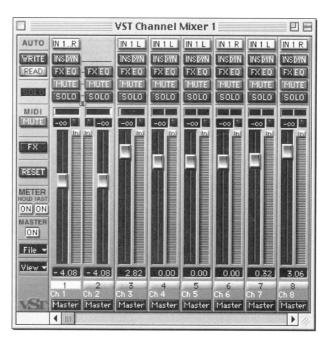

VST Channel Mixer. To make fine volume adjustments, hold down the Shift key when you move the faders

On mixdown, as well as during recording, the output level of each audio channel is controlled either with the faders in the VST Channel Mixer or with the Dynamic Volume Events control in the Audio Editor. In the Channel Mixer, each audio channel has a fader to control volume, and you can also use the Mute and Solo buttons to silence one or several channels, although the faders determine the final output level of your stereo mix. If you want to hear only the audio, click on the MIDI Mute button to the left of the VST Channel Mixer. This will mute all MIDI playback, letting you concentrate on mixing the audio.

The volume fader for an audio channel is "mirrored" in the Inspector, so any volume changes made in the Inspector are reflected in the Channel Mixer and vice versa. (Incidentally, only the left channel volume for stereo audio tracks is displayed in the Inspector.) You can use the channel, group and master faders to set up a volume balance between the audio channels and perform a manual mix by moving the faders and other controls while playing back, and you can also use the Write function to automate fader movements and other VST Channel Mixer actions. This means that nearly every action in the Channel Mixer window can be automated by writing it into a special *audiomix part*. When you play this back, the part will repeat your fader movements and button-presses just as if you performed them in real time, and you'll see the faders and buttons move on the screen, just like on expensive commercial mixers equipped with motorised controls. While the Write button is lit, every volume, pan, mute or solo movement you make will be recorded.

The Write button also works in Stop mode, as well as during playback, so if you activate Write when Cubase is stopped, all changes made to the mixer's parameters are recorded at the current Song Position. You can use this functionality quite creatively if you need, say, initial mixer settings or abrupt changes. To see what you've actually done, activate the automated playback by clicking on the Read button in the upper-left-hand corner of the Channel Mixer. (Cubase allows you to have Write and Read activated simultaneously so that you can watch and listen to your recorded mixer actions while you're recording fader movements for another channel.)

If you select Undo from the Edit menu, all actions recorded since you last activated Write will be undone, so it's a good idea to get into the habit of always deactivating Write after each recording "pass" and listening to what you've recorded. If you find all of this a little daunting, you can make separate audiomix parts for the different audio channels or record passes and then edit or delete these afterwards.

Although Cubase only creates one dedicated audiomix track, you can structure your mixer automation into different parts for different channels. You might find that this makes it easier to edit and redo those mixer recordings with which you aren't particularly satisfied. To use this method, record your fader movements and other mixer actions for the first audio channel, then deactivate the Write function and go to the Arrange window and make a new mixer track. (It's probably a good idea to name it after the audio channel you've just mixed in order to avoid any confusion later on.) After you've done that, move the entire audiomix part to the new track, then open the Channel Mixer again, activate the Write function and record your mixer actions for the next audio channel. When you do this, Cubase creates a new audiomix part on the original empty audiomix track. If you activate the Read function, the part that you recorded earlier will be played back from its new track, so you can watch your recorded fader movements while you continue working with any new audio channels, and you can repeat these steps for as many channels as you like. You'll eventually end up with a number of mixer tracks, all playing back at once and affecting different audio channels in the Channel Mixer. From here, you can either keep it like this or, if you want to clean up your Arrange window, you can merge the parts into one or put all of the tracks in a folder track.

Mixdown in Cubase VST can be completely automated, and the following parameter settings can be recorded with the Write function for each channel:

- Volume
- Pan
- Mute
- EQ Bypass switch
- Settings for 4 EQ modules
- Eight Effect Send Active switches
- Eight Effect Send levels
- Eight Effect Send PRE switches
- Effect Send Bypass switch
- Four Insert Effect Program selections
- Four Insert Effect parameters (ie the first 15 parameters for each effect).

panning

When you're mixing, you've got to decide where in the mix you want each of your instruments, vocals or sounds to be positioned. This involves panning sounds and instruments to appropriate positions in the stereo mix to achieve the desired level of depth and texture. Although panning can be used quite creatively, as a general rule vocals, bass drum, bass instruments and often snare drum are usually panned in the centre, although in some types of music you might want to pan the snare slightly off centre. Vocals can also be panned a little to the left or right, but they tend to sound better if there's a balancing vocal or similar instrument panned to the opposite side. Instruments such as guitars, brass, keyboards and backing vocals can be panned to either side, and don't forget to pan stereo effects – such as reverb – fully left and right in the mix, if you want to create a sense of width.

Of course, you can pan any instrument, vocal or pad sound back and forth in your mix to achieve the effect and "movement" you're after. As with volume, the pan or stereo position of each audio channel can be controlled with the Pan control in the Channel Mixer or with the Dynamic Pan Events control in the Audio Editor. The pan control in the Channel Mixer pans sound between the left and right side of the assigned stereo output bus, and if you want to make fine pan adjustments using this then hold down the Shift key when you move the control. If you want to select the central pan position, hold down the Command key and click on the control. Or, if you want to select whether volume or pan should be shown in the Events window, select your audio part in the Arrange window and double-click on it to open the Audio Editor. Pull down the pop-up menu immediately to the right and select the Pan option.

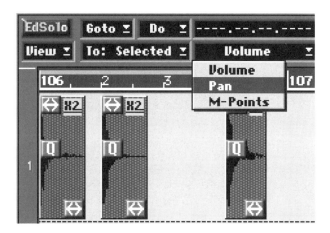

Remember that dynamic data affects the segment played by the event, so even if you have ghost events that play the same segment, any changes made to the volume/pan curve for one of the events will be reflected in the others.

A helpful tip is not to rely on the pan controls to keep your sounds separate. Try to get your mix working in mono first and then start panning the various elements. After you get a rough balance in mono using no EQ, you can then start to play around with the fine-tuning.

When you're actually recording, try to make your up-front sounds slightly brighter while at the same time keeping your background and supporting sounds less bright. Since it's always easier to cut frequencies using EQ than to boost them later, make sure that you've got enough top end in your various recordings. Also, to make sure that you keep a sense of contrast in your mix, don't process everything, or you'll end up with a muddy cacophony of competing sounds. Or something that sounds vaguely like hip-hop.

Remember that most digital editing in Cubase is non-destructive (ie the original data remains intact). In other words, nothing is deleted from your hard drive until you want it gone, even the bits of audio you may have chopped off and forgotten about. This could mean that you end up using more and more space on your hard drive – often up to 50% more – until you delete the unwanted audio. Of course, it's best not to do this until your track is completed.

effects – send, insert or master?

In Chapter 8 we looked at how Cubase handles effects and briefly touched on some points to consider before adding effects to your tracks or final mix. Although Cubase allows you to apply effects in three different ways (with the exception of EQ), for most musicians the Send Effects option is probably the most common choice for applying effects to a mix. You can use up to eight effects, and when you use Send Effects, audio is routed through the effects processors via independent effect sends for each channel, just like on a physical mixing desk. The output from each effects processor is then routed to one of the buses or to the master faders, where you can mix it with your dry (ie effect-free) signal if you desire. You'll probably find that the Effect Send option is a good choice for adding effects like echo, reverb and chorus, where you'll want to be able to balance the mix of dry and effected signals. When you use this option, effects are mono in/stereo out.

The Insert Effects option is also readily available on all audio channels in the Channel Mixer, and this inserts effects into the signal chain of an audio channel. This means that the whole channel signal passes through the effect, which makes inserts suitable for effects for which you don't need to mix dry or direct and wet (processed) sound. A good example of this would be using distortion, filters, EQ, noise gating or some other effect that changes the tonal or dynamic characteristics of a sound. Unlike with the Send Effects, because of the way in which the signal is routed, the signal level going into the inserted effects isn't affected by the level of the channel fader. The Cubase manual says that you can have up to four different insert effects per channel, but the number of effects you can actually use is restricted only by the processing power of your machine.

The Master Effects option is primarily designed for the processing you might want to undertake in a final stereo mix. Up to four stereo-in/stereo-out effects processors can be added to the signal on the final stereo mix, but there is no facility for mixing dry/effected signals here like there is with Send Effects. You'll find that you use the Master Effects option for compressor/limiter effects, noise-suppression units, loudness maximisers, etc, and you can get a whole assortment of these plug-ins (described in Chapter 8) from third-party suppliers.

Some effect plug-ins may have a certain delay, which will be particularly noticeable when you use them as insert effects. If you experience a delay in audio playback from tracks with insert effects, you should activate Plug-In Delay Compensation in the Audio System Setup dialog box, which will adjust the playback timing of the delayed tracks in order to compensate for the delay caused by the plug-ins. (You may also need to activate this option if you're using the Channel Settings VST Dynamics panel. Even though these aren't accessed as insert effects, technically they are just that, and they may also cause an audible delay.)

EQ again

Although some people insist on adding EQ while recording, as a general rule it's best not to. One good reason for this is that, when you create a mix and find out that it's not what you were hoping for, you can go back to a blank sound canvas by resetting your EQ and starting again. Another reason is that there's no way that you can really know what EQ a sound finally needs until you hear it in context with the rest of your mix. Also, trying to EQ a sound that already has EQ applied to it can create some really ugly noises. Remember that some sounds in your mix will have to take a back seat and won't be heard on their own, so in this case why record them with heavy EQ, as if they were up-front solos?

As any producer will tell you, EQ can make or break a mix. Just as a painter will mix primary colours to accentuate certain areas of a painting and draw the eye across the canvas, so too will the producer mix high, low and mid-range frequencies to achieve subtle colourings of tone that all good mixes demand. Often, when you listen back to one of your mixes, two or more sounds operating in the same frequency can combine in synergy to create a new sound which is greater than the sum of its parts. This blending of sound creates new timbres as well as distance between sounds, and this separation is particularly important in most dance music, as a lot of low frequencies infringe on each other's wavelength (ie bass lines and kick drums). In fact, a lot of producers of jungle music will pitch up their drum loops in order to allow low basses to sit comfortably in the mix. The same applies to mid-range sounds – snares, hi-hats and bongos all tend to occupy a similar wavelength and will need to stand out from each other.

EQ can vastly affect the character of a sound, but if used subtly it can change the presence of a sound without altering its tonal quality, and this is the key to achieving the spacious mixes that we're all accustomed to. With EQ, just as it is with effects, less is more, so always try cutting frequencies before boosting them.

Here are some general tips for getting a better overall sound:

- Always listen to the whole track dry, with no effects, no EQ, nothing. This will help you to determine where things should sit in the mix. Of course, if the song you're mixing utilises processed samples, this can't be done. A relatively effective way of reducing effects on pre-processed samples is to use a limiter or some form of compression. You can also target the frequency band where the sample is most effected by reducing the gain, although this can lead to unwanted tonal change;

- Thin out pads, backing vocals and acoustic guitar parts with EQ. Perversely, this dramatises the dynamics rather than diminishing them;

- Next door is were it's at. Try going into a different room and occupying yourself with something totally unrelated to music. Leave your track running. Now see what needs doing.

- Smooth the curve. Although this isn't to everyone's taste, it's definitely familiar as the radio-friendly "pro" sound of most modern recordings. The polished feel seems to rest in the mid band of the EQ, and producers tend to cut frequencies between 200Hz and 4Hz, chopping out the most in the 600Hz-1kHz region.

OK, forget the techie crap. On a graphic equaliser, like the one you have in Cubase, EQ carried out like this forms a smooth, upside-down curve, which you can just draw in graphically. Professional producers take down the mid range, as middle frequencies have a habit of tiring the ear and blocking the finer frequencies. This holds especially true on tracks that have a profusion of guitar. The "edge" that's apparently so desirable is achieved not by boosting the mid range (which seems natural) but by tweaking the top and bottom frequencies so that they interact with contrast.

I know I said I wasn't going to get into a lot of techie detail here, but when it comes to EQ, it's worth knowing a little about frequency settings for particular instruments. This will at least give you an idea of where to start with your EQ settings in Cubase, although you don't have to worry too much about whether or not you actually understand the science. To begin with, an instrument's sound is made up of a fundamental frequency, the musical note itself and harmonics, even when only a single note is played, and it's these harmonics that give the note its unique character. If you use EQ to boost the fundamental frequency, you simply make the instrument louder and don't bring it out in the mix. You should also note that a particular frequency on the EQ – 440Hz, say – corresponds directly to a musical note on the scale (which, in the case of 440Hz, is the A above middle C, hence the tuning reference "A-440"). Boosting the harmonic frequencies, on the other hand, boosts the instrument's tonal qualities, and can therefore provide it with its own space in the mix. Below are some useful frequencies for various instruments:

- Voice – Presence, 5kHz; sibilance, 7.5-10kHz; boominess, 200-240kHz; fullness, 120Hz;
- Electric guitar – Fullness, 240Hz; bite, 2.5kHz; air/sizzle, 8kHz;
- Bass guitar – Bottom, 60-80Hz; attack, 700Hz-1kHz; string noise, 2.5kHz;
- Snare drum – Fatness, 240Hz; crispness, 5kHz;

- Kick drum – Bottom, 60-80Hz; slap, 4kHz;
- Hi-hat and cymbals – Sizzle, 7.5-10kHz; clank, 200Hz;
- Toms – Attack, 5kHz; fullness, 120-240Hz;
- Acoustic guitar – Harshness/bite, 2kHz; boominess, 120-200Hz; cut, 7-10kHz.

TrueTape

TrueTape is a new feature in Cubase VST version 5.0 which is a unique Steinberg technology that emulates the behaviour of a professional analogue tape recorder. While digital audio recording has many benefits, some musicians have expressed the opinion that digital sound always tends to be somewhat sterile and cold when compared to high-quality analogue recordings, and indeed, a few years ago, Neil Young was particularly outspoken about the evils of digital sound. However, TrueTape claims to remedy this problem by recreating that good old "open-fire" sound of analogue tape saturation at the recording stage. If you're particularly into acoustic music, you might want to play around with this, if your system can handle it.

TrueTape produces 32-bit *float files*, and all of the hard-disk and processor-speed considerations of the regular 32-bit format apply here. Unlike the regular 32-bit mode, however, you can make use of the TrueTape mode even if your audio hardware only supports 16-bit resolution, because the TrueTape feature converts the signal to 32-bit float format and adds audio information in the floating-point domain. However, keep in mind that only Cubase VST/32 can play back TrueTape audio files.

Once you've selected the TrueTape 32-bit format, you can make settings by selecting VST TrueTape from the Panels menu, which brings up a control panel for TrueTape. You can then use the Drive control to adjust the amount of tape saturation to your liking, and if you're monitoring through Cubase VST you'll hear how the changes colour the sound of the monitored signal, allowing you to try out the settings before actually recording. There's a pop-up menu below the TrueTape panel which allows you to select one of four Drive presets to effect quick changes. These contain no "hidden parameters", so selecting the 24dB Super Saturation preset is the same as moving the Drive control all the way to the right. (Note that any adjustments made to the Drive control are automatically applied to the selected preset.) You can also rename a preset by double-clicking and typing in a new name, and if you raise the Drive level, you'll also raise the level in the audio file. If Input Level Metering is selected in the Channel Mixer, you may find that the clip indicators light up, although, unlike when recording in 16-bit format, this is nothing to worry about – Steinberg say that it's virtually impossible to get digital distortion in a 32-bit float file.

integrating audio and MIDI tracks

More often than not, when you're mixing audio tracks, you'll also want to use a number of MIDI tracks. Probably the easiest way of doing this – and the one you'll probably use most often – is the one mentioned in Chapter 5, where the sounds from the MIDI instruments are simply recorded onto one or more audio channels in Cubase, or perhaps onto stereo pairs. After you've done this, mute your original MIDI tracks, leaving the complete, inclusive version as audio only. You can then mix down all of the audio tracks and master the final results to DAT or CD via the analogue outputs on your Mac, via the digital outputs of your sound card or by simply exporting the lot as an audio file within your Mac using Cubase's Export Audio function.

The Export Audio function in Cubase allows you to create stereo files of your whole mix, which you can later transfer to audio CD using a normal Mac-compatible CD-R burner. It also provides a convenient way of mixing down several tracks onto one audio channel or onto stereo pairs, thus freeing up space in your audio arrangement or on your hard drive so that you can extend your recording capacity.

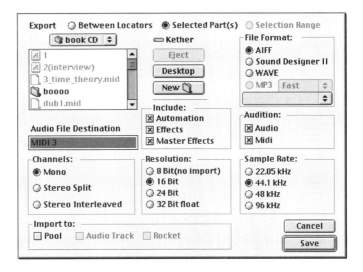

Make sure that you've already set your locators to the segment or completed tracks in the Arrange window and that you've had a good listen to make sure that the mix is exactly the way you want it. If you're happy, pull up the Export Audio dialog box and set your sample rate, channel options, resolution, etc. (You can also decide to automatically import your new file back into the Audio Pool and use automation, as well as other functions.) When you're happy with all of your settings, select a folder and a name for your new file and click the Create File button. You'll find that a new audio file is automatically created as a new part in the Arrange window.

Incidentally, you can also use this same procedure to create a stereo file of your whole mix, which will give you a digitally clean file that shows none of the signs of degradation traditionally displayed when audio is transferred from one medium to another.

and then...

There are a few more things to keep in mind at all times during the mixing phase of your project, and if I'm repeating myself here then it's probably because it's important...although a touch of early senility isn't out of the question. To begin with, don't constantly mix at high volume. For that matter, don't constantly mix at the same volume, either. Check your mix frequently, using a very low volume and at various mid-level volumes, and every now and then crank it up so that you can really hear how things hit hard. Look at your speakers when you do this to make sure you're not overdriving them.

When the mix is finished, you should listen to it from start to finish at a high level, turning it down again if you need to make further alterations. Your ears can get tired, woolly and even damaged if you listen to loud music for long periods, and you might end up hearing a muffled version of the sound that's actually being produced. OK, maybe that sounds like your parents blathering on about the evils of rock music, but believe me, you don't want to mess with your ears. If you're a musician, you'll need to keep them in the best condition possible.

One final note: a well-arranged and well-tracked song shouldn't require a great deal of fader-riding. You may have to bring up a lead instrument here and there, but that should be about it.

chapter 11

generic recording styles

"Verbal art, like poetry, is reflective; it stops to think. Music is immediate; it goes on to become."
     – WH Auden

Trying to understand the subtle nuances and permutations of musical genre can stimulate a level of philosophical angst that is remarkably similar to trying to grasp the significance of why kamikaze pilots wore helmets or agonising over whether or not illiterate people get the full effect of alphabet soup. The dictionary definition of genre settles for "kind, category, or sort…especially of literary, musical or artistic work". Not the most lucid or enlightening of definitions, you'll agree, but at least it's somewhere to start.

Although Cubase can be used to record anything in any style of music, from bluegrass to hard house, your whole approach and the level of functionality that you'll need to access will vary considerably depending on the kind, category or sort of music that you want to record. In a book like this, it's impossible to detail all of the various permutations for each and every musical genre, or to even begin to list the pitfalls and problems that you may end up encountering along the way, so instead I've just picked a few general generic areas where I know that Cubase is being used successfully and tried to add in a few extras that you probably wouldn't pick up just from reading the Steinberg manuals. If you want to get into the real nitty-gritty of studio technique and mad sound science, there are a number of other Sanctuary books on the subject covering every conceivable aspect of the process and practice. (See page 288 for a full list of these titles.)

dance

Sequencers and dance music are happy bedfellows, and Cubase VST is the ideal recording environment for this kind of stuff. Unfortunately, a generic boundary is a tiny cot to dance's super-king-sized double bed. It's impossible to cover all approaches to all styles of dance music in a single chapter – there are books devoted to the dance genre and all its beat-influenced brethren – so I'll try to provide only a rough outline of some of the more notable categories.

It's an interesting notion that dance music as it is today wouldn't exist if it weren't for Cubase. Back when music was first becoming computer-based, it was Cubase and Atari that blazed the frontier, with well over 90% of the classic tunes of the day emerging from smoky bedrooms equipped with a Groovebox and an ST. As a general rule, dance exists in the realms of MIDI, drawing its sounds from a vast array of synths, and so sequencers like Cubase are an obvious choice. It's very possible to create dance music entirely on MIDI, but as horizons and CPU power expand so audio is also becoming an integral tool.

So, at the risk of sounding old and stupid, here's a very simplistic breakdown of the main dance genres and how, on the whole, they are approached.

house

This is probably the great-grandaddy of dance, the blind, idiot godfather of limitless permutations. However, house itself is not a single genre but rather a broad heading under which dozens of hybrids shelter.

Trance

This is the sharpened product of rave which emerged as synth potential grew. In many respects, it's simply a four-to-the-floor rhythm layered with electronica and soaring pads. It usually focuses around a breakdown, with either side of the song working on the plus/minus build ethic. A simple riff is repeated and built upon, with the exception of bass breaks and key changes.

The integral factor to trance is the depth of the melodies. Trance always attempts the epic, and is designed to extract the maximum serotonin at desired intervals.

To get the trance sound you need, start with the drums. Most house music uses either the Roland 808 or 909 drum machine. These maps are available from the inventors, but most manufacturers offer similar kits. With the LM-9

VST plug-in, it's possible to load in multisamples and create your own drum kits, and 808 samples are readily available over the Internet.

So now you have the drum sound. Like its father, house, trance uses a 4/4 rhythm with syncopated claps or hits, and laid over the drums dances an arpeggiated bass line. (You can create your own bass line with one of VB's synth basses and Cubase's Arpeggiator.) The bass line itself need not be too bottom-end heavy, as the floor tom carries the really low frequencies.

On top of the bass line you need lots of lushly orchestrated pads, and with a bit of time and effort Neon can actually create satisfactory results. For a quick pad, choose a triangle wave, assign a heavy attack and pump the release. Now play with VST's bounteous effects to acquire depth. A common mistake with pads is to saturate them with reverb, which is bad, as they already occupy a huge frequency band and reverberation just expands their range.

For the main melody, use either a synth lead or piano, the trusty guns of trance. The Universal Sound Module actually has a very convincing "cheese" piano, which is perfect for those floating arpeggios. To obtain a synth-lead overdrive on Neon, employing a square wave and maximum LFO can have pleasing results.

Hard House

Here's another style that can happily thrive in the oxygen-starved world of MIDI. Hard house follows a similar structural path to house but is sped up and, as the name implies, is generally harder, so add some mild distortion to your synth sounds and phase your hi-hats. Hard house tends to be driven by the bass line, which means that you want a grooving bass melody instead of the floating lead of trance. Experiment with VST. You'll be surprised at the results.

House doesn't end there, of course. Tech trance, deep house and disco all enter in at some point, for which similar production rules apply. House is a good entry into dance production, offering accessible drum programming and simple melodies. It's also a genre that can be fully creatable with a stand-alone version of Cubase 5.0. In terms of EQ, a gentle curve that knocks out the middle is the standard rule, since this helps to imply depth.

drum and bass

The clever naming continues. Drum and bass relies on…wait for it… drums and bass to convey its essence. Born out of jungle – which itself was born out of rare groove and Motown – drum and bass relies on a solid, fast, two-step rhythm rolling in at between 160 and 180 bpm. This two-step is driven by a snare that falls on the beat and a bass drum that falls behind every second stroke. Unfortunately, the standard drum sounds on the LM-9 aren't adequate for drum and bass; practitioners favour instead real drums time-stretched and pitched up. As well as giving the desired speed, this pitching up allows room for the spleen-shattering bass frequencies.

acoustic instruments

At the opposite end of the spectrum from the thunder of dance music is good old acoustic music. This is the melodic and soulful stuff that stretches back to the likes of Bob Dylan, Paul Simon and James Taylor and runs through to the likes of Dave Matthews, Ben Harper, David Gray and Badly Drawn Boy. Although working with audio can be slightly trickier than working exclusively with MIDI, Cubase is powerful enough to allow you to make some stunning recordings of acoustic music. However, there are some things that you'll need to consider.

First, the acoustic guitar is a rather difficult instrument to record well. The subtle quality of the overtones and suchlike make it a very complex sound to capture. Most musicians and good producers tend to agree that you should never record the piezo pick-up mounted in some guitars. Yes, I know, I've heard it done on major-label productions, too, but I still think it sounds thuddy, thin and metallic. Your best bet is to use a good condenser mic or two. However, if all you have is a choice between an SM-57 or the pick-up, I'd use the SM-57 every time. Avoid aiming the mic directly at the soundhole, as this tends to produce a particularly boomy result, so instead position it between eight and twelve inches away and aim it at the spot where the neck and the body meet (usually around the 14th fret). I normally use just one mic, but for a larger-than-life sound try placing one mic in the way described above and a second mic an equal distance away and aimed at the bridge. This will pick up more of the mid range and bite, and the two signals can then be blended to taste in the mix. This tends to work for things like mandolins, banjos, etc, although with banjos you really need to watch your levels and make sure that the sound isn't too tinny.

As with any recording, the quality starts with the instrument itself, and no amount of EQ or effects will inject life into strings that are old and dull. I always put new strings on my guitar before gigging or recording. Also, there's no way to totally disguise fret buzz, and it's true that, while a certain amount of fret and finger noise will add to the "organic" sound, too much can spoil a performance.

If you're a singer/guitarist and you want to record both bits in one take, you'll end up with a certain amount of spill between the guitar and vocal mics. You can minimise this by using a good directional cardioid mic placed as close to the guitar as possible while positioning a directional vocal mic fitted with a pop shield no more than twelve inches from your mouth. Although there will still be some spill, it won't be all that serious, and you can even create an illusion of stereo by panning the guitar to one side and the vocal mic to the other.

For something a bit more exotic, such as an acoustic bass guitar, place your mic about six inches above the bridge and aim it slightly toward the soundhole. For an upright bass, an Audio Technica ATM25 placed just outside the f-hole, along with a large- or small-diaphragm condenser just above the bridge, also works well on two separate tracks. The bridge mic can then be blended to taste in the mix until you achieve the desired amount of attack, string vibration, etc. Keep the mics within twelve inches of the instrument or you're likely to get phase cancellations from the reflections of the sound coming from the floor. You don't really want a lot of room ambience on a bass track, anyway, and if you decide to put some outboard reverb on a bass track, your mix will instantly turn to mush.

With other instruments – such as violins, flutes, whistles, etc – start by positioning the mic at around six inches from the sound source and then adjust it accordingly. Even moving the mic a few inches or centimetres can affect the sound quite considerably, while the acoustic environment can also play a considerable part in giving the recorded sound particular characteristics. Acoustic sound changes constantly, and the level of recording difficulty is increased when you use more than one mic. As with everything, don't be afraid to experiment until you get the mic placement and the sound right.

Don't be afraid to use EQ, compression, etc, but don't overuse it. Try to set EQ within the ambient range of the instrument – ie guitar and vocals are usually around the mid range, while bass is mid to low, etc. Also, you should always try to record acoustic instruments clean. If you want reverb, add it later, but don't overdo it, and don't expect to fix an atrociously bad sound in the mix. Always try to get the best and cleanest recording possible at source.

vocals

Since you can't, unfortunately, tune a singer, the place to start with is his or her environment. For example, although it may sound a bit new age, a room with dim lights can relax a singer about to sing a song with a mellower mood. Conversely, a brightly lit room can support a high-energy song.

Temperature also affects a vocalist's performance, and a cold room can cause his vocal chords to tense up. You'll therefore want to make sure that the room in which you'll be recording vocals is at a comfortable temperature.

The standard mic position for recording vocals is about nine inches away from and slightly above the singer's mouth, so angle the mic down a bit in order to avoid pops. Also, if you have one, a pop shield is a very useful tool, but don't worry if you don't have one, as they're quite easy to make.

Compression is a very useful tool when it comes to recording vocals, and vocals will almost always benefit from being compressed a little. When using compression in Cubase, a good place to start is with a -10dB threshold, 3:1 ratio, a fast attack time and a moderately fast release time. Bring the threshold down until the reduction meters are almost always lit and adjust the ratio until you get around 6dB of reduction.

EQ is usually helpful to pull the sound of a vocalist out of a mix. Use narrow bandwidths, if possible, as this will reduce the chance of boosting the same frequency as that of another instrument.

For all vocals, use suitable compression. Even well-disciplined vocalists tend to sound uneven against the very controlled dynamics of a pop mix, so it helps to apply a little compression while you're recording. Err on the side of caution and use less compression than you think you'll finally need, but don't be afraid to use more compression on the vocal track once it's been recorded. When the performance is in the can, you can try both subtle and heavy compression within Cubase to see which works best with the track, although, if you're using a lot of compression, you may need to gate the vocal track first, which will prevent a build-up of noise in the pauses between phrases.

It's at the mixing stage that a compressor with an obvious character can be used to make a vocal seem larger than life. However, don't gate the vocal while recording, as a badly-set-up gate can ruin an otherwise perfect take, so save gating until the mixing stage. Use the gate before any further compression, but don't gate so hard that you remove all of the breath noises preceding words, as these are part of the character of a vocal performance and the recording will sound unnatural without them.

Take care not to run amok with the EQ. Mid-range boosting usually results in a nasal or phasey sound, so use as little EQ as you can. If you've picked the right mic and taken the time to fine-tune its position during recording, you shouldn't need much corrective EQ, anyway, although of course there are times when EQ is used for creative purposes.

Make sure that reverb is used sparingly. Vocals recorded in a dry acoustic environment need reverb to give them a sense of space and reality, but don't use any more than the song really needs. As a general rule, busy songs need less reverb and slower ballads with lots of space in the arrangement can afford to have a little more. If the vocals are recorded very brightly, they may cause any added reverb to sound sibilant, but instead of de-essing the vocals (which often produces an unnatural sound) try instead de-essing just the feed to the reverb unit. You can also experiment with the type of reverb and tonality to help minimise sibilance and spitting.

The chances are that the "keeper" vocal track will be recorded as an overdub after the basic tracks are cut. You'll also find that the ability to punch in vocals in Cubase to fix phrasing and bum notes will be invaluable. You'll want to apply limiting to the vocal on the way down, using the highest ratio you have, the fastest attack time possible and a threshold setting that just grabs the peaks. If the singer refuses to sing without some reverb then send them a little over their headphones, but record it dry. Apart from eating memory and CPU power, reverb is notorious for masking pitch problems.

electronic instruments

Although instruments like electric guitars often sound better with the amp miked up, you can DI (Direct Inject) any electronic instrument that you can plug into an amp. In some instances, you might find that you'd like to use a combination of DI'd and miked sounds. You should be aware, however, that plugging your instrument directly into your Mac or mixing desk may not work properly, because the impedances won't match, which is particularly true if your instrument doesn't have a pre-amp. However, DI boxes can be very useful, as they allow signals from either instruments, pre-amps or power amps to be used as recording sources without producing the usual hum and mismatch of impedances.

Miking amps isn't really all that difficult, but the position of a mic relative to the amp speaker can make a big difference in overall sound. In your studio, don't use huge stacks of amps for recording purposes; it's easier to get a good, manageable sound out of a small combo, and this will even produce a more natural overdrive when pushed than a humongous Marshall stack would. Close-miked or DI'd guitars also tend to need a bit of reverb to give the illusion of space, but don't overdo it.

Like guitars, electronic instruments can generate noise themselves, and hiss from the amp can create noise interference in your recording. Using Cubase's Gate at the mixing stage, you can minimise this noise and maintain true silence during pauses or between phrases.

As far as your desired sound goes…well, that depends on whether you're using electronic instruments for heavy metal or for '80s TV-theme-tune music. Plugging in all of your instruments and getting a track laid down is relatively easy, but what you do with it once it's recorded is the proverbial horse of a different colour.

production tips and random esoteric nonsense

"It is a new art form, a new kind of instrument. I'm not saying were the masters of a new art form, because were just toddling around in the playground. What we are doing is saying, 'The playground is open,' and I'm absolutely confident that people will, you know, come in and play."
– Matt Black, Coldcut/Ninja Tune

According to Hunter S Thompson, when the going gets weird, the weird turn pro. Maybe the music business and the record industry won't stop getting weirder, but when it comes to producing your own music the way you want to, in your own time and in your own way, the Macintosh is still the best option for empowering anyone and everyone with the creative tools with which to turn pro. As I mentioned at the beginning of this book, professional musicians overwhelmingly choose the Macintosh, because of its ease of use and its true "plug and play", combined with excellent professional and amateur music software and reliable MIDI implementation. As a matter of fact, over 60% of professional musicians and untold thousands of amateurs and wannabes all use the Mac, and that usage isn't confined to any one particular genre or style. Artists using the Mac as the heart of their music systems for producing an eclectic range of musical styles include the likes of:

Bryan Adams	vocals/guitar	rock
Aerosmith	band	metal
Tori Amos	vocals/piano	soft rock
Laurie Anderson	vocals/effects	experimental
The Beastie Boys	band	rap
Bjork	vocals	weird pop

Bono/U2	vocals/band	clever rock
The Chemical Brothers	band	electronica/dance
David Crosby	band	acoustic folk/rock
(Crosby, Stills, Nash And Young)		
Sheryl Crow	vocals	mellow pop
David Darling	cello	classical
Art Davis	bass	jazz
Brooks And Dunn	vocals	country (use PowerBooks onstage)
Danny Elfman	composer	*The Simpsons*
Brian Eno	composer/musician	ambient/experimental
Enya	vocals	rushy Celtic folk
Fatboy Slim	samples/beats	popular dance
Gina G	whatever	British pop
Herbie Hancock	piano	jazz
Ice T	rap/vocals	rap
Michael Jackson	vocals	pop
Quincy Jones	musician/producer	jazz
BB King	vocals/guitar	blues
Courtney Love	vocals/guitar	grunge
Reba McEntire	vocals	country
Madonna	vocals	pop
Marilyn Manson	vocals	gothic rock
Paul McCartney	vocals/bass	rock-ish
Sarah McLachlan	vocals/piano	ambient/acoustic/folk
Metallica	band	metal
George Michael	vocals	pop
Prince	vocals/guitar	R&B
Public Enemy	band	rap
The Rolling Stones	band	rock (use a Mac onstage)
Carlos Santana	vocals/guitar	Latin rock
Sting	vocals/bass	rock
Michael Stipe	REM	mellow rock
Luther Vandross	vocals	soul
Paul Winter	consort	jazz/world
Neil Young	vocals/guitar	folk rock

And the list just goes on and on. OK, not everything currently being produced on a Mac displays the highest standards of artistic creativity. And, yes, I know that Paul Joyce produced his complete recording of the insipid 'Bob The Builder' in his Nottingham home studio, a song which is based around Cubase VST running on a Mac G4. But you get the general picture.

"Macs seemed to be an easier thing to do. The PC thing seemed to be more for suits than musicians."
– Warren McRae, bass player for Tina Turner

Throughout this book, I've tried to emphasise the fact that, in music, creativity is – or, at least, should be – considerably more important than technology. Great technology like a Mac and Cubase can take your music wherever you want to go, as long as you actually have some music and a reasonable idea of where it is you want to go. Accept the fact that Cubase probably has more features and functionality than you'll possibly ever need, or even need to know about, and just get on with making music. You don't have to get hung up on all the techie blue smoke and mirrors, and if you really want a taste of all that weird-science stuff then just sit yourself down and read the glossary at the end of this book, which is a guaranteed bluffers' guide to all things audio.

"I couldn't do a show like this without the Mac. It's so flexible. I can throw audio from one medium into the Mac, import it into Cubase, edit it any way I need to, throw it back into 'the box' and we're good to go."
– Paul Mirkovich, Cher's music director

Remember that some of the most successful artists using Macs and Cubase are openly unapologetic about their relatively thin grasp of all things technical. In an interview in *MacAddict*, Moby – popular dance mogul and king of advert music – freely admitted, "I don't know that much about the intricacies of computers, to be honest with you. My goal with the computer is to have something I can turn on and it just works. I've got some friends who know their computers inside and out. The slightest little quirk, they can go into the system folder and find out which extension needs to be enabled or disabled or whatever. I just want to turn it on and have it work. So I'm not a tech-head, in that sense."

The same tends to go for hard-and-fast tips. Since everyone works differently towards different ends, trying to get a detailed explanation of exactly what the ideal process would be if you were to sit down in front of your Mac right now and just start a new composition would be about as productive and as specific as trying to get the Pope to reveal the more technical aspects of how you'd go about turning water into wine. (But then again, it's always interesting to ask.) According to Moby, who still uses a IIci, as well as a G3, to produce that elusive musical miracle, "Well, sit down at the computer and go to Cubase and just start playing. The way Cubase works – or most sequencing software works – is, you generate tracks, and the tracks are specific to different instruments in the MIDI set-up. One danger with sequencing on a computer is this visual element, that's quite interesting, in and of itself. Sometimes you can be working on a piece of music and sort of get seduced by the computer screen, and so, instead of devoting 100% of your attention to what you're hearing, you're devoting 80% of your attention to what you're hearing [and] another 20% watching the cute little cursor move across the screen."

"The ability to use digital-audio-editing tools on Macs gives more power to musicians. It allows a guitar-based band like ours to do our own sampling and producing."
– Jeff Robbins, guitarist with Orbit

portrait of an artist with a young Mac

Although I tend to slag off the record industry at every opportunity, there are still a few labels out there who haven't lost the plot completely and are continuing to produce credible and interesting artists without losing their senses of humour. No, you won't see many of them on *Top Of The Pops*, or even looking for charlie backstage at the Brits, but you can find their albums if you look really hard, and you can hear many of their groups and artists touring live all over the world.

The kind of label I'm talking about is personified by companies like Ninja Tune. Ninja Tune is the brainchild of Matt Black and Jonathan More, who were better known as Coldcut, when they were on tour in Japan. At the time, they were also at the ends of relationships with a variety of major labels that had led to their classic remix of Eric B And Rakim's 'Paid In Full', as well as forgivable anomalies such as launching the careers of Yazz and Lisa Stansfield. All of this had led to the usual heartache, pain, misunderstanding and annoyance, and the duo decided that they wanted to go back to their roots and release whatever they wanted, whenever they wanted. After 13 dates in ten days, soaking in Japanese media and living on a diet of sushi, the pair found the idea of a new label congealing with the idea of a ninja, characterised by stealthy movement and physical and psychic camouflage. They gravitated to the image of ninja as a trickster, joker or juggler (an archetype with which I'm all too familiar, and one that I used as the centre for the one and only commercial LP I ever recorded). Out of this vision of tricknology, Ninja Tune, the "technicolour escape pod", was born. This was back in 1990, and by 1994, with the label's reputation firmly established on the club, dance and experimental jazz scenes, they released an album by a band called The Herbaliser.

The Herbaliser is a conglomeration of sample-driven hip-hop beats carefully combined with live funk grooves and scratching at a thoroughly orchestrated level. A crew of between seven and nine musicians, led by Jake Wherry and Ollie Teeba, The Herbaliser makes it all sound so simple. Whatever your mood, whatever your moment, they've manifested it with inspirational instrumentals that elevate your soul, while lyrical tracks featuring the likes of Roots Manuva (UK), Dream Warriors (Canada), Blade (UK), What What (US) and Bahamadia (US) motivate your goals.

Jake Wherry, the computer whizzing beatworm of jazz/funk/soul bands The Propheteers and The Meateaters, had his ears accustomed to artists such as James Brown, Leroy Huston, Quincy Jones, Leon Thomas and David Axelrod at an early age. Naturally, his interests progressed into rare groove and hip-hop, and his dreams of forming a group seemed oh so tantalising. Although these days much of his time in the studio is consumed by production, you can always catch him onstage playing bass at a Herbaliser show.

Jake's been using a Mac and Cubase for over nine years. His first Mac was a Classic II with 8MB of RAM running Cubase 2.5 with an Akai S1000 sampler. That was from 1992 until around 1996, so in fact the first two LPs on Ninja Tune (*Remedies* and *Blow Your Headphones*) were all done on this set-up. I asked Jake why he chose the Mac and what he saw as its main advantages.

> JAKE: Hmm. At that time, 90% of people I spoke to said that PCs had major timing problems, and they all used Macs, so essentially a Mac was the second thing on my studio shopping list after my Akai S1000. Now one can do so much on a Mac that, whenever I'm asked what one ought to buy to get started, the first thing I would say now is, 'A G4.'

> MP: What sort of music system do you use now? Have you encountered any problems with set-up, usage, etc?

> JAKE: The studio is currently based around our new, dual-processor G4 500, with 512 megs of RAM and a 7200 IDE internal audio drive, with a MOTU 2408 system optically linked to an Akai DR16 for 16 outputs,

plus two S3000 XL samplers, two 24-soundtrack ghost desks, quested VS2108 monitors and a fair bit of outboard instruments/mikes, running Cubase VST 5.0 as our main program.

MP: Tell me a bit about The Herbaliser.

Jake: Maybe vez@ninjatune.net would send you a bio, plus herbaliser.com has all the info you could need. To be honest, I would vomit right now if I had to recount our tale again. Sorry.

MP: Are there plans for a *Session Two*?

JAKE: *Session One* covers tracks from all three CDs that we've put out on Ninja Tune [*Remedies*, *Blow Your Headphones*, *Very Mercenary*]. The tracks we've done live over the years are the ones that were made from the sort of samples that we felt we could replace with live musicians, and we even chose the best tracks from the three records. So, yes, there will be a *Session Two*, but probably after having done at least two more new studio CDs on Ninja. Then we'll pick the best of those, gig them for maybe 200 shows, then go in the studio when we're totally tight and bust the tracks down in two days, like we did with *Session One*.

MP: What do you see as being the essential process in the music that you write?

JAKE: Turning up in the morning helps, I think.

MP: How has translating sample-based music into a live setting changed your approach to writing and producing?

JAKE: It hasn't, really. Having played guitar for ten years and been in many bands before I first got a sampler and Mac, in '92, I feel that I set out to use a sampler with a lot of musical empathy. Inspirations such as The Young Disciples [who employed a perfect blend of programmed beats, singing, rapping and sampling]. However, now that we are where we are with our band, and with the improved recording equipment we have, we're using live musicians a lot more on current stuff we're working on, whereas the first two CDs on Ninja Tune are almost 99% made entirely from samples.

MP: How do you approach sequencing? Do you loop up audio directly or trigger samples with MIDI?

JAKE: We're in an evolutionary process. In the old days, when I had the Mac Classic II and an Akai S1000, I always liked to chop up my samples (usually I chop a bar into at least four parts, if not eight), and so I would sit for hours at my S1000 manually splicing my beats and loops into individual bits. Then, in 1996, I got a Power Mac 7600, which I upgraded to a 200MHz 604e card, and we started to use ReCycle. Like, wow! A software that literally did a job that would take about ten minutes in seconds. So we used ReCycle without using the REX export option for a few years, and now I have 16 outputs on my MOTU sound card. We have the option of sending samples as REX files, etc, straight to audio. So, depending on what I imagine we're going to do with a sample, from ReCycle I will either send it by SCSI back to an Akai sampler – usually drums – or I will send it as an audio REX file in Cubase.

MP: Do you ReCycle or cut up by hand?

JAKE: Blowing my trumpet, I must claim to be one of the first to be a true sample-chopper. With reference to what I said in the last paragraph, now I use ReCycle all of the time. But I *don't* rely on the chop points that ReCycle sets. Most of the time, I chop the sample by inserting my own chop points, and most of this chopping is based on the way I used to chop by hand, on my Akai S1000. But, oh yes, do we chop!

MP: What sampler do you use? And what do you think of software samplers?

JAKE: Currently, two Akai S3000 XLs. I think Unity is a good idea, but it always seems buggy on the systems I've seen it on. I think the EXS24 on Logic is brilliant, mainly because I did a beat on my mate's G4 with Logic Platinum and the EXS24 and I was amazed at how tight it was. I'm dying to see what Steinberg come up with as a Cubase equivalent, as well as dying to get one of those Midex MIDI systems, because, let's face it, timing is the issue that people moan the most about Cubase on a Mac/PC these days.

MP: What are some of the main features of Cubase that you use regularly?

JAKE: Audio – the Play button! We don't dig deep, really. It's kids stuff isn't it? Like building blocks with colours. Seriously, the audio side is amazing, especially the audio-editing capabilities, which I think are far more powerful than Logic's.

MP: Any comments on the way in which the whole process of making music is changing? How do you see the use of home-based digital studios and the Internet changing the music industry?

JAKE: Already major record companies have lost their clout, because, since the late '80s, people wanting to make this type of music have been able to get a little bedroom set-up together without having had to convince a record company that they're the future big thing. And at the same time, little record companies have set up happy with selling maybe a few thousand twelve-inches rather than a minimum of, say, 15,000 units.

MP: Any hints or suggestions for musicians wanting to set up their own desktop digital studios?

JAKE: Get a Mac. And lots of time.

Apart from their adventures with Cubase and the Mac, The Herbaliser also tours, in its entirety. Recently, they've journeyed from Prague to Montreal, playing over 200 live performances, and they don't stop. Also, like the best musicians, they're constantly reinventing themselves. No, they're not trying to save the world from poverty or starvation (yet) or prove that they surpass all the rest; they're simply trying to make good music that reflects the quality and versatility of their taste.

"You could cut a whole album on a PowerBook and no one would know you weren't in a studio costing $2,500 a day."
– The Dust Brothers

epilogue

Steve Jobs, Apple's co-founder and current sometime CEO, used to be fond of the Zen paraphrase "The journey is its own reward". Making music on your Mac can be the start of a beautiful journey that can take you nearly anywhere you can imagine, while using Cubase and the various other music tools available on the Mac can bring you a lot of personal and creative pleasure and can allow you to produce finished recordings that will easily stand comparison with commercial or "professional studio" music. However, don't forget that you're dealing with a lot of powerful and sophisticated stuff here, and that, as in cooking, sex or brewing Grolsch, the result is always better and more satisfying if you don't rush things. As a musician, you'll already know that, no matter how experienced you are, there's always something more to learn. The same is true when it comes to using your virtual digital studio – sometimes the journey is far more exciting than the final destination, and that journey is what keeps music interesting and alive.

In Michelangelo Antonioni's wonderful film *Beyond The Clouds*, a girl in a Parisian cafe tells a stranger the story of a group of explorers travelling through the jungle to find a lost Incan city. One day, at the foot of a mountain, the porters simply stop and refuse to go any further. When asked why, they refuse to speak, and nothing can persuade them to go on. After a few days, the porters suddenly pick up their packs and carry on with their journey. When one of the explorers asks the chief why they had stopped, he replies simply, "They were waiting for their souls to catch up." Enjoy your adventure, trust your ears and remember to stop once in a while to let your soul catch up.

good housekeeping

A fter you've put all that time and effort into recording and mixing your songs, make sure that you save and back up your files regularly. Audio files are particularly large by nature and can quickly clog up all of the available space on your hard disk. If you record audio regularly, you'll probably want to back up your files onto another drive or onto removable media, such as Zip or Jaz drives. Like most Mac programs, Cubase can read and write a variety of different file formats that contain different types of information, although some formats support specific Cubase functions and can only be read by Cubase, while others are designed for importing or exporting information between different programs, so making yourself familiar with these different formats will help you to decide which is the right option for saving, opening or moving your own music.

Essentially, Cubase offers two main formats for you to use for saving your music: the song file and the arrangement file. When you save a song, your file will include the following:

• all of the arrangements;

• the Audio Pool, including all audio settings and audio file references, but not the actual audio files themselves;

• the entire set-up, including settings in dialog boxes, menus, groove maps, Transport bar settings and even drum maps;

• all preferences with the Save With Song option activated.

However, song files take up more disk space than regular files, even if you only have one arrangement in the song. And while song files contain all audio references, they don't contain the actual audio files, and so, if you want to transfer a song containing audio to another Mac, you'll need to move your audio files as well.

When you save an arrangement file, you will include:

• all of the things you see in one Arrange window, including the tracks, the parts, Inspector settings and tempo;

• the audio-file references for the audio parts used in the arrangement.

You'll probably find that the arrangement format is generally adequate for saving most of your music. Arrangement files take up little disk space, can be saved and opened in another song and, when opened, don't affect settings in dialog boxes or menus. However, these files also don't contain any audio settings, other than the audio-file references used in the arrangement and won't give you a complete "snapshot" of the program's state.

These file formats are called *native files*, because they're designed for use in Cubase exclusively and generally can't be read by other programs. For example, although arrangement files and MIDI files both contain MIDI data, MIDI files can be read by other computer programs, while arrangement files can't. Only import and export files can be read by other programs. Other native files include part files, which contain individual parts or several parts or tracks. When you save in this format, your required parts must be selected or all parts in the current track will be saved. Part files contain audio or MIDI events and audio parts also include audio-file references for these events, which makes it possible to import audio parts into other songs without having to import their audio files separately in the Audio Pool.

Additional file formats, which are more or less self-explanatory, include drum-map files, set-up files, window sets, keyboard lay-out, score set and preferences files. Like most Mac applications, native file formats are usually opened and saved using the Open and Save commands in the File menu – ie when you choose Save As, your song will be saved under whatever name you choose. If you've already saved your song once using this option and then choose Save Song from the File menu, Cubase will save your song without asking for a file name or location and will simply overwrite the earlier version.

Since MIDI files usually come in two formats, type zero and type one, Cubase provides a MIDI file format for importing or exporting standard

MIDI files. Type zero files will always contain only one track, which plays back on many MIDI channels, while type one files will contain your original track structure and include two or more tracks on separate MIDI channels.

Cubase also has an Autosave feature, which can be set in the General Preferences dialog box. If you select this option, you can decide how often Cubase saves your work automatically. There's also a Save Backup feature in the File menu, which enables you to save a back-up copy of your current song, giving you a complete replica of the original song, with the same name but with an additional number that corresponds to the number of back-ups you've made. (Back-up copies are normally placed in the same folders as your original files.) There is also a Revert To Saved option, which restores the song to your last saved version, so that any changes you made since you last-saved are undone. You can use this command as a way of undoing many changes at the same time. Save your song, experiment with it, and then, if you don't like the results, revert to the last-saved version.

MP3

MP3 files are compressed files that are popular for posting and exchanging music on the Internet. Unfortunately, even in version 5.0, Cubase won't let you play these back, as such. However, if you import an MP3 file, Cubase will create a copy of that file and convert it to WAV format. This converted file will be placed in the Audio Files folder that you've selected for your song from the Audio Setup option from the Options menu. (If you haven't specified an Audio Files folder before converting an MP3 file, you'll be asked to do so when you import it.) Just remember that, while MP3 is an efficient method of compression, the converted WAV file will probably be considerably larger than the original MP3 file, no matter how small it was originally.

customising Cubase

One of the great things about Cubase is that you can customise nearly the entire program to look, feel and work the way you want it to. Here's a run-down of some of the things you can customise or personalise.

Preferences

This is a really good place to start, since the various Preferences dialog options on the Edit menu contain many very useful functions that allow you to make Cubase VST look and behave the way you want it to.

Key Commands, MIDI Remote And Toolbar

If you prefer to invoke commands from the computer keyboard or via MIDI, it's worth noting that a huge number of commands can be set up for key or remote MIDI control, by which you can connect any key and practically any MIDI message to any function. If you'd rather use your mouse, you can set up your own toolbar that will allow you to use graphical "buttons" for all of the same functions that can be accessed from the computer keyboard and via MIDI.

Window Settings And Sets

You can move and change the sizes of the windows, open various types of windows, move dividers and set magnification to tailor the windows to your needs. Saving these settings in the start-up song will make the program appear as you want it to. In addition to this, you can create window sets that allow you to quickly switch between various window configurations.

Tracks

You can create and name tracks and set them to different track classes, etc. For example, if you know that you always want a drum track that plays on MIDI channel 10, simply create it. A more advanced option is to prepare empty folder tracks – for example, for various sections in your orchestra. You can also rearrange, hide and resize track columns as you like.

Parts

You can even have parts in your start-up song which could, for example, contain libraries of often-used drum patterns or riffs, or they could contain system-exclusive dumps of settings that load your instruments with certain sounds. Put the parts onto muted tracks and drag them onto other tracks when you need them.

Transport Bar Settings

You might, for example, prefer to record in Replace mode, or you might always want to AutoQuantize your recordings. If this is the case, simply set this up on the Transport bar.

Editor Settings And Drum Maps

If you prefer certain settings in the editors – for loops, quantizing, etc – set them up and save them with the start-up song. A perfect candidate for customising is the drum map, and the start-up song will include which drum maps to use and how they should be set up.

MIDI Track Mixer

You can modify the MIDI Track Mixer to include various "custom control panels". Preparing such maps and including them in the start-up song will allow you to access many important control functions in your MIDI instruments from the MIDI Track Mixer.

Mixer Maps

Cubase allows you to have up to eight mixer maps loaded in a song. You might, for example, have different "editors" for various MIDI instruments in your rig.

Audio Settings

There are a number of things that you can prepare that are related to audio:

- System settings. These are mainly prepared to optimise the number of audio channels, EQs and effects;

- Initial mix settings, channel naming, effect settings, etc, as found in the VST Channel Mixers and in the various effects windows. This allows you to start with a basic tracking set-up every time you begin a new song;

- Audio buses, sends, etc. This is mainly for those of you using audio hardware with multiple outputs. Preparing all of these ensures that all outputs are used for their right purposes for every new project;

- The Pool window allows you to determine how you want the files and segments listed.

Grooves And Other Quantize Settings

If you've created a few favourite grooves or have made settings for Iterative Quantize, make these part of your start-up song.

Metronome, MIDI Setup And MIDI Filter

Do you want a click track at all? Do you want it via the computer speaker or via MIDI? How long do you want the count-in to be? All of this is set in the

Metronome dialog box in the Options menu. The MIDI System Setup dialog box – found in the MIDI Setup sub-menu in the Options menu – contains information about your MIDI interface, among many other things. Since you don't want to have to set this every time you launch Cubase, you should save this setting in the start-up song. If you have equipment that generates MIDI data that you don't want to record, use the MIDI Filter dialog box, also found in the MIDI Setup sub-menu in the Options menu.

Sync

Most often, you'll synchronise to the same external equipment – for example, the tape recorder in your studio. To set up the Synchronisation dialog box as you want it, activate Sync on the Transport bar and save this with the start-up song. Cubase will then automatically synchronise as soon as you hit Play on the tape recorder.

web sites

Here's an assortment of Web sites that may or may not be of interest. Unfortunately, the Internet can all too often seem more like a digital dirt track than an information super-highway, when it comes to finding the music stuff you're really interested in. But, as the *I Ching* says, perseverance furthers, and if you keep at it, there's a wealth of samples, production info and interviews for the finding.

general

www.ninjatune.net (a superb site and home to great music)
www.timespace.com (the ultimate sample supplier for the UK)
www.progression.co.uk
www.hyperreal.com
www.disinfo.net (the ultimate knowledge resource)
www.djdownfall.co.uk
www.cybersales.co.uk/music/indie/abuse
www.sospubs.co.uk (*Sound On Sound* magazine's home page)
www.macworld.co.uk (**Macworld** magazine's home page)

MIDI file sites

www.prs.net (a huge archive of classical MIDI files)
www.newtronic.com (contains dance-orientated MIDI programming and software)
www.themidicity.com
www.midifarm.com
www.keyfax.com

software and plug-in sites

www.rhime.com
www.d-lusion.com/products/mj/index.html
www.mixman.com
www.groovemaker.com
www.dspstudio.de
www.sonicfoundry.com
www.antarestech.com
www.digidesign.com
www.waves.com
www.arboretum.com

sequencing software sites

www.steinberg.net/www.steinberg.de (main German site)
http://dspace.dial.pipex.com/steinberg-uk (main UK site)
www.clubcubase.com
www.cubase.net
www.opcode.com

company home pages

Midiman
www.midiman.net

Time & Space
www.timespace.com

Yamaha
www.yamaha.com

Korg
www.korg.com

Novation
www.nova-uk.com

glossary

absorption

Short for the term acoustical absorption, the quality of a surface or substance that takes in a sound wave rather than reflecting it.

AC

Abbreviation of the term *alternating current*, ie an electric current that flows back and forth in a circuit. All studio signals running through audio lines are AC.

acoustic(al)

Having to do with sound that can be heard by the ears.

acoustical absorption

The quality of a surface or substance that allows it to take in a sound wave rather than reflect it or pass it through, or an instance of this.

acoustic amplifier

The portion of an instrument that makes the vibrating source move more air or move air more efficiently, making the sound of the instrument louder. Examples of acoustic amplifiers include the body of an acoustic guitar, the soundboard of a piano, the bell of a horn and the shell of a drum.

acoustic echo chamber

A room designed with very hard, non-parallel surfaces and equipped with a speaker and microphone. Dry signals from the console are fed to the speaker and the microphone will have a reverberation of these signals that can be mixed in with the dry signals at the console.

A/D

Abbreviation of either *analogue-to-digital conversion* (ie the conversion of a quantity that has continuous changes into numbers that approximate those changes) or *analogue-to-digital converter*.

ADAT

A trademark of Alesis for its modular digital multitrack recording system, released in early 1993.

ADSR

Abbreviation for *attack, decay, sustain* and *release*, the various elements of volume changes in the sounding of a keyboard instruments, and also the four segments of a common type of synthesiser envelope. The controls for these four parameters determine the duration (or, in the case of sustain, the height) of the segments of the envelope.

AES/EBU

A standard professional interface for sending and receiving digital audio adopted by the Audio Engineering Society and the European Broadcast Union.

AIFF

Abbreviation of *audio interchange file format*, a common format for Macintosh audio files. It can be mono or stereo, and at a sampling rate of up to 48kHz. AIFF files are compatible with QuickTime.

algorithm

A set of procedures designed to accomplish something. In the case of computer software, the procedures may appear to the user as a configuration of software components – for example, an arrangement of operators in a Yamaha DX-series synthesiser – or as an element (such as a reverb algorithm) that performs specific operations on a signal.

algorithmic composition

A type of composition in which the large outlines of the piece, or the procedures to be used in generating it, are determined by the human composer, while some of the details, such as notes or rhythms, are created by a computer program using algorithmic processes.

aliasing

Undesired frequencies that are produced when harmonic components within the audio signal being sampled by a digital recording device or generated within a digital sound source lie above the Nyquist frequency. Aliasing differs from some other types of noise in that its pitch changes radically when the pitch of the intended sound changes. On playback, the system will provide a signal at an incorrect frequency, called an alias frequency. Aliasing is a kind of distortion.

All Notes Off

A MIDI command, recognised by some (but not all) synthesisers and sound modules, that causes any notes that are currently sounding to be shut off. The panic button on a synth or sequencer usually transmits All Notes Off messages on all 16 MIDI channels.

ambience

The portion of a sound that comes from the surrounding environment, rather than directly from the sound source.

ambient field

The same as *reverberant field*, ie the area away from the sound source where the reverberation is louder than the direct sound.

ambient miking

Placing a microphone in the reverberant field in order to take a separate recording of the ambience or to allow the recording engineer to change the mix of direct to reverberant sound in the recording.

amp

1. Abbreviation of *amplifier*. 2. Abbreviation of *ampère*, the SI unit of current. 3. Abbreviation of *amplitude*, the height of a waveform above or below the zero line.

ampère

The SI unit of current, abbreviated to amp.

amplification

An increase in signal strength.

amplifier

A device that increases the amplitude (level) of an electrical signal, in effect making it louder.

amplitude

The height of a waveform above or below the zero line, or the amount of a signal. Amplitude is measured by determining the amount of fluctuation in air pressure of a sound, the voltage of an electrical signal or, in a digital application, numerical data. When the signal is in the audible range, amplitude is perceived as loudness.

analogue

Representative, continuous changes that relate to another quantity that has a continuous change. Capable of exhibiting continuous fluctuations. In an analogue audio system, fluctuations in voltage correspond in a one-to-one fashion with (that is, are analogous to) the fluctuations in air pressure at the audio input or output. In an analogue synthesiser, parameters such as oscillator pitch and LFO speed are typically controlled by analogue control voltages, rather than by digital data, and the audio signal is also an analogue voltage.

analogue recording

A recording of the continuous changes of an audio waveform.

analogue-to-digital converter

A device which converts a quantity that has continuous changes (usually of voltage) into numbers that approximate those changes. Alternatively, a device that changes the continuous fluctuations in voltage from an analogue device (such as a microphone) into digital information that can be stored or processed in a sampler, digital signal processor or digital recording device.

assign

To choose the destination of an output.

attack

The first part of the sound of a note. In a synthesiser ADSR envelope, the attack segment is the segment during which the envelope rises from its initial value (usually zero) to the attack level (often the maximum level for the envelope) at a rate determined by the attack-time parameter.

attack

The rate at which a sound begins and increases in volume.

attenuation

Making something smaller. A reduction of the strength of an electrical or acoustic signal.

attenuator

A potentiometer (pot) that is used to lower the amplitude of a signal passing through it. The amplitude can usually be set to any value between full (no attenuation) and zero (infinite attenuation). Pots can be either rotary or linear (sliders), and can be either hardware or virtual sliders on a computer screen.

audio

Most often refers to electrical signals resulting from a sound wave being converted into electrical energy.

automatic gain (volume) control

A compressor with a very long release time. Used to keep the volume of audio material constant.

automation

In consoles, automation is a feature that allows the engineer to program control changes (such as fader level) so that, on playback of the multitrack recording, these changes happen automatically.

aux send

Abbreviation of *auxiliary send*, which adjusts the level of a signal sent from the console input channel to the auxiliary equipment through the aux bus.

auxiliary equipment

Effects devices separate from but working with a recording console.

axis

A line around which a device operates. In a microphone, for example, this would be an imaginary line coming out of the front of the mic in the direction of the diaphragm's motion.

baffles

Sound-absorbing panels used to prevent sound waves from entering or leaving a certain space.

balance

1. The relative level of two or more instruments in a mix, or the relative level of audio signals in the channels of a stereo recording. 2. To even out the relative levels of audio signals in the channels of a stereo recording.

balance control

A control on a stereo amplifier that, when moved clockwise, makes the right channel louder and the left channel softer and will do the reverse when moved anticlockwise.

balanced

1. Having a pleasing amount of low frequencies when compared to mid-range frequencies and high frequencies. 2. Having a pleasing mixture of the various instrument levels in an audio recording. 3. Having a fairly equal level in each of the stereo channels. 4. A method of interconnecting electronic gear using three-conductor cables.

bandwidth

1. The range of frequencies over which a tape recorder, amplifier or other audio device is useful. 2. The range of frequencies affected by an equalisation setting – ie the available "opening" through which information can pass. In audio, the bandwidth of a device is the portion of the frequency spectrum that it can handle without significant degradation taking place. In digital communications, the bandwidth is the amount of data that can be transmitted over a given period of time.

bank

1. A collection of sound patches (data concerned with the sequence and operating parameters of the synthesiser generators and modifiers) in computer memory. 2. A number of sound modules grouped together as a unit.

baud rate

Informally, the number of bits of computer information transmitted each second. MIDI transmissions have a baud rate of 31,250 (31.25 kilobaud), while modems typically have a much lower rate of 2,400, 9,600 or 14,400 baud.

bar

The same as the American term *measure*, ie the grouping of a number of beats in a music (most often four).

barrier miking

A method of placing the head of a microphone as close as possible to a reflective surface, thus preventing phase cancellation.

basic session

The first session in recording an audio production to record the basic tracks.

bass

1. The lower range of audio frequencies, up to approximately 250Hz. 2. Abbreviation of bass guitar.

bass roll-off

An electrical network built into some microphones to reduce the amount of output at bass frequencies when close-miking.

beat

1. A steady, even pulse in music. 2. The action of two sounds or audio signals mixing together and causing regular rises and falls in volume.

beats per minute

The number of steady, even pulses in music occurring in one minute and therefore defining the tempo of a song.

bi

A prefix meaning two.

bi-amplification

The process of having low-frequency and high-frequency speakers driven by separate amplifiers.

bi-directional pattern

A microphone pick-up pattern that has maximum pick-up directly in front and directly to the rear of the diaphragm and least pick-up at the sides.

binary

A numbering system based on two. In the binary system, there are two numbers used: one and zero.

bit

The smallest unit of digital information, representing a single zero or one. Digital audio is encoded in words that are usually eight, twelve or 16 bits long (ie the bit resolution). Each additional bit represents a theoretical improvement of about 6dB in the signal-to-noise ratio.

blending

1. A condition where two signals mix together to form one sound or give the sound of one sound source or one performance. 2. Mixing the left and right signal together slightly, which makes the instruments sound closer to the centre of the performance stage. 3. A method of panning during mixing where instruments are not panned extremely left or right.

board

1. Another, less formal, term for console or desk. 2. A set of controls and their housing which control all signals necessary for recording and mixing. 3. A slang shortening of the term *keyboard instrument*.

boom

1. A hand-held, telescoping pole used to suspend a microphone above a sound source when recording dialogue in film production. 2. A telescoping support arm attached to a microphone stand which holds the microphone. 3. Loosely, a boom stand.

boom stand

A microphone stand equipped with a telescoping support arm to hold the microphone.

boost

To increase gain, especially at specific frequencies with an equaliser.

BPM

Abbreviation of *beats per minute*.

brick-wall filter

A low-pass filter at the input of an analogue-to-digital converter. Used to prevent frequencies above the Nyquist frequency from being encoded by the converter.

buffer

Memory used for the recording or editing of data before it is stored in a more permanent form.

bulk dump

Short for *system-exclusive bulk dump*, a method of transmitting data, such as the internal parameters of a MIDI device to another MIDI device.

bus(s)

A wire carrying signals somewhere. Usually fed from several sources.

byte

A grouping of eight information bits.

cancellation

A shortening of the term *phase cancellation*, which occurs when the energy of one waveform significantly decreases the energy of another waveform because of phase relationships at or close to 180°.

capacitance

The property of being able to oppose a change in voltage or store an electrical charge.

capacitor

An electronic device comprising two plates separated by an insulator.

capsule

1. The variable capacitor section of a condenser microphone. 2. In other types of microphone, the part of the microphone that includes the diaphragm and the active element.

card

1. A plug-in memory device. RAM cards, which require an internal battery, can be used for storing user data, while ROM cards, which have no battery, can only be used for reading the data recorded on them by the manufacturer. 2. A circuit board that plugs into a slot on a computer.

cardioid pattern

A microphone pick-up pattern which picks up most sound from the front, less from the sides and the least from the back of the diaphragm.

carrier

A signal that is modulated by some other signal, as in FM synthesis.

cascade

To set and interconnect two mixers so that the stereo mixing bus(es) of a mixer feed(s) the stereo bus(es) of a second mixer.

CD

Abbreviation of the term *compact disc*, a small optical disc with digital audio data recorded onto it.

CD-ROM

Abbreviation of the term *compact disc, read-only memory*, a compact disc used to store digital data, such as large programs, that can be read by a computer. Many programs, libraries of sound samples and graphics are distributed on CD-ROM, because each CD can store hundreds of megabytes of information and yet costs about the same to manufacture as a floppy disk, which only stores about 1MB.

centre frequency

That frequency of an audio signal that is boosted or attenuated the most by an equaliser with a peak equalisation curve.

chamber

1. An echo chamber, ie a room designed with very hard, non-parallel surfaces equipped with a speaker and microphone so that, when dry signals from the console are fed to the speaker, the microphone picks up a reverberation of these signals, which can then be combined with the dry signals at the console. 2. A program in a delay/reverb effects device that simulates the sound of an echo chamber.

channel

1. In multitrack tape machines, the same as *track* (ie one audio recording made on a portion of the width of a multitrack tape). 2. A single path that an audio signal travels or can travel through a device from an input to an output.

charge

The electrical energy of electrons. The energy is in the form of a force that is considered negative and repels other like forces (other electrons) and attracts opposite (positive) forces.

chase

The action of a recorder or sequencer whose speed has been automatically adjusted to be in time with another recorder.

chip

1. A slang term with the same meaning as *IC* (Integrated Circuit), ie a miniature circuit of many components that is in a small, sealed housing with prongs to connect it into equipment. 2 The thread cut away from the master lacquer to make the groove while recording onto disc.

chord

Two or more musical pitches sung or played together.

chorus

1. The part of a song that is repeated and has the same music and lyrics each time. The chorus usually gives the point of the song. 2. A musical singing group that has many singers. 3. A delay effect that simulates a vocal chorus by adding several delays with a mild amount of feedback and a medium amount of depth. 4. A similar effect created in some synthesisers by detuning (reducing the pitch slightly) and mixing it with a signal that has regular tuning and a slight delay.

chorusing

A type of signal processing. In chorusing, a time-delayed or detuned copy of a signal is mixed with the original signal. The mixing process changes the relative strengths and phase relationships of the overtones to create a fatter, more animated sound. The simplest way to achieve chorusing is by detuning one synthesiser oscillator from another to produce a slow beating between them.

circuit

1. One complete path of an electric current. 2. Similar to definition 1 but including all paths and components to accomplish one function in a device.

clangorous

Containing partials that aren't part of the natural harmonic series. Clangorous tones often sound like bells.

clicking

Pressing and immediately releasing the switch on a computer's mouse.

clip

To deform a waveform during overload.

clock signal

The signal put out by a circuit that generates the steady, even pulses or codes used for synchronisation.

close miking

A technique involving placing a microphone close to (ideally within a foot of) a sound source being recorded in order to pick up primarily the direct sound and to avoid picking up leakage or ambience.

co-ax

Twin-conductor cable consisting of one conductor surrounded by a shield.

coincident microphones (coincident pair)

An arrangement by which the heads of two microphones are placed as close as possible to each other so that the path length from any sound source to either microphone is, for all practical purposes, the same.

comb filter

1. The frequency response achieved by mixing a direct signal with a delayed signal of equal strength, especially at short delays. 2. Also loosely used to describe effects that can be achieved with comb filtering as part of the processing.

compander

1. A two-section device used in noise-reduction systems. The first section compresses the audio signal before it is recorded and the second section expands the signal after it's been recorded.

2. In Yamaha digital consoles, a signal processor that applies both compression and expansion to the same signal. Digital companding allows a device to achieve a greater apparent dynamic range with fewer bits per sample word (see *digital word*).

compression driver

In a horn loudspeaker, a unit that feeds a sound-pressure wave into the throat of the horn.

compression ratio

In a compressor or limiter, the number of decibels that an input signal has to rise above a threshold to achieve one more decibel of output.

compressor

A signal-processing device that allows less fluctuation in the level of the signal above a certain adjustable or fixed level.

condenser

An old term meaning the same thing as *capacitor*, ie an electronic device that is composed of two plates separated by an insulator and can store charge. The term is still in common use when used to refer to a microphone's active element.

condenser microphone

A microphone that converts changes in sound pressure into changes in capacitance. The capacitance changes are then converted into variations in electrical voltage (ie an audio signal).

console

A set of controls and their housing that control all of the signals necessary for recording and mixing.

consumer format (consumer DIF)

A standard adopted by the IEC for the sending and receiving of digital audio, based on the AES Professional Interface.

contact microphone

A device that senses vibrations and puts out an audio signal that is proportional to the vibrations.

controller

1. Any device – for example, a keyboard, wind synth controller or pitch-bend lever – capable of producing a change in some aspect of a sound by altering the action of some other device. 2. Any of the defined MIDI data types used for controlling the ongoing quality of a sustaining tone. (Strictly speaking, MIDI continuous controllers are numbered from 0 to 127.) In many synthesisers, the controller-data category is more loosely defined in order to include pitch-bend and aftertouch data. 3. Any device generating a control voltage or signal fed to another device's control input.

corner frequency

Same as *cut-off frequency*, ie the highest or lowest frequency in the pass band of a filter.

CPU (central processing unit)

1. The main "brain" chip of a computer, which performs the calculations and execution of instructions. 2. The main housing of a computer containing the "brain" chip, as opposed to other pieces of the computer system, such as keyboards, monitors, etc.

critical distance

The point a distance away from the sound source at which the direct sound and the reverberant sound are equal in volume.

crossfade looping

A sample-editing feature found in many samplers and most sample-editing software in which some portion of the data at the beginning of a loop is mixed with some portion of the data at the end of the same loop in order to produce a smoother transition between the end and the beginning of the loop.

crossover (crossover network)

A set of filters that "split" the audio signal into two or more bands, or two or more signals, each of which have only some of the frequencies present.

crossover frequency

1. The frequency that is the outer limit of one of the bands of a crossover. 2. In the Lexicon 480L delay/reverberation effects unit, the frequency at which the bass-frequency reverb time is in effect rather than the mid-frequency reverb time.

crosstalk

Leakage of an audio signal from an adjacent or nearby channel into a channel that isn't intended to carry the signal.

cue

1. The signal fed back to musicians over headphones. 2. To set a tape or disc so that the intended selection will immediately play when the tape machine or player is started. 3. A location point entered into a computer controlling the playback or recording of a track or tape. 4. In MCI tape machines, a term meaning the same thing as *sync playback*, where the record head is used as a playback head for those tracks already recorded.

current

The amount of electron charge passing across a point in a conductor per unit of time.

cut

1. One selection (song) on a pre-recorded music format. 2. A term with the same meaning as *mute* (ie to turn off a channel or a signal). 3. To reduce the gain of a particular band of frequencies with an equaliser. 4. To deny the passing of a particular band of frequencies (said of a filter).

cut-off frequency (turnover frequency)

1. The highest or lowest frequency in the pass band of a filter. 2. The highest or lowest frequency passed by an audio device. The cut-off frequency is usually considered to be the first frequency to be 3dB lower than a reference frequency in the middle of the bandwidth of the device.

cut-off rate/slope

The number of decibels that a filter reduces the signal for each octave past the filter's cut-off frequency (ie outside the pass band).

cycle

1. An alternation of a waveform that begins at a point, then passes through the zero line and ends up at a point with the same value and moving in the same direction as the starting point. 2. On a Solid State Logic console, a command that tells the console's computer to control the tape machine and make it play and replay a certain section of a tape.

cycles per second

A unit used in the measure of frequency, equivalent to Hertz. Cycles per second is an outdated term that was replaced by Hertz in 1948.

cyclic redundancy checking code

A digital error-detection code used in digital recording.

D/A

Abbreviation of *digital-to-analogue converter*, a device which changes digital data numbers (digital audio signal) into discrete voltage level.

daisy chain

1. A hook-up of several devices where the audio signal has to pass through one device to reach the second device and through the second device to reach the third device. 2. In MIDI, a hook-up of MIDI devices where the MIDI signal has to pass though each device in order to reach the next device.

DAT

An abbreviation of *digital audio tape* and a standard format for recording digital audio on small, specially designed cassette tapes.

data

1. Information (usually letters, words and commands). 2. An analogue signal in early console automation systems made from the control voltages feeding VCAs (Voltage-Controlled Amplifiers).

DAW

Abbreviation of *digital audio workstation*, a dedicated device that is both a recorder and mixer of digital audio.

dB

Abbreviation of the term *decibel*, a unit used to compare signal strengths.

dBm

1. Decibels of audio power present compared to one milliwatt of power in a 600-ohm load. 2. Very incorrectly and too-commonly-used term designating the reference voltage of .775 volts of audio signal strength, regardless of impedance.

dBSPL

The sound-pressure level present compared in decibels to the standard sound-pressure reference level representing "no" sound (ie a sound-pressure level that about 50% of people would say that they couldn't hear).

dBu (dBv)

The audio voltage present compared in decibels to the level of .775 volts of audio voltage in a circuit of any impedance.

DBX

A brand of noise reduction systems, dynamic processing equipment and other audio gear.

DC

Abbreviation of *direct current*, ie electric current flowing in one direction only.

dead

1. An acoustically absorbent area or space. 2. A slang term for "broken".

decay

1. The rate of reduction of an audio signal generated in synthesisers from the peak level to the sustain level. (See also *ADSR*.) 2. The fade-out of the reverberation of a sound.

decibel

A unit of measurement used to indicate audio power level. Technically, a decibel is a logarithmic ratio of two numbers, which means that there is no such thing as a decibel measurement of a single signal. In order to measure a signal in decibels, you need to know what level it's referenced to. Commonly used reference levels are indicated by such symbols as dBm, dBV and dBu.

de-esser

1. The control circuit of an audio compressor or limiter that is made more sensitive to the sounds made by a person pronouncing the letter S. 2. Any device that will reduce the high-frequency energy present when the letter S is pronounced loudly.

definition

1. The quality of a sound that allows it to be distinguished from other sounds. 2. In Lexicon reverb units, a parameter that sets a decrease in reverberation density in the later part of the decay.

degauss

A term with the same meaning as *demagnetise*, ie to remove the magnetism from something.

delay

A signal that comes from a source and is then delayed by a tape machine or delay device and can then be mixed with the original (non-delayed) signal to make it sound fuller, create echo effects, etc. 1. The first stage of a five-stage DADSR envelope, which delays the beginning of the envelope's attack segment. 2. A control function that allows one of the elements in a layered sound to start later than another element. 3. A signal processor used for flanging, doubling and echo which holds its input for a period of time before passing it to the output, or the algorithm within a signal processor that creates delay.

delay effects

Any signal processing that uses delay as its basis for processing, such as echo, reverb delay and special effects, such as flanging and chorusing.

demo

1. A cheaply-made recording that gives an idea of some of the musical performances that could be used in a final music production. 2. To make a demo. 3. Any demonstration or trial use of equipment that may be purchased in the future. 4. The equipment being demonstrated.

detune

1. A control that allows one oscillator to sound a slightly different pitch than another. 2. To change the pitch of one oscillator relative to another in order to produce a fuller sound.

DI

Abbreviation of *direct injection* or *direct input*.

dialogue

The spoken word recorded in film/video sound, commercials and instructional recordings.

diaphragm

The part of the microphone which moves in response to fluctuations in the sound-pressure wave.

digital

Literally "of numbers". Digital music equipment uses microprocessors to store, retrieve and manipulate information about sound in the form of numbers, and typically divides potentially continuous fluctuations in value – such as amplitude or pitch – into discrete quantized steps.

digital controls

1. Controls that have changing number displays when the control is changed. 2. Controls that change the digital control signal information bits to change the value of some functions.

digital delay

A delay line or delay effects unit that converts audio signal into digital audio signal, delays it and then converts it back to analogue audio signal before sending it out of the unit.

digital domain

The realm where data is expressed as a series of binary numbers or binary number signals rather than analogue signals.

digital error

Caused by lost bit information from the digital words of the digital audio signal.

digital interface format (DIF)

A specification of the number of bits, their meaning, the voltage and the type of connector used with digital audio connections.

digital multimeter

A small, hand-held, battery operated testing device that tests levels of voltage, current, resistance and continuity. The results are showed on a digital display.

digital recording

The process of converting audio signals into numbers representing the waveform and then storing these numbers.

digital signal processing (DSP)

Any signal processing done after an analogue audio signal has been converted into digital audio.

digital-to-analogue converter (DAC)

A device that changes the sample words put out by a digital audio device into analogue fluctuations in voltage that can be sent to a mixer or amplifier. All digital synthesisers, samplers and effects devices have DACs (pronounced to rhyme with fax) at their outputs to create audio signals.

digital word

A number of information bits that will communicate one value, with each word being a standard length.

dip

To reduce the levels of signals in a specific band of audio frequencies.

direct

1. Using a direct pick-up. 2. Using a direct output. 3. Recording all musicians to the final two-track master without using a multitrack tape.

direct box

An electronic device utilising a transformer or amplifier to change the electrical output of an electric instrument (for example, an electric guitar) to the impedance and level usually obtained from a microphone.

direct current

Electric current flowing in one direction only. Usually abbreviated to DC.

directional pattern

1. In microphones, the same as *pick-up pattern*, ie a description or graphic display of the level that a microphone puts out in response to sounds arriving from different directions. 2. In speakers, the pattern of dispersion (the area that the sound from a speaker will cover evenly in a listening area).

direct inject

The same as *direct pick-up*.

direct input

The same as *direct pick-up*, ie to feed the signal from an electrical output of an electric instrument to a recording console or tape recorder without using a microphone but instead by changing the electrical output of the instrument to the same impedance and level as a microphone.

direct output

1. On most consoles, an output of the console activated by the Direct Output switch, which connects a numbered input module to a same-numbered track – for example, the direct output on input module one feeds to track one of the tape recorder. 2. On some consoles, a jack that is the output of a console input module which can be used to patch the signal from this module to any track input of a tape machine.

direct pick-up

Feeding the signal from an electrical instrument to the recording console or tape recorder without using a microphone.

direct sound

The sound that reaches a microphone or listener without hitting or bouncing off any obstacles.

disk/disc

1. A round, flat object (usually housed in a protective sleeve) coated with material that can be magnetised in a similar manner to tape. 2. Any round, flat object capable of storing audio signals (digital or analogue) or digital data, including phonograph records and compact discs.

distant miking

The technique of placing a mic far from a sound source so that reflected sound is picked up with the direct sound.

distortion

1. The audio garble that can be heard when an audio waveform has been altered, usually by the overloading of an audio device like an amplifier. 2. The similar garbled sound that can be heard when the sound-pressure level is too loud for the waveform to be accurately reproduced by the human hearing mechanism.

diversity

A system in wireless microphone receivers that switches between two or more antennae to prevent drop-outs in the audio signal.

Dolby

The name and trademark of a manufacturer of noise-reduction systems and other audio systems. These systems improve the performance and fidelity of devices that record, play back and transmit audio material.

Doppler effect

A change in frequency of a delayed signal caused by changes in the delay time while the cycle is being formed.

DOS

Abbreviation of *disk operating system*, ie the function of storing and handling data by a computer.

double

1. To record a second performance, ie double-tracking (recording a second track with a second performance closely matching the first). 2. To use a delay line with medium delay to simulate this.

drive

1. To control something else, especially the mechanical movement of a recording or playback device. 2. The mechanical mechanism used to drive something, as in definition 1. 3. To feed a

signal to a device. 4. Short for *disk drive*, the mechanism that writes and reads digital data to and from a floppy disk.

driver

In a horn loudspeaker, the unit that feeds a sound-pressure wave into the throat of the horn.

drop-out

A very short absence of signal in magnetic recording, usually caused by dirt or defects in the magnetic coating of tapes and discs, or any very short loss of an audio signal.

drum machine

A sample playback unit or sound module with drum sounds that can be sequenced by an internal sequencer to play drum patterns.

drum pattern

A sequence of drum sounds played by a drummer or sequenced into a drum machine, especially a short pattern used in part of a song.

dry signal

A signal consisting entirely of the original, unprocessed sound. The output of an effects device is 100% dry when only the input signal is being heard, ie with none of the effects created by the processor itself, with no reverberation or ambience. The term is more loosely used to describe an audio signal free of signal processing.

DSP

Abbreviation of *digital signal processing*, ie any signal processing performed after an analogue audio signal has been convened into digital audio. Broadly speaking, all changes in sound that are produced within a digital audio device – other than those caused by the simple cutting and pasting of sections of a waveform – are created via DSP. A digital reverb is a typical DSP device.

dub

1. To copy a recording. 2. A copy of a recording. 3. A recording made in time with another recording so that the final result is a combination of the first recording and the second recording. 4. To add dialogue to a picture after the picture has been filmed or recorded on videotape.

dynamic microphone

1. A microphone in which the diaphragm moves a coil suspended in a magnetic field in order to generate an output voltage proportional to the sound-pressure level. 2. Occasionally used to mean any microphone that has a generating element which cuts magnetic lines of force in order to produce an output, such as a dynamic microphone (definition 1) or a ribbon microphone.

dynamic (signal) processing

An automatic change in level or gain effected to change the ratio in level of the loudest audio to the softest audio.

dynamic range

1. The level difference (in decibels) between the loudest peak and the softest level of a recording, etc. 2. The level difference between the level of clipping and the noise level in an audio device or channel.

dynamics

1. The amount of fluctuation in level of an audio signal. 2. In music, the playing of instruments loudly or softly.

dynamic voice allocation

A system found on many multitimbral synthesisers and samplers that allows voice channels to be reassigned automatically to play different notes (often with different sounds) whenever required by the musical input from the keyboard or MIDI.

early reflections

1. The first echoes in a room, caused by the sound from the sound source reflecting off one surface before reaching the listener. 2. A reverb algorithm whose output consists of a number of closely spaced, discrete echoes, designed to mimic the bouncing of sound off nearby walls in an acoustic space.

earth

The British version of the American term *ground* (in electronics, a place that has zero volts).

echo

1. One distinct repeat of a sound caused by the sound reflecting off a surface. 2. Loosely used to mean reverberation (ie the continuing of a sound after the source stops emitting it, caused by many discrete echoes closely spaced in time).

echo chamber

1. A room designed with very hard, non-parallel surfaces and equipped with a speaker and microphone. 2. Any artificial or electronic device that simulates the reverberation created in a room.

echo return

An input of the console which brings back the echo (reverberation) signal from the echo chamber or other echo effects device.

echo send

The output of a console used to send a signal to an echo chamber or delay effects device.

echo send control

A control to send the signal from the input module to the echo chamber or effects device via the echo bus.

edit buffer

An area of memory used for making changes in the current patch. Usually the contents of the edit buffer will be lost when the instrument is switched off and a Write operation is required to move the data to a more permanent area of memory for long-term storage.

editing

1. Changing the sequence of a recording by cutting the recording tape and putting the pieces together in the new sequence with splicing tape. 2. Punching in and then punching out on one or more tracks of a multitrack tape recorder to replace previously recorded performances. 3. Changing the sequence of a digital recording's playback by using a computer program.

effects

1. An effect is a device that modifies an audio signal by adding something to the signal to change the sound. 2. Short for the term *sound effects* (sounds other than dialogue, narration or music added to film or video shots, such as door slams, wind, etc).

effects track

1. In film production, a recording of the mixdown of all of the sound effects for the film ready to be mixed with the dialogue and music. 2. In music recording, one track with a recording of effects to be added to another track of a multitrack recording.

electret condenser

A condenser microphone that has a permanently polarised (charged) variable capacitor as its sound-pressure-level sensor.

electric current

A more formal term for *current*, ie the amount of electron charge passing across a point in a conductor per unit of time.

electric instrument

Any musical instrument that puts out an electrical signal rather than an acoustic sound.

electricity

Electrical current (the amount of electron charge passing across a point in a conductor per unit of time) or voltage (the force pushing electrons in order to obtain electrical current).

electromagnetic field

Magnetic energy put out because of current travelling through a conductor.

electromagnetic induction (electromagnetic pick-up)

The generation of electrical signal in a conductor moving in a magnetic field or being close to a changing magnetic field.

electromagnetic theory

A statement of the principles behind electromagnetic induction, ie when a conductor cuts magnetic lines of force, current is induced in that conductor.

electronics

1. On a tape machine, the housing for and the channel circuitry that processes the signal to be fed to the heads in order to provide bias and playback. 2. The branch of science dealing with the behaviour of electrons/charges in vacuums, gases, semiconductors and special conductors.

electrons

Negatively charged particles which revolve around the centres of atoms. The movement of such electrons down a conductor causes electrical current.

electrostatic charge

The excess or deficiency of electrons in a given area.

engineer

1. A technician in charge of a recording session, also called the *recording engineer*. 2. A person with an engineering degree. 3. A person with sufficient experience in the field to be equivalent to the education one would receive on an engineering degree course.

envelope

1. Description of the way in which a sound or audio signal varies in intensity over time. 2. How a control voltage changes in level over time, controlling a parameter of something other than gain or audio level. The shape of a synthesiser's envelope is controlled by a set of rate (or time) and level parameters. The envelope is a control signal that can be applied to various aspects of a synth sound, such as pitch, filter cut-off frequency and overall amplitude. Usually, each note has its own envelope(s).

envelope generator

A device that generates an envelope. Also known as a *contour generator* or *transient generator*, because the envelope is a contour (shape) that is used to create some of the transient (changing) characteristics of the sound. (See *ADSR*.)

envelope tracking

Also called *keyboard tracking*, *key follow* or *keyboard rate scaling*. A function that changes the length of one or more envelope segments, depending on which key on the keyboard is being pressed. Envelope tracking is most often used to give the higher notes shorter envelopes and the lower notes longer envelopes, mimicking the response characteristics of percussion-activated acoustic instruments, such as guitar and marimba.

equal loudness contours

A drawing of several curves showing how loud the tones of different frequencies would have to be played for it to be said that they were of equal loudness.

equalisation

Any time that the amplitudes of audio signals at specific set of frequencies are increased or decreased more than the signals at other audio frequencies.

equipment rack

A cabinet with rails, or free-standing rails, that have holes to accept screws at standard spaces. Used to house outboard gear.

error concealment

Replacing information in a digital audio signal to replace lost bits when the digital recording or processing system cannot verify whether the lost bits were ones or zeros but can make a good guess by comparing the known bits that were close in position to the lost bits.

error correction

Replacing exactly information lost from a digital audio signal.

error detection

The process of discovery that sonic information has been lost in a digital audio signal.

error message

A prompt on a computer screen telling the operator that an error has occurred.

expander

A device that causes expansion of an audio signal.

expansion

The opposite of compression. For example, an expander may allow the signal to increase 2dB every time the signal input increases by 1dB.

expansion ratio

The number of decibels that the output signal will drop for every decibel that the input signal falls below the threshold.

fade

1. A gradual reduction of the level of an audio signal. 2. A gradual change of level from one preset level to another.

fader

A device to control the gain of a channel on a console, thereby determining the level of a signal in that channel.

far field

The area covering the distance from three feet away from the sound source up to the critical distance.

fat

Having more than a normal amount of signal strength at low frequencies or having more sound than normal by the use of compression or delay.

feed

To send an audio or control signal to a device.

feedback

1. The delayed signal sent back to the input of a delay line, used in repeat-echo effects. 2. The pick-up of the signal out of a channel by its input or the howling sound that this produces. 3. In an amplifier, the phase-reversed output signal sent back to its input, reducing gain but also causing distortion and noise.

feedback control

The control on a delay line or delay effects device that controls the amount of feedback present in a signal.

fidelity

The recording or reproduction quality of an audio device.

figure-of-eight pattern

Another name for a bi-directional pattern, a microphone design that picks up best from the front and rear of the diaphragm and not at all from the side of the diaphragm.

file

A collection of digital data stored in a computer's memory bank or on a floppy disk.

filter

1. A device that removes signals with frequencies above or below a certain point, known as the *cut-off frequency*. 2. An equaliser section, used in this sense because filters are used with other components to give an equaliser its frequency response characteristics. 3. The action of

removing signals of some frequencies and leaving the rest. 4. A mechanical device that smoothes out speed variations in tape machines, known as a *scrape flutter filter* or, more usually, a *scrape flutter idler*.

final mix

A two-track stereo master tape mixed from the multitrack master.

FireWire

The popular name for a high-speed digital standard connection for linking up peripherals such as digital video cameras, audio components and computer devices. FireWire was originally developed by Apple Computers as a replacement for the SCSI bus. IEEE 1394 is formal name for the standard. Vendors must obtain a licence from Apple in order to use the term FireWire.

first generation

A descriptive term meaning original, as opposed to a copy.

flange

An effect caused by combining an approximately even mix of a modulated (varying) short delay with the direct signal.

flat

1. Lower in musical pitch. 2. A slang term used to describe the sensitivity to frequency of a microphone, amplifier, etc, as being even at all frequencies (usually within 2dB).

Fletcher Munson effect

A hearing limitation shown by Fletcher Munson equal-loudness contours that, as music is lowered in volume, it's much more difficult to hear bass frequencies and somewhat harder to hear very high frequencies.

floor

1. An alternative term to *range* (ie a limit on the amount that a signal is reduced when the input signal is lowered by an expander or gate). 2. A shortening of the term *noise floor* (ie the level of noise).

flutter

1. High-frequency variations in pitch of a recorded waveform due to rapid variations in speed of a recorder or playback machine. 2. Originally, and more formally, any variations – fast or slow – in the pitch of a recorded tone due to speed fluctuations in a recorder or playback unit.

fly in

1. To add sounds into a mix or recording that have no synchronisation. 2. An application of this is where a performance from one part of a tune is recorded and then recorded back into the recording at a different time in the recording.

foldback

A European term for the signal sent to the stage monitors in a live performance.

foot switch

A switch placed on the floor and pressed by a musician to trigger various functions.

formant

An element in the sound of a voice or instrument that doesn't change frequency as different pitches are sounded. Can also be described as a resonant peak in a frequency spectrum. The variable formants produced by the human vocal tract are what give vowels their characteristic sound.

format

1. The number, width, spacing and order of tracks for the purposes of tape recording. 2. To prepare a digital storage medium so that it will accept and store digital information.

frame

1. The amount of time that one still picture is shown in film or video. 2. A division of one second in synchronisation and recording, coming from definition 1.

FreeMIDI

A Macintosh operating system extension developed by Mark Of The Unicorn that enables different programs to share MIDI data. For example, a sequencer could communicate with a librarian program to display synthesiser patch names – rather than just numbers – in the sequencer's editing windows.

frequency

The number of cycles of a waveform occurring in the space of a second.

frequency range

The range of frequencies over which an electronic device is useful or over which a sound source puts out substantial energy.

frequency response

The measure of sensitivity shown by an electronic device (microphone, amplifier, speaker, etc) to various frequencies. Often communicated via a graph.

FSK (frequency shift key)

A simple clock signal that can be used to run a sequencer in time with an audio tape.

full

Used to describe a sound that has all frequencies present, especially the low frequencies.

full step

A change in pitch that occurs when one moves up or down two piano keys.

fundamental

The tuned frequency and, almost always, the lowest frequency that is present in the sounding of a pitch by a musical instrument.

gain

An increase in the strength of an audio signal, often expressed in decibels.

gain control

A device that changes the gain of an amplifier or circuit. Often appears as a knob that can be turned or a slider that can be moved up and down.

gain reduction

A reduction in gain during high-level passages, effected by a limiter or compressor.

gain structure

The way in which gain changes at the various stages or sections of an audio system.

gate

A dynamics-processing device that turns a channel off or down when a signal drops below a certain level.

General MIDI (GM)

A set of requirements adopted by manufacturers of MIDI devices and used to ensure the consistent playback performance on all instruments bearing the GM logo. Some of the requirements include 24-voice polyphony and a standardised group and location of sounds. For example, patch 17 will always be a drawbar organ sound on all General MIDI instruments.

generating element

The portion of a microphone that actually converts the movement of the diaphragm into electrical current or changes in voltage.

generation

A term used here to describe the number of times that a recorded audio signal has been copied.

generation loss

The amount of clarity lost in an audio copy due to added noise and distortion.

glide

A function where the pitch slides smoothly from one note to the next instead of jumping over the intervening pitches. Also called *portamento*.

golden section

A ratio of exact height to width to length of a room in order to achieve good acoustics. First recommended by the ancient Greeks. The ratio is approximately the width of a room x 1.6 times its height and its length x 2.6 times its height.

gigabyte

One billion bytes.

global

Pertaining to or governing all of the operations of an instrument.

graphic editing

A method of editing parameter values using graphical representations (for example, of envelope shapes) displayed on a computer screen or LCD.

graphic equaliser

A device equipped with several slides to control the gain of an audio signal present within one of several evenly spaced frequency bands, spaced according to octaves.

ground

US equivalent of British *earth*. In electronics, a place (terminal) that has zero volts.

ground lift

A switch that breaks the connection between the ground points in two different circuits.

ground lifter

An adapter that takes a three-pronged power cord and plugs into a two-pronged outlet, used to disconnect the third (ground) pin of the power outlet. It can be *very* dangerous to have no ground connection to the casing by using a ground lifter and not grounding the unit by other means.

ground loop

A double grounding of a line or electronic device at two different "ground" points of differing voltage.

group

1. A number of channels or faders that can be controlled by one master VCA slide. 2. A shortening of the term *recording group* (ie a bus or the signal present on a bus).

group faders

The VCA faders of a number of individual channels that are all controlled by a group master fader (ie a slide control used to send out a control voltage to several VCA faders in individual channels).

grouping

1. Controlling the gain of several individual channels with a group fader. 2. The mixing together of several individual audio signals to send a mixed signal out of the console to record a track on a multitrack tape machine.

group master

A slide control used to send out a control voltage to several VCA faders in individual channels, thus controlling the gain of several channels.

guitar controller

An electric guitar or device played like an electric guitar that produces MIDI signals which can be used to control synthesisers and sound modules.

guitar processor

A unit that adds effects to a direct guitar signal, including a simulated instrument amplifier sound and, often, delay and reverb effects.

Haas effect

Simply stated, a factor in human hearing where delay has a much bigger effect on the human perception of direction than level does.

half step

A difference in pitch present between adjacent keys on a piano.

hall program

A setting of a digital delay/reverb effects unit that approximates concert halls. Hall programs are characterised by a pre-delay of up to 25ms.

harmonic

A frequency that is a whole-number multiple of the fundamental frequency. For example, if the fundamental frequency of a sound is 440Hz, the first two harmonics are 880Hz and 1,320Hz (1.32kHz). Harmonics are whole-number multiples of the frequency that determines the timbre recognition of an instrument's sound.

harmonic distortion

The presence of harmonics in the output signal of a device that weren't present in the input signal.

head amp

Alternative name for pre-amplifier, a low-noise amplifier designed to take a low-level signal, such as the output of a tape head, and bring it up to normal line level.

headphones

Devices that can be worn on the head fitted with small speakers that fit over the ears or, sometimes, into the ears.

headroom

1. The level difference (in decibels) between normal operating level and clipping level in an amplifier or audio device. 2. A similar level difference between normal tape-operating level and the level at which the distortion would be 3%.

hearing limitation

An inability of the human ear to hear important characteristics of sound under certain conditions. Characteristics that can be affected include pitch, level, clarity, presence and direction.

Hertz

The basic unit of frequency, equivalent to *cycles per second*. The term is usually abbreviated to Hz.

high frequencies

Audio frequencies at 6,000Hz and above.

high impedance

Impedance of 5,000 ohms or more.

high-impedance mic

A microphone designed to be fed into an amplifier with an input impedance greater than 20,000 ohms.

high-pass filter

A device that rejects signals below a certain frequency (known as the *cut-off frequency*) and passes signals with frequencies that are higher than this.

highs

Abbreviation of *high frequencies* (ie audio frequencies of 6,000Hz and higher).

hi-z

Abbreviation of *high impedance* (ie an impedance of 5,000 ohms or more).

horn

A speaker or speaker enclosure where sound-pressure waves are fed through a narrow opening (by a speaker cone or driver) and where the narrow opening flares out into a larger opening.

hum

Produced when 60Hz power-line current is accidentally induced or fed into electronic equipment.

hypercardioid pattern

A microphone pick-up sensitivity pattern demonstrating that the least-sensitive pick-up point is more than 90° but less than 150° off axis (usually 120°).

Hz

Abbreviation of *Hertz*, the unit of frequency.

IC

Abbreviation of *integrated circuit*, ie a miniature circuit comprising many components in small, sealed housing equipped with prongs to connect it to other equipment.

icon

A visual picture or symbol on a computer screen that represents a file, program, disk or folder that can be used or opened.

ID

An index signal (ie digital data that provides a machine with information concerning the starting points and selection numbers of sections, etc) on a DAT or CD.

IM distortion

Abbreviation of *intermodulation distortion*, which is caused by one signal beating with another signal and producing frequencies that are both the sum and the difference of the original frequencies present.

impedance

The opposition to alternating current (AC).

impedance matching

Having or converting the output impedance of a device so that it matches the impedance of the input that it will feed.

in

Short for "in the circuit". In other words, active.

infinite baffle

A baffle so large that the sounds coming from one side don't reach the other.

infinite repeat

A function on some delay lines that cause enough feedback for the repeat echo to last forever but not enough to cause a howling sound.

information bits

The bits in a digital signal that make up actual values or commands being communicated, as opposed to bits that are used for the checking and correction of data or for other purposes.

initialise

To prepare a digital storage medium, such as a hard disk, so that it will accept and store digital information bits.

in-line console

A console equipped with modules that have all of the controls for all of the sections in one long strip.

in port

A jack on a MIDI device or computer that will accept an incoming data signal.

input

1. The jack or physical location of the point at which a device receives a signal. 2. A signal being received by a device. 3. To feed a signal from one device to another.

input impedance

The opposition to current flow exerted by the first circuits of a device.

input/output module

A set of controls on one housing for an in-line console that has two channels – one for recording and one for monitoring – and which has controls for all console sections.

input overload

Sending too high a signal level into a device, so that the first amplifier of the device overloads.

insert

1. A punch in performed on all of the tracks being recorded in a recording session. 2. On Solid State Logic consoles, to place an outboard piece of gear in a channel by patching and activating a switch.

instrument amplifier

A device that has a power amplifier and speaker in a case (or in separate cases) to reproduce the signal put out by an electric instrument (such as an electric guitar) and to allow the instrument to be heard.

instrument out direct

The action of feeding the output of an electric instrument, such as an electric guitar, to a recording console or tape recorder without using a microphone.

insulator

A substance that, for all practical purposes, won't conduct electricity, such as glass, air or plastic.

integrated circuit (IC)

A miniature circuit comprising many components in a small, sealed housing fitted with prongs to allow it to be connected to equipment.

interface

Any device that allows one unit to work, drive or communicate with another unit when they can't do so by just feeding each other, often because the units are manufactured by different companies.

intermodulation distortion

Form of distortion caused by one signal beating with another signal and producing frequencies that are both the sum and the difference of the original frequencies.

inverse square law

This expresses the fact that, in an unobstructed area (such as an open field), the sound-pressure level will drop to half pressure (-6dB) every time the distance to a sound source is doubled.

I/O

Abbreviation of *input/output,* referring to: 1. an in-line console module that contains controls for the input section, output section and monitor section; 2. a module in electronic gear containing input and output amplifiers for the device; and 3. a digital port (connector) able to both receive digital data and output digital data.

isolation

A containing of the sound wave in a certain area so that it won't leak into other areas and/or unintended mics.

isolation booth/room

A room that prevents loud sounds produced by other instruments from leaking in.

jack

A connector mounted on the casing of a device or on a panel.

jack bay

A series of jacks that have connections for most of the inputs and outputs of the equipment in a control room.

jam sync

A generation of new SMPTE according to the input SMPTE signal.

joystick

1. A quad pan pot that determines the percentage of a signal sent to each of four outputs. 2. A control that separately controls two functions at once.

k

Abbreviation of *kilo*, a prefix for 1,000.

K

Abbreviation of *kick drum*.

key

The control of a dynamics-processing device via an external audio signal.

keyboard

1. Any musical instrument controlled by pressing a key. 2. The part of the computer that has the keys.

keyboard controller

A device that has the standard music keys of piano but transmits MIDI signals.

keyboard scaling

A function by which the sound can be altered smoothly across the range of a keyboard by using key numbers as a modulation source. Level scaling changes the loudness of the sound, while filter scaling changes its brightness.

keying input/key input

An input on a dynamics-processing device used to control the device via an external audio signal.

key note number

A number assigned to each key of a synthesiser or controller keyboard that is transmitted in the MIDI signal.

kHz

Abbreviation of *kiloHertz* (1,000 Hertz).

kilo

A prefix meaning 1,000.

kilobyte (KB)

Linguistically, 1,000 bytes. In practice, a kilobyte generally contains 1,024 bytes.

layering

The recording or playing of a musical part with several similar sound patches playing simultaneously.

lead

The musical instrument or vocal that plays or sings the melody of a tune.

lead sheet

A written chart showing the melody, lyrics and chords of a tune, complete with full musical notation.

leakage

Sounds from other instruments and sources that weren't intended to be picked up by a microphone.

LED (light-emitting diode)

A light that allows current to flow in one direction only and emits light whenever a voltage of a certain level or beyond is applied to it.

level

The amount of signal strength (ie the amplitude, especially the average amplitude).

LFO

Abbreviation of *low-frequency oscillator*.

lift

To boost the gain of an audio signal at a particular band of frequencies with an equaliser.

limiter

A device that reduces gain when the input voltage exceeds a certain level.

line

1. Abbreviation of *line level*. 2. A cable.

linear

The condition of obtaining a change at the output of the device which is proportional to the change occurring at the input.

line input

An input designed to take a line-level signal.

line level

An amplified signal level put out by an amplifier and used as the normal level that runs through the interconnecting cables in a control room.

line out(put)

Any output that sends out a line-level signal, such as the output of a console that feeds a recorder.

link

A term used with reference to compressors and dynamic-processing units meaning to combine the control input signals of two channels of a compressor (or dynamic-processing unit) so that both channels always have the same gain and are triggered to change gain by the signal of either channel.

listen circuits

A type of solo circuit that allows you to listen to a channel before the fader or after the fader.

live

1. Refers to the sound produced by instruments during a performance to an audience. 2. Having a large portion of reverberant or reflected sound.

live recording

1. The practice of recording where all musicians are playing at once and no overdubbing takes place. 2. Recorded material with a lot of natural reverberation.

load

1. The opposition to an audio output signal of a device by the input of the device being fed. 2. A resistor that would have the lowest impedance that a device was designed to feed into used during the testing of a device. 3. To copy the digital data on a storage medium into the RAM of a computer. 4. To put tape onto a tape machine and activate the computer-controlled constant-tension system.

load impedance

The opposition to the flow of output current caused by the input that it feeds.

Local (mode) On/Off

A switch or function in a synthesiser that connects (On) or disconnects (Off) the keyboard control of the synthesiser's sound module.

long delay

Delay times greater than 60ms.

loop

1. The same as *anti-node*, ie the points of maximum displacement of motion in a vibrating, stretched string. 2. A piece of material that plays over and over. In a sequencer, a loop repeats a musical phrase. In a sampler, loops are used to allow samples of finite length to be sustained indefinitely.

loud

Causing equal volume changes at all frequency ranges, including frequency response changes at lower operating levels in order to compensate for the Fletcher Munson effect.

loudness

A measure of how loud something sounds to the ear.

loudness control

A knob that changes the level and adjusts the frequency response of the circuit controlling the speakers in order to compensate for the inability of the ear to hear low frequencies and extremely high frequencies at low volumes.

low end

A slang term for bass-frequency signals (ie those below 250Hz).

lower toms

Large toms that sit on the floor, mounted on metal feet, with heads up to approximately 20 inches in diameter.

low frequencies

1. Audio or audible frequencies below 1kHz. 2. The range of bass frequencies below approximately 250Hz.

low-frequency oscillator

An oscillator that puts out an AC signal between .1Hz and 10Hz, used for a control signal. Especially devoted to applications below the audible frequency range, and typically used as a control source for modulating a sound to create vibrato, tremolo, trills and so on.

low impedance

Impedance of 500 ohms or less.

low-pass filter

A device that rejects signals above a certain frequency and passes those that are lower in frequency.

lo-z

Abbreviation of *low impedance*, ie an impedance of 500 ohms or less.

magnetic

1. Emitting magnetic energy. 2. Able to be magnetised.

magnetic lines of force

The magnetic field that exists between poles of a magnet.

map

A table in which input values are arbitrarily assigned to outputs by the user on an item-by-item basis.

mapper

A device that translates MIDI data from one form to another in real time.

margin

The amount of decibels between the highest peak level of a program and the point at which overload occurs.

masking

The characteristic of hearing by which loud sounds prevent the ear from hearing softer sounds of similar frequency.

master

1. A control to set the level going out of a console, especially the stereo output to a two-track machine at mixdown. 2. A term with the same meaning as *sub-master*, ie a control that adjusts the level of a signal mixed together and sent out to one track of a multitrack recorder. 3. A term with the same meaning as *VCA master*, ie one slider that controls the control voltage sent to several VCA faders. 4. A machine used as a speed reference when synchronising two or more machines to run together. If the master tape transport changes speed, the other machines synced to it will change speed with it. 5. The original recording, used for making copies. 6. To make an original recording which will be used to make commercial copies, especially making a master lacquer (for record manufacturing) or a master CD.

master fader

1. The fader which controls the main output(s) of a console during mixdown. 2. In some

consoles, faders which control outputs to a multitrack tape recorder during recording. 3. Occasionally used to mean a VCA master (ie one slide that controls the control voltage sent to several VCA faders).

MCI

Abbreviation of *media control interface*, a multimedia specification designed to provide control of onscreen movies and peripherals, such as CD-ROM drives.

MDM

Abbreviation of the term *modular digital multitrack*, ie a multitrack digital recorder with (usually) eight tracks that can be run in synchronisation with other machines (of the same type) in order to attain more tracks. An example of this type of machine is the ADAT (Alesis' modular digital multitrack recording system).

measure

The grouping of a number of beats in music.

medium delay

Delay times of 20-60ms.

meg(a)

1. A prefix for 1,000,000. 2. A slang abbreviation of megaHertz (1,000,000Hz) or megabytes (1,024,000 bytes).

memory

The components in a computer or devices that can be connected to a computer that store digital data. In the case of musical devices, this data comprises information about patches, sequences, waveforms and so on.

merger

A MIDI accessory that allows two incoming MIDI signals to be combined into one MIDI output.

meter

A device which measures or compares electrical signals, often used to read the voltage levels of audio signals.

mic

Abbreviation of *microphone*.

mic gain control

A level control on a mic pre-amp that sets gain and is used to prevent the overload of that pre-amp.

mic input

The input of a console or other device into which a microphone can be plugged.

mic level

The very low audio voltage level that comes out of a studio microphone.

mic/line switch

The selector switch on the input of a console channel that chooses which input jack feeds the console.

mic pad

A device that reduces the level of a signal, placed just before a microphone pre-amplifier to prevent overloading of the pre-amplifier.

mic pre-amp

An amplifier that boosts the low-level audio signal produced by a microphone up to line level.

microphone

A transducer that converts sound-pressure waves into electrical signals.

microprocessor

One IC (Integrated Circuit) that performs the core of activities in a computer.

MIDI

Abbreviation of *musical instrument digital interface*, a digital signal system (ie a system of number signals) used to send and receive performance information to and from musical instruments.

MIDI channel

A grouping of data concerning the performance of one synthesiser or device separate from the data concerning other synthesisers or devices. MIDI commands contain all of the information that a sound board needs to reproduce the desired sound.

MIDI clock

Time data in a MIDI signal that advances one step each $1/24$ of a beat and can be used to sync two sequencers together.

MIDI clock with song pointer

A MIDI clock that which also has a number signal for each measure or bar to indicate the number of measures or bars into the tune.

MIDI controller

A device that can be played by a musician that transmits MIDI signals to control synthesisers or sound modules.

MIDI echo

A function in a synthesiser that causes the output of a sequencer to send a MIDI signal out of the out port matching the MIDI signal coming in for the track being recorded.

MIDI interface

A device that converts a MIDI signal into the digital format used by a computer so that the computer can store and use the MIDI signal.

MIDI mode

Any of the ways in which devices respond to incoming MIDI data. While four modes – Omni Off/Poly, Omni On/Poly, Omni Off/Mono and Omni On/Mono – are defined by the MIDI specification, Omni On/Mono is never used. There are also at least two other useful modes that have been developed: Multi mode, for multitimbral instruments, and Multi-Mono mode, for guitar synthesisers.

MIDI patch bay

A device that has several MIDI inputs and outputs and allows any input to be routed to any output.

MIDI sample dump

The copying of a digitally recorded sample without converting it to analogue between different storage units or sound modules through a MIDI transmission.

MIDI sequencer

A computer that can record and play back MIDI data in such a way as to control the performance of MIDI-controlled musical instruments or devices in a series of timed steps.

MIDI Thru

There are two types of MIDI Thru. One, a simple hardware connection, is found on the back panels of many synthesisers. This Thru jack simply duplicates whatever data is arriving at the MIDI In jack. Sequencers have a second type, called Software Thru, where data arriving at the In jack is merged with data being played by the sequencer, and both sets of data appear in a single stream at the Out (rather than the Thru) jack. Software Thru is useful because it allows you to hook a master keyboard to the sequencer's MIDI In and a tone module to its Out. You can then play the keyboard and hear the tone module, and the sequencer can also send its messages directly to the tone module.

MIDI time code

All of the information contained in SMPTE time code that has been converted into part of the MIDI signal.

mid-range frequencies

Audio frequencies from around 250Hz through to 6,000Hz.

milli

A prefix meaning a thousandth – for example, milliwatt.

MiniDisc

A small, recordable compact disc that can be used by general consumers, introduced by Sony at the end of 1992.

mix

1. To blend audio signals together into a composite signal. 2. The signal made by blending individual signals together. 3. A control or function on a delay/reverberation device that controls the amount of direct signal that is mixed into the processed signal.

mix down

To combine the signals from the tracks of a multitrack tape onto a master tape. Reverberation and other effects may be also added.

mixer

1. A console or other device that blends audio signals into composite signals and has a small number of outputs. 2. A section on a console that performs this function. 3. In Europe, a fader. 4. An engineer or technician who mixes, especially a live-sound mix during a live performance.

mixing console/desk

A device that can combine several signals into one or more composite signals in any proportion.

mixing solo

A button that turns off all other channels, thus allowing the signal to be heard in the stereo perspective and the level used at mixdown, and with reverberation also applied.

modulation

The control of one signal by another AC signal.

modulation noise

Noise that is present only when the audio signal is present.

module

A group of circuits and controls that are mounted on a removable housing. On consoles, this often means all of the controls and circuits for one or two channels.

monitor

1. To listen, in the context of audio. 2. To indicate with a meter or light the conditions in a circuit, especially level and overload. 3. A device designed to listen or observe.

monitor mixer

1. A console or other device that blends audio signals into composite signals and has a small number of outputs. 2. The section of a console that is used to complete a rough mix so that an engineer can hear what's being recorded without effecting the levels being fed to the multitrack recorder. 3. The audio technician who mixes the signals sent to the stage monitor speakers.

monitor pot

A rotary control used to set the level of the track signal in the monitor (ie the signal to or the signal back from one track of a multitrack tape recorder).

monitor (mixer) section

The section of a console that is used to complete a rough mix so that an engineer can hear what's being recorded without effecting the levels being fed to the multitrack recorder.

monitor selector

1. On consoles, a switch that allows you to hear various things over the control-room monitor speakers, such as the main console outputs (for mixing purposes), the monitor mixer section (for recording and overdubbing), the disc player, tape machines and other devices. 2. On tape machines, a switch that, in one position, sends the signal from the tape to the meters and the output of the machine's electronics or, in a second position, sends the input signal being fed to the machine to the meters and the outputs of the electronic devices.

mono

Abbreviation of *monophonic*.

monophonic

1. More formal term for mono and meaning that there is only one sound source, or that the signal was derived from one sound source. 2. In synthesisers, a term meaning that only one pitch may be sounded at a time.

moving-coil microphone

The same as *dynamic microphone*, ie a mic in which the diaphragm moves a coil suspended in a magnetic field in order to generate an output voltage proportional to the sound-pressure level.

moving-fader automation

In consoles, a feature that enables an engineer to program changes in fader levels so that these changes happen automatically upon playback of a multitrack recording, because the fader positions actually change. The faders are driven by tiny motors.

MP3

Abbreviation of MPEG 1, audio layer 3. MPEG stands for Moving Picture Experts Group, and is used to describe a number of file-compression formats used for audio and video files. The idea of MP3 is that it disregards repeated information and also ignores any fluctuations or inaudible harmonics. OK, it's a bit more complicated than that, but you get the idea. Despite the current hype, MP3 doesn't really deliver sound quality that's even close to that of CD or even MiniDisc, but it does create relatively small files (ie around a tenth of the size of normal audio files).

ms

Abbreviation of *milliseconds* (thousandths of a second). Not usually capitalised.

MS miking

A method of placing stereo microphones so that one cardioid microphone points directly at the middle of the area to be miked and a bi-directional microphone is as close as possible to the first mic, with its rejection pointing the same way as the axis of the first mic.

MTC

Abbreviation of *MIDI time code*, ie all of the information of SMPTE time code that has been converted into part of the MIDI signal.

multi(jack)

Abbreviation of the term *multiple jack(s)*. 1. A jack at the output of a device which is not normalised so that plugging into the jack socket will allow the output to be sent to a different input and the output will also feed the place that it normally it feeds. 2. A set of jacks (or one of a set of jacks) with each terminal wired to a corresponding terminal of another or other jacks.

Multi mode

A MIDI reception mode in which a multitimbral module responds to MIDI input on two or more channels and maintains musical independence between the channels, typically playing a different patch on each channel.

multisample

The distribution of several related samples at different pitches across a keyboard. Multisampling can provide greater realism in sample playback (wavetable) synthesis, since the individual samples don't have to be transposed over a great distance.

multitasking

The running of more than one program at the same time by a computer.

multitimbral

A synthesiser that is able to send out several signals of different sound patches (and often playing different parts) or has several sound modules is said to be multitimbral.

multitrack recording

1. Recording various instruments separately on different portions of the same tape in time with each other so that final balancing of the sound may be accomplished later. 2. Digitally recording various instruments onto a hard disk in different data files so that they may be played in time with each other and so that the final balancing of the sound may be accomplished later.

multitrack tape

A magnetic tape that can be used to store two or more discrete signals in time with each other.

Mute switch

A switch that turns off a channel, takes out a track signal from the monitors or turns off the entire monitor signal.

nano

A prefix meaning one billionth.

nanowebers per metre

The standard unit in measuring magnetic energy.

Napster

A popular Internet site for the exchanging or "swapping" of MP3 files. Napster has recently been the subject of considerable legal action brought about by the US recording industry for alleged breach of copyright. At this point in time, as they say, the jury is still out.

narrow-band noise

Noise (random energy) produced over a limited range of frequencies.

near field

The area up to one foot away from the sound source.

negative feedback

Used to describe an out-of-phase portion of an output signal that is fed into the input of an amplifier.

noise

1. Random energy that contains energy at all audio frequencies. 2. Any unintentional or objectionable signal added to an audio signal.

noise filter

A filter that passes only signals with the intended audio frequencies, thus eliminating noise signals at other frequencies.

noise floor

The level of noise below the signal, measured in decibels.

noise gate

A gate used to turn off an audio channel when noise but no signal is present.

noise reduction

Any device designed to remove noise in a device or system.

non-directional

Used with microphones to mean the same thing as *omni-directional* (ie picking up sound from all directions).

non-linear

The condition of obtaining a change at the output of the device that is not proportional to the change occurring at the input, therefore causing distortion.

normalise

1. To provide normalised switches on a jack. 2. To reset a synthesiser, sound module or sample-playback unit to the original factory settings. 3. To adjust the level of a selection so that the highest peak is at the maximum recording level of the medium. 4. To boost the level of a waveform to its maximum amount without experiencing clipping (distortion), thus maximising resolution and minimising certain types of noise.

normalising jacks/normals

Switches on patch jacks that connect certain jack sockets together until a patch cord is inserted.

notch

A narrow band of audio frequencies.

notch filter

A device that rejects signals that have frequencies within a narrow band of audio frequencies and passes all other signals.

null

1. A condition of zero energy or movement. 2. In console automation, the position of a slide or fader at the exact point at which it was originally positioned when the automated mix was made.

nW/m

Abbreviation of *nanowebers per meter*, the standard unit in measuring the amount of magnetic energy.

nybble

Half a byte (ie four information bits).

Nyquist frequency

The highest frequency that can be recorded and reproduced properly by a particular sampling rate. Theoretically, the Nyquist frequency is half of the sampling rate. For example, when a digital recording uses a sampling rate of 44.1kHz, the Nyquist frequency is 22.05kHz. If a signal being sampled contains frequency components that are above the Nyquist frequency, aliasing will be introduced in the digital representation of the signal, unless those frequencies are filtered out prior to digital encoding.

Nyquist rate

The lowest sampling rate that can be used to record and reproduce a given audio frequency.

octave

A difference of pitch where one tone has a frequency that is double or half that of another tone.

off axis

1. Away from the front or axis of the mic. Measured in degrees. 2. 180º from the front.

offset/offset time

1. SMPTE time that triggers a MIDI sequencer. 2. The amount of position difference needed to get two reels to play music in time.

ohm

The unit of resistance (opposition to current flow).

Ohm's law

Formula used to describe the mathematical relationship between voltage, current and resistance.

omni

A prefix meaning "all".

omni-directional

1. Used to describe microphones that pick up evenly from all directions. 2. Used to describe

speakers that send out evenly in all directions.

Omni mode

When Omni mode is activated in a MIDI device, all MIDI messages are recognising and acted on, no matter what their channel.

OMS

Abbreviation of *open music system* (formerly *Opcode MIDI system*), a real-time MIDI operating system for Macintosh applications. OMS allows communication between different MIDI programs and hardware so that, for example, a sequencer could interface with a librarian program to display synthesiser patch names in the sequencer's editing windows, rather than just numbers.

on axis

The position directly in front of the diaphragm of a microphone, in line with its direction of movement.

op amp

Abbreviation of the term *operational amplifier*, an amplifying circuit used in most audio devices.

open circuit

1. A break in a conductor or an incomplete path of electron flow for some other reason. 2. Said of an amplifier that has nothing feeding the input.

operating level

The maximum level of operation, which should not be exceeded.

operational amplifier

An amplifying circuit used in most audio devices.

oscillator

1. A device that puts out test tones at various frequencies in order to align a tape machine or for other testing purposes. 2. In a digital synth, an oscillator more typically plays back a complex waveform by reading the numbers in a wave table.

outboard equipment

Equipment that is used with, but is not part of, a console.

out of phase

1. Being similar to another signal in amplitude, frequency and wave shape but being offset in time by part of a cycle. 2. Having the opposite polarity (ie being 180° out of phase).

out port

A jack that sends out digital data from a computer or digital device.

output

1. The jack or physical location at which a device sends out a signal. 2. The signal put out by a device.

output impedance

The opposition to current flow by the output circuits of an amplifier or some other device.

output level

The signal level at the output of a device.

output selector

The switch on a tape machine which, when activated, allows the VU meter and audio output of the circuits of a tape machine to monitor and send out either the input signal to the tape machine, the playback of what was being recorded or the level of bias currently being fed to the record head.

overdub

To record additional parts alongside or merged with previous tracks. Overdubbing enables "one-man band" productions, as multiple synchronised performances are recorded sequentially.

Over-Easy

DBX's trademark term for the gradual change of compression ratio around the threshold, thus making it difficult to detect when compression is taking place.

overload

To put out too much signal level, thereby causing distortion.

overload indicator

An LED on a console channel that lights up when the input or some other part of the circuit is receiving an overload.

oversampling

A process where the analogue audio (or the digital audio, for playback) is sampled many times more than the minimum sampling rate.

overtones

The harmonics of an instrument's sound minus the fundamental frequency.

pad

1. An attenuator usually used to prevent the overloading of the amplifier that follows it. 2. A device with a surface that can be hit by a drum stick, whereby hitting the pad produces an output signal pulse (or MIDI command) which causes a drum machine or synthesiser to produce a drum sound.

pan pot

An electrical device that distributes one audio signal to two or more channels or speakers.

parallel

1. A circuit interconnection where the source feeds several branched circuit components and where interrupting the current flow in one component doesn't stop current flow in another. 2. A method of sending data where each digit of a digital word is sent at the same time over separate connections.

parallel jacks

Several jacks that are wired together so that each connection is wired to the corresponding connection of other jacks.

parallel port

A jack that sends out or receives digital data where several bits are being sent or received at the same time through different pins.

parameter

A user-adjustable quantity that governs an aspect of a device's performance. Normally, the settings of all of the parameters that make up a synthesiser patch can be changed by the user and stored in memory, but the parameters themselves are defined by the operating system and cannot be altered.

parametric EQ

An equaliser in which all of the parameters of equalisation can be adjusted to any amount, including centre frequency, the amount of boost or cut in gain and bandwidth.

partial

1. In acoustic instruments, a term with the same meaning as *overtone*. 2. In synthesisers, the term means literally "part of a sound patch", ie circuitry in the synthesiser that generates and/or modifies elements of a sound in order to provide a particular tone with timbre. 3. The sound element generated by definition 2.

pass band

The frequency range of signals that will be passed by a filter, rather than reduced by it.

passive device

A piece of signal-processing gear or other device that doesn't use an amplifier as part of its design.

patch

To connect together – as in the inputs and outputs of various modules – generally with patch cords. Also applied to the configuration of hook-ups and settings that results from the process of patching and, by extension, the sound that such a configuration creates. Often used to denote a single tone colour or the contents of a memory location that contains parameter settings for such a tone colour, even on an instrument that requires no physical patching.

patch bay

A series of jacks with connections for most of the inputs and outputs of a console, the console sections, tape machines and other pieces of equipment.

patch editor

A computer program that allows the creation or the changing of sound patch parameters, thereby creating or modifying a specific synthesised sound outside a synthesiser.

patch field

A series of jacks that has connections for most of the inputs and outputs of the console, console sections, tape machines and other pieces of equipment.

patch lead

A cable with two plugs on it used to interconnect two patch jacks in the patch bay.

patch librarian

A computer program that allows the storing of sound patches outside a synthesiser.

patch map

A map with which any incoming MIDI Program Change message can be assigned to call up any of an instrument's patches (sounds).

patch panel

A series of jacks with connections for most of the inputs and outputs of the console, console sections, tape machines and other pieces of equipment.

patch point

One jack in a patch bay.

path

Short for *signal path*, the course that current follows or may follow in a circuit or across a device.

PCM

Abbreviation of *pulse-code modulation*, ie the use of amplitude pulses in magnetic tape to record the digital information bits comprising digital audio data.

peak

1. The highest point in an audio waveform. 2. Short for *peak detecting* (ie responding to a peak) or *peak indicating* (ie showing a peak). 3. Having a frequency response that would draw something similar to a mountain peak on a frequency response graph.

peak detecting

Recognising and responding to peak values of a waveform, rather than average values.

peak indicating meter

A meter that reads the absolute peak level of a waveform.

peaking filter

An EQ circuit which exhibits a peak response.

peak level

The same as *peak value*, ie the maximum positive or negative instantaneous value of a waveform.

peak responding

Recognising and responding to (or indicating) a peak value, rather than the average or effective value.

peak response

1. The same as *peak*. 2. A raising or lowering of the amplitude of signals at the centre frequency more than signals at any other frequency.

peak-to-peak value

The difference in amplitude between positive and negative peaks. Equal to twice the peak value for a sine wave.

peak value

The maximum positive or negative instantaneous value of a waveform.

percentage quantization

A method of quantization by which notes recorded into a sequencer with uneven rhythms aren't shifted all the way to their theoretically perfect timings but are instead shifted part of the way, with the degree of shift being dependent on a user-selected percentage (quantization strength). (See *quantization*.)

phantom powering

A system used to supply condenser microphones with power, thus eliminating the need for external power supplies.

phase

A measurement (expressed in degrees) of the time difference between two similar waveforms.

phase addition

Phase addition occurs when the energy of one waveform increases the energy of another waveform because the two waveforms have similar phase relationships.

phase cancellation

Phase cancellation occurs when the energy of one waveform decreases the energy of another waveform because of phase relationships at or close to 180°.

phase distortion

A change in a sound because of a phase shift in the signal.

phase-distortion synthesis

A method of altering a wave shape in order to add harmonics by phase-shifting while a cycle is being formed.

phase linear

The quality of not having phase shift.

phase lock

1. A method of keeping tape machines synced together by sensing phase differences in the playback of pilot tunes by the two machines and adjusting their speeds to eliminate the phase difference. 2. In synthesisers, the control of one tone generator so that it begins its waveform in phase with the signal from another tone generator.

phase reversal

A change in a circuit effected in order to cause a waveform to shift by 180°.

phase shift

A delay introduced into an audio signal, measured in degrees delayed.

phase sync

1. The same as *phase lock*. 2. A method of keeping machines synced together by sensing phase differences in the playback of pilot tones by the two machines and adjusting their speeds to eliminate the phase difference.

phasing

An effect sound created by the variable phase-shifting of an audio signal mixed with the direct signal.

phon

1. A unit of equal loudness for all audio frequencies. 2. The phon is numerically equal to dBSPL (Sound-Pressure Level) at 1,000Hz but varies at other frequencies according to ear sensitivity.

phone plug (jack)

A plug (or its mating jack) with a diameter of a quarter of an inch and a length of one and a quarter inches used for interconnecting audio devices.

phono cartridge

1. A device which changes the mechanical vibrations stored on records into electrical signals. 2. A transducer that changes sound stored as mechanical vibrations to sound in the form of electricity.

phono plug

1. The same as *RCA plug*. 2. A common audio connector found on most stereo systems, with a centre pin as one connection and an outer shell as the second connection.

photo-electric cell

A device that generates a small electric current when it receives light.

pick-up

1. A device on an electric guitar (or other instrument) that puts out an audio signal according to the motion of the strings on the instrument. 2. A device that puts out an audio signal according to the vibration of something. This term means the same thing as *contact microphone*.

pick-up pattern

The shape of the area from which a microphone will evenly pick up sound, giving similar but less detailed information than a polar pattern.

pilot tone

1. The same as *neo-pilot tone*. 2. A system of recording a 60Hz tone, used for syncing on a quarter-inch tape developed by Nagra.

pink noise

Noise that has equal energy per octave or portion of an octave.

pin plug

1. The same as *RCA plug*. 2. A common audio connector found on most stereo systems, with a centre pin as one connection and an outer shell as the second connection.

pitch

1. The ear's perception of frequency (ie music sounding higher or lower). 2. A control on a tape

machine which increases or decreases speed slightly, thus changing the pitch and time of the music. 3. The spacing of the grooves on a phonographic record.

pitch bend

1. In a synthesiser, the pitch-bend control makes the pitch smoothly glide upwards slightly. 2. The wheel controller or MIDI command used to bring this about.

pitch change

1. A characteristic of human hearing where bass frequencies sound lower in pitch at high levels of sound pressure, often as much as 10% lower. 2. A function of a delay device where the pitch of the output signal is different to that of the input signal.

pitch ratio

The percentage of pitch change in a delay line's pitch-change program.

pitch shift

To change the pitch of a sound without changing its duration, as opposed to *pitch transpose*, which changes both. Some people use the two terms interchangeably.

pitch-to-MIDI converter

A device that converts audio signals into MIDI information.

pitch-to-voltage converter

A device that converts the frequency changes of audio signals into proportional voltage changes.

plate

1. A type of reverb device in which a large metal sheet is suspended on spring clips and driven like a speaker cone. 2. An electrode in a tube that receives electrons.

plate program

A setting in a digital delay/reverb device that simulates the sound of plate reverberation.

playback equalisation

A reduction of the amplitude of those signals with high frequencies during the playback of a tape in order to compensate for the record equalisation.

playback level

1. The same as *reproduction level*. 2. A control that determines the output levels of signals played back from recorded tracks.

playlist

A series of computer commands sent to a disk recording of digital audio material where the playback of the digital audio is to comprise certain portions of the material and not others.

plug

A connector (usually on a cable) that mates with a jack.

plug-in

A software program that acts as an extension to a larger program, adding new features.

point source

A design in speaker systems where separate speakers are made, reproducing different frequency ranges, so that the sound appears to come from one place.

polarising voltage

Voltage applied to the plates of the variable capacitor in a condenser microphone capsule.

polarity

The direction of current flow or magnetising force.

polar pattern

1. A graphic display of the audio output levels caused by sound waves arriving at a microphone from different directions. 2. A graphic display of a speaker's dispersion pattern.

Pole mode

A MIDI mode that allows voices of controlled synth to be assigned polyphonically by incoming key-note numbers. The more poles a filter has, the more abrupt its cut-off slope. Each pole causes a slope of 6dB per octave. Typical configurations are two-pole and four-pole (12dB and 24dB per octave).

polyphonic

Used to describe a device capable of producing more than one note at a time. All synthesisers place a limit on how many voices of polyphony are available. General-MIDI-compliant synthesisers are required to provide 24 voices of polyphony.

polyphony

The number of voices (notes) that a device can produce at once.

poly(phonic) pressure

Also called key pressure. A type of MIDI channel message by which each key senses and transmits pressure data independently.

pop shield/filter

A device placed over a microphone or between the microphone and singer to prevent loud popping sounds – caused by breath on the microphone – from being picked up.

port

1. An opening in a speaker case or just behind the diaphragm in a microphone casing. 2. A jack that accepts or sends digital data.

portamento

1. A pitch change that glides smoothly from one pitch to another. 2. The synthesiser mode or MIDI command that allows or causes this to happen.

ported-case microphone

A microphone with at least one port (opening behind the diaphragm) in its casing.

post-echo

The positioning of an echo send control after the main channel fader.

post-production

Production carried out after a film or video has been shot, including the recording of replacement dialogue, the addition of sound effects and the mixing of dialogue, effects and music.

pot

Abbreviation of *potentiometer*, a device that outputs part of the input voltage according to the position of the control's knob.

power

1. Measurement of the ability of an electrical current to produce light, produce heat or do other work. 2. Similar measurement of another form of energy to perform work. 3. The name of the switch which turns on a device.

power amplifier

A device that takes a line-level signal and amplifies it to the level at which it can drive a speaker.

power supply

An electrical circuit that supplies voltage and current to electrical devices so that they can operate.

pre-amp

A low-noise amplifier designed to take a low-level signal and bring it up to normal line level.

precedence effect

A factor in human hearing where delay has a much bigger effect on the human perception of the location of the sound source than level does.

pre-delay

Delay circuits at the input of a reverb device that produce a delay before the reverberation is heard.

pre-echo

1. A repeating of the sound before the reverberation is heard. Used to simulate reflections found in a stage environment. 2. In tape recording, a low-level leakage of sound coming later, caused by print-through (ie data leaking through onto the other side of the tape). 3. In disc recording, a similar sound caused by a groove deforming a later groove. 4. The positioning of an echo send control before the main channel fader.

pre-emphasis

A boosting of high frequencies during the recording process in order to keep the signal above the level of noise at high frequencies.

pre-fader

The positioning of a send or other control before the main channel fader.

pre-fader listen

A solo circuit that allows a channel signal to be heard (and often metered) before the channel fader.

pre-mix

1. The same as *pong* (ie to play several recorded tacks with sync playback through a console in order to mix them together and record them on an open track). 2. To mix together the audio of several devices before sending the composite mix to the main console. 3. The composite mix of definitions 1 or 2.

pre-/post-switch

A switch on an input module which determines whether the echo send control comes before or after the main channel fader.

presence

The quality in an instrument (or sound source) that makes it sound like it's right there next to you.

presence frequencies

The range of audio frequencies between 4kHz and 6kHz that often, when boosted, increase the sense of presence, especially with voices.

preset

1. A sound programmed into a device at the factory by the manufacturer. 2. A factory-set

parameter that gives one effect on a signal-processing device. Some manufacturers distinguish between presets, programs and patches, each of which may contain a different set of parameters.

pressure-gradient microphone

A microphone whose diaphragm that is exposed at the front and at the back and whose diaphragm movement is caused by the difference in pressure between its front and back.

pressure microphone

A microphone whose diaphragm moves because the pressure of a sound wave causes one side of the diaphragm to work against the normal or controlled air pressure inside the mic case.

pressure-operated microphone

The same as *pressure microphone*.

pressure sensitivity

The feature in a synthesiser or keyboard controller of aftertouch (a control or operational function of a synthesiser where the exerting of pressure on a key after it has been pressed, and before it is released, will activate a control command that can be set by the player).

pressure zone microphone (PZM)

Barrier microphone manufactured by Crown. The head of the mic is attached closely to a plate designed to be attached to a larger surface and which has a half-omni pick-up pattern.

preview

1. To play an edit in a digital-audio editing system before committing to save it. 2. In a computer-assisted punch in, to have the computer play over the area while switching the monitoring so that the effect of the punch in can be heard before it is performed. 3. Short for *preview signal*.

preview signal

A signal in disc recording that matches and occurs earlier than the signal being recorded.

processing

1. Function carried out by a computer performing its tasks as programmed. 2. Short for *signal processing*, ie changing the sound of an instrument or other sound source with equalisers, limiters, compressors or other devices and thereby "processing" them to be recorded onto a master.

processor

The part of a computer that actually performs task and calculations.

producer

The director of an audio-recording project and the person responsible for obtaining a final product of desired quality within a budget.

production

1. The recording of a tune, collection of tunes, video or film performance. 2. The action of directing an audio recording project to obtain a final product of desired quality within a budget.

program

1. The instructions, the action of instructing or the action of recording instructions for a computer or computer-controlled device in order to compel it to perform certain functions. 2. A sound patch, ie the sequence of tone generators and modifiers in a synthesiser designed to obtain a particular sound. 3. The settings (especially those set at the factory) that will obtain a certain effect in an effects processor. 4. One selection of recorded music on a CD or DAT. 5. The audio that is recorded in general.

program change

A MIDI message sent to a receiving device that will change its presets, causing a synthesiser or other device to switch to a new program (also called a preset or patch) contained in its memory.

program equalisation

Changing the level of any signal in a certain range of frequencies to emphasise or de-emphasise certain elements in the frequency of an instrument or sound source and change its tone.

programmable

A device – especially a computer-controlled device – is described as programmable if its parameters can be changed by the user.

Program mode

An operational mode of a monitor section of a console where the monitor inputs are connected to the console outputs feeding the multitrack tape machine (used during a recording session).

program number

The number of a pre-recorded selection on a CD or DAT.

program switch

A switch that activates the Program mode (Record mode) of the monitor section connecting the monitor inputs to the console outputs feeding the multitrack tape recorder (used during the recording session).

program time

In DAT recording, the time indication from the top of one selection.

prompt

A set of instructions that appear on a computer screen as a guide for the user to follow.

proprietary

Describing a function, feature or characteristic owned by one company and available only in units manufactured by that company.

protocol

A system of digital data where the positioning of the data, and the significance of each bit in the data stream, is determined according to a standardised format so that all devices can properly interpret the data.

proximity effect

In directional microphones, this is the boost in the microphone's output for bass frequencies as the mic is moved closer to the sound source.

psychoacoustics

The study of how things sound to individuals because of mental or emotional factors.

puck

Any circular piece of metal, fibre, rubber, etc, which drives something from a rotating power source.

pulse

A rise and then fall in amplitude, similar to a square wave, but one which stays up for less time than it stays down.

pulse-code modulation

The use of amplitude pulses in magnetic tape to record the digital information bits of digital audio.

pulse-wave modulation

Moving smoothly from a square wave to a pulse wave, in response to a control-voltage input (usually from a LFO).

pulse width

The amount of time that a pulse is at maximum voltage.

pumping breathing

The sound of noise changing volume as a limiter or compressor operates.

punching in

Putting a recorder/sequencer in Record mode on a previously-recorded track while the track is playing in Sync Playback mode and the singer or musician is singing or playing along.

pure tone

A tone without harmonic frequencies (except for the fundamental frequency) and with a sine-wave shape.

PZM

A trademark belonging to Crown for its barrier microphone. (See *pressure zone microphone.*)

Q

The sharpness of the peak response in an equalisation circuit.

quality factor

The ratio of reactance to resistance in a coil which affects Q.

quantization distortion error

A modulation noise (also perceived as a distortion) that occurs in digital processing and recording and is caused by the sample levels being altered to conform to standard quantization levels.

quantization/quantizing levels/increments

A standard level that can be recognised by a digital recording system.

quantization noise

A modulation noise (also perceived as a distortion) that occurs in digital processing and recording and is caused by the sample levels being altered to conform to standard quantization levels. This is one of the types of error introduced into an analogue audio signal by encoding it in digital form. The digital equivalent of tape hiss, quantization noise is caused by the small differences between the actual amplitudes of the points being sampled and the bit resolution of the analogue-to-digital converter.

quantize

The conversion of the values of an analogue wave or random occurrence into steps. Quantizing is a function found on sequencers and drum machines and causes notes played at odd times to be "rounded off" to regular rhythmic values.

rack

1. The physical setting of a head in the direction toward or away from the tape, therefore affecting how much pressure is applied on the head by the tape. 2. Short for *equipment rack*, a cabinet with rails, or free-standing rails, that have holes in them to accept screws at standard spaces. Used to house outboard gear.

rack ears/flanges

Mounting brackets that can be attached to equipment to allow it to be housed in a standard equipment rack.

rack mount

To mount in an equipment rack.

rack space

A standardised size of the front mounting plate in outboard gear, equal to approximately one and three quarter inches tall by 19 inches wide.

radiation

The angle and pattern of a speaker's coverage.

radiation pattern

A polar graph of the coverage of a speaker.

radio frequencies

Frequencies higher than 20kHz (usually above 100kHz).

RAM

Abbreviation of *random access memory*. Used for storing user-programmed patch parameter settings in synthesisers and sample waveforms in samplers. A constant source of power (usually a long-lasting battery) is required for RAM to maintain its contents when the main power is switched off.

ramp wave

A waveform that is similar to a sawtooth waveform but differs in that it starts at zero level and gradually rises to its peak level and then instantly drops back to zero level to form one cycle.

random-note generator

A device that generates unpredictable pitches at a set rate. Used in synthesisers.

random phase

The presence of many signals or reflections where some of the signals are in phase and some out of phase. The overall effect is that of being between in phase and out of phase.

rap

To perform a spoken rhythmic part to a music or percussion performance. Considered by some to be people talking bollocks.

rarefaction

The spreading apart of air particles in the formation of a sound-pressure wave.

rated load impedance

The input impedance (ie the opposition to current flow by a device's input) that a piece of equipment is designed to feed.

RCA plug/jack

Common audio connector, found on most stereo systems.

R-DAT

Abbreviation of *rotating-head digital audio tape*, a standard format for the recording of digital audio. Comprises a very small tape cassette and the recording process employs a rotating head.

reactance

Opposition to the flow of electrical current that changes with the frequency of the current.

read

To retrieve information bits from a storage device. Equivalent to reproducing digital signals.

read head

The digital audio reproduction head in a digital recorder or a similar device that converts magnetic pulses on a storage medium to voltage pulses.

ready

The control state of one track of a multitrack tape recorder where the track will go into Record mode when the Record function of the tape recorder is activated.

real time

Occurring at the same time as other, usually human, activities. In real-time sequence recording, timing information is encoded, along with the note data, as the computer analyses the timing of the input. In real-time editing, changes in parameter settings can be heard immediately, without the need to play a new note or wait for computational processes to be completed.

recognise

To be able to take in and respond to incoming digital control data.

reconstruction filter

A low-pass filter on the output of a digital-to-analogue converter that smoothes the staircase-like changes in voltage produced by the converter in order to eliminate clock noise from the output.

recording chain

All of the transducers and changes of energy form in a recording and reproducing system listed in order.

recording session

Any period where music is being recorded, especially the first such period, where the rhythm instruments are being recorded.

recording solo

A switch or function which routes the signal of a channel to the monitor system by itself, and yet the signals out of the console to the recorder are uninterrupted.

reference level

1. A standard value used to describe the amount of level present in decibels above or below this reference. 2. The same as *operating level* (ie the maximum average level, which should not be exceeded in normal operation).

reflected sound

Sound that reaches a mic or listener after reflecting once or more from surrounding surfaces.

regeneration

1. The same as *jam sync*, ie a generation of a new SMPTE time-code signal according to the input SMPTE signal, giving an identical SMPTE signal out as the one that came in. 2. Feedback, especially around a delay line.

register

A user-modified program, with changed parameters, that is stored in the memory of an effects unit or sound module.

regulated power supply

A device that supplies power to electronic equipment to ensure that the output voltage won't fluctuate when more equipment is turned on or if there is a change in voltage of the power line.

relay

An electric switch in a device. When activated – ie when a control voltage is applied to the device – two terminals are connected or disconnected.

relay rack

An older term for *equipment rack*.

release

1. The rate at which the volume of a synthesiser drops to silence once a key is released. 2. The portion of an envelope that begins after a key is lifted.

release time

The time it takes for a dynamics-processing device to change gain when the input signal crosses the threshold level while decreasing.

release velocity

The speed with which a key is raised and the type of MIDI data used to encode that speed. Release-velocity sensing is found on some instruments, although it is rare. It's usually used to control the rate of the release segments of an envelope or envelopes.

remote

1. Short for *remote control*, a device with which an operator can control a tape machine some distance away. 2. The recording taken at the site of a performance, rather than in a recording studio.

repeat echo

An echo effect caused by discrete repetitions of a program source by using a long delay time and feedback on a delay line. Also called *space echo*.

resistance

Opposition to the flow of current in one direction or which does not represent different opposition for signals of different frequencies.

resistor

A device that opposes the flow of electrical current and does so evenly at all frequencies.

resonance

1. The prolonging of a sound at a certain frequency and the tendency of something to vibrate at a particular frequency after the source of energy is removed. 2. A function on a filter in which a narrow band of frequencies (the resonance peak) becomes relatively more prominent. If the resonance peak is high enough, the filter will begin to oscillate and produce an audio output, even in the absence of input. Filter resonance is also known as *emphasis and Q*, and on some older instruments is also known as *regeneration* or *feedback* (because feedback was used in the circuit to produce a resonance peak).

resonant

1. Term used to describe equipment that tends to pass signals of a certain frequency or narrow range of frequencies more than signals of other frequencies. 2. Physical properties that tend to reinforce the energy at certain frequencies of vibration are described as being resonant.

resonant frequency

The frequency at which a physical item tends to vibrate after the source of energy (which causes the vibration) is removed.

resonate

1. To vibrate at the resonant frequency. 2. To linger on, as in reverberation. In this respect, the term is used in terms of sound in a room or is used to describe a room or other area that produces reverberation with a long reverb time.

return

Short for *echo return* or *auxiliary return*, ie the input of a console which brings the effect signal back from an echo chamber or other reverberation device.

reverb

1. The persistence of a sound after the source stops emitting it. 2. A function on a filter in which a narrow band of frequencies (the resonance peak) becomes relatively more prominent. If the resonance peak is high enough, the filter will begin to oscillate and produce an audio output, even in the absence of input. Filter resonance is also known as *emphasis and Q*, and on some older instruments is also known as *regeneration* or *feedback* (because feedback was used in the circuit to produce a resonance peak).

reverb(eration) time

The time it takes for the reverberation or echoes of a sound source to decrease by 60dB after the direct sound from the source stops.

reverberant field

The area away from a sound source at which reverberation is louder than the direct sound from the sound source.

reverberation envelope

Literally, the attack, decay, sustain and release of the reverberation volume. In other words, the time it takes for the reverberation to reach its peak level and its rate of decay. (See also *ADSR*.)

reverb-time contour

A graph of reverberation time for signals of different audio frequencies.

RF

Abbreviation of *radio frequencies*, ie frequencies higher than 20kHz (usually above 100kHz).

RF interference

The induction of RF signals (usually broadcast by television and radio stations) into audio lines causing noise, buzzing and static.

rhythm track

The section of recording that features rhythm instruments.

ribbon microphone

A microphone with a thin, conductive ribbon as both the diaphragm and the generating element (the device that generates the electricity).

riding the faders

Moving the faders up at quiet passages so that the signal will be recorded well above the noise and taking the faders back down during loud passages in order to prevent distortion.

riff

A short melody repeatedly played in a tune, sometimes with variation and often between vocal lines.

ringing

An undesirable resonance at the cut-off frequency of a filter that has a high rate of cut-off.

ringing out a room

A test often carried out at the setting-up stage before a performance, where pink noise is sent through the speakers and the microphones are turned up until feedback occurs.

ring modulator

A special type of mixer that accepts two signals as audio inputs and produces their sum-and-difference tones at its output but doesn't pass on the frequencies found in the original signals themselves. (See *clangorous*.)

rise time

The time it takes for an audio waveform to jump suddenly to a higher level.

RMS

Abbreviation of *root mean square*, the effective average value of an AC waveform.

RMS detector

A control circuit that recognises and responds to the RMS level, rather than to the peak level.

roll-off

The reduction of signal level as a signal's frequency moves away from the cut-off frequency, especially when the cut-off rate is mild.

ROM

Abbreviation of *read-only memory*, a type of data storage where the contents can't be altered by the user. An instrument's operating system and, in some cases, its waveforms and factory presets are stored in ROM. (See also *RAM.*)

room equalisation

An equaliser inserted in a monitor system that attempts to compensate for changes in frequency response caused by the acoustics of a room.

room sound

The ambience of a room, including reverberation and background noise.

room tone

The background noise in a room where there are no people speaking and there is no music playing.

rotary control

A level or other control in a device that has a circular movement rather than a linear movement.

round sound

A pleasingly balanced sound, ie one that has a pleasing mixture of high-frequency to low-frequency content.

RT

Abbreviation of *reverb time*, ie the time it takes for the reverberation or echoes of a sound source to decrease by 60dB after the direct sound from the source stops.

rumble

A low-frequency noise, especially that caused by earth/floor vibration or by uneven surfaces in the drive mechanism of a recorder or playback unit.

run

In computer terminology, the term to run is applied to the performing of a function or command.

run-off

A quick reference mix recorded on cassette or some other format after a multitrack recording or overdubbing session so that the client can listen to what was recorded.

run through

Musicians run through a tune before the recording process begins so that the engineer can calibrate levels and check the sound quality.

sample

1. In digital recording, to measure the level of a waveform at a given instant. 2. To record a short segment of audio for the purpose of playback later. 3. The short recording made in definition 2.

sample and hold

1. In digital recording, a term used to describe the measuring of the level of a waveform at a given instant and then converting it to a voltage at that level, which will then be held until another sample is taken. When triggered (usually by a clock pulse), a circuit on an analogue synthesiser looks at (samples) the voltage at its input and then passes it on to its output unchanged, regardless of what the input voltage does in the meantime (the hold period), until the next trigger is received. In one familiar application, the input was a noise source and the output was connected to oscillator pitch, which caused the pitch to change in a random staircase pattern. The sample-and-hold effect is often emulated by digital synthesisers through an LFO waveshape called "random".

sample dump

The copying of a digitally recorded sample without converting it to analogue between different storage units or sound modules through a MIDI transmission.

sample playback

The reproduction (in analogue signal form) of a recorded sample, the pitch and sustain of which is controlled by a MIDI signal.

sampler

A device that records and plays samples, often including features for the editing and storage of the samples, usually by allowing them to be distributed across a keyboard and played back at various pitches.

sample rate

In digital recording, this refers to the number of times that samples are taken each second.

sample-rate conversion

The conversion of digital audio data at one sample rate to digital audio data at a different sample rate without first converting the signal to analogue.

sampling

The process of encoding an analogue signal in digital form by reading (sampling) its level at precisely spaced time intervals.

sampling frequency

The same as *sample rate*, ie the number samples taken each second. Typical sampling rates are usually between 11kHz and 48kHz.

sampling synchronisation signal

A stream of synchronisation pulses that are generated by a digital audio tape recorder, recorded onto tape and then used as a clock signal to time the sampling of the sampling circuits.

saturation

The point at which the tape is fully magnetised and will accept no more magnetisation.

save

To store the digital data in the RAM onto a permanent storage device, such as a hard disk.

sawtooth waveform

A waveform that jumps from a zero value to a peak value and then gradually diminishes to a zero value to complete the cycle.

schematic

A diagram that shows the signal paths and electronic components of a device.

scratch

1. A descriptive term meaning "temporary". 2. A scratch vocal is taken during a basic recording session to help the other musicians play their parts. At a later date, the final vocal track is overdubbed. 3. The action of a musician or disc jockey quickly moving a record back and forth with a phono cartridge reproducing the stylus motion in order to create a rhythmic pattern of sound.

scrub

1. To shuttle (ie move the sound track) either forward or backward when a control is moved off a centre point either left or right. 2. To move backward and forward through an audio waveform under manual control in order to find a precise point in a wave (for editing purposes).

SCSI

Abbreviation of *small-computer systems interface*, a high-speed communications protocol that allows computers, samplers and disk drives to communicate with one another. Pronounced "scuzzy".

SDII

Abbreviation of *Sound Designer II*, an audio file format and the native format of Digidesign's Sound Designer II graphic audio waveform editing program for the Macintosh.

SDS

The standard MIDI sample dump. SDS is used to transfer digital audio samples from one instrument to another over a MIDI cable.

sealed case

Describes the enclosure of a microphone diaphragm which is sealed so that the back of the mic can't receive sound-pressure changes.

select

1. A switch which controls the location at which an input receives its signal. 2. To choose the location at which an input receives its signal.

semiconductor

1. A material that conducts more than an insulator but less than a conductor. 2. Any device constructed primarily from semiconductor material, such as a transistor.

send

A control and bus designed to feed signals from console channels to an outboard device, such as a reverberation unit.

send level

A control determining the signal level sent to a send bus.

sensitivity

In microphones, the output level produced by a standard amount of sound-pressure level.

separation

A term used to describe the pick-up of a desired signal compared to that of an undesired signal.

sequence

1. An automatic playing of musical events (such as pitches, sounding of samples and rests) by a device in a step-by-step order. 2. The action of programming a computer to play musical events automatically, in a stepped order.

sequencer

1. A computer which can be programmed to play and record a stepped order of musical events. 2. A device or program that records and plays back user-determined sets of music-performance commands, usually in the form of MIDI data. Most sequencers also allow this data to be edited in various ways and stored on disk.

serial data

Digital data where all of the bits are transmitted one after another over a single wire/connection.

serial interface

A plug and cable for a computer that sends and receives data one bit after the other.

serial port

A jack that sends out or receives digital data one bit after another through a single pin.

series connection

Equipment (especially circuit elements) connected so that the electrical signal flows from one device to the next and to the next and so forth.

servo control

A motor used in a control circuit where the actual speed of the motor is sensed and compared to a reference, such as a pulse timing signal.

set up

To position microphones, instruments and the controls on recorders/consoles etc prior to recording.

set-up

An arrangement where microphones, instruments and controls on recorders, consoles, etc, are positioned for recording.

shelf

The frequency response of an equalisation circuit where the boost or cut-off frequencies form a shelf on a frequency response graph. A high-frequency shelf control will affect signal levels at the set frequency and all higher frequencies, while a low-frequency shelf control will affect signal levels at the set frequency and at all lower frequencies.

shelf filter

The circuit in an equaliser used to obtain the shelf.

shield

1. The outer, conductive wrapping around an inner wire or wires in a cable. 2. To protect the inner wire or wires in a cable from picking up energy given off by such things as fluorescent lights.

shielded cable

Cable that has a shield around an inner conductor or conductors.

shock mount

An elastic microphone mount that reduces the microphone's movement when the stand vibrates in response to floor vibrations from footsteps, etc.

short (circuit)

A direct connection between two points in a circuit that (usually) shouldn't be connected.

short delay

Delay times under 20ms.

shortest digital path

The routing of a digital-audio signal so that there is a minimum amount of digital-to-analogue, analogue-to-digital or sample-rate conversion.

shortest path

A technique in recording by which a signal is routed through the least amount of active (amplified) devices during recording.

shotgun microphone

A microphone with a long line filter (a tube that acoustically cancels sound arriving from the side), thus allowing the microphone to pick up sound in one direction much better than in any other direction.

shuttle

1. A technique used in older tape machines of stopping the fast winding (either fast-forward or rewind) of tape in older tape machines, where the engineer would put the tape machine in the opposite fast mode and press stop after the machine had just started to reverse direction. 2. Moving reels of a tape machine by hand so that the tape moves past the desired point first in one direction and then in the other, back and forth. 3. A control that moves the sound track either forward or backward when the control is moved off a centre point, either left or right.

sibilance

Energy from a voice centred at around 7kHz, caused by pronouncing "s", "sh" or "ch" sounds.

side bands

Frequency components outside the natural harmonic series, generally introduced to a tone by using an audio-range wave for modulation. (See *clangorous*.)

side chain

The control circuit of a dynamics-processing device.

signal

1. In audio, an alternating current or voltage matching the waveform of, or being originally obtained from, a sound-pressure wave. 2. In audio, an alternating current or voltage between 20Hz and 20kHz. 3. A digital-audio bit stream.

signal flow

The path that a signal follows through an audio system, such as a console.

signal generator

The same as *audio oscillator*, a device which emits test tones at various frequencies.

signal path

The way in which current travels or may travel across a circuit or through a device.

signal processing

Changing the sound of an instrument or some other sound source with equalisers, limiters, compressors and other devices, thereby "processing" the sound ready to be recorded onto a master.

signal-to-error ratio

The difference in level between the signal and the noise and distortion caused by converting analogue audio signals into digital audio and then back into analogue.

signal-to-noise ratio

The difference in decibels between the levels of signal and noise.

sine wave

The waveform produced by a sound source vibrating at just one frequency (ie making a pure tone).

single D

Abbreviation of *single port distance*, used to describe a microphone in which there is one distance between the port and the diaphragm.

Single-Step mode

A method of loading events (such as notes) into memory one event at a time. Also called *step mode* and *step time*, compared with real time.

slap echo

One distinct repeat added to one or more instrument sounds in a mix that creates a very live sound, similar to what you'd hear in an arena.

slate

1. The voice recorded onto the beginning of a master tape to identify the tune and take, or the action of making it. 2. The circuit or control that allows you to slate masters.

slave

The transport that adjusts speed so that it's in time with the master transport when two machines are synced together.

slide

A control that has a knob which moves in a straight line and which outputs part of an input voltage according to the position of the knob.

smart FSK

An FSK (Frequency Shift Key) sync signal where the beginning of each measure has an identification message giving the measure number.

SMDI

Abbreviation of *SCSI musical data interchange*, a specification for sending MIDI sample dumps over the SCSI bus.

SMPTE

1. Society of Motion Picture and Television Engineers, a professional society. 2. A term loosely used to mean *SMPTE time code*, a standardised timing and sync signal specified by the aforementioned society.

SND

Sound resource, a Macintosh audio file format.

soft key

Abbreviation of *software key*, another name for a function key (ie a key that has a different function depending on the programming of a computer and as shown on a menu screen), especially when it's on a device that has an internal computer.

soft knee

Generic name for the DBX Corporation's registered trade name of Over-Easy, named for the gradual change of compression ratio around the threshold, which makes it difficult to detect when compression is taking place.

soft knob

Abbreviation of *software knob*, a knob used in a computer-controlled device which has a different function depending on the programming of the computer.

soft sound source

A low-volume instrument, such as an acoustic guitar.

solid state

In electronics, solid-state devices use transistors and semiconductors rather than tubes.

solo

1. A circuit in a console that allows just one channel (or several selected channels) to be heard or reach the output. 2. In music, an instrument or section where an instrument is the featured instrument for a short period, often playing a melody. 3. An original Copy Code (protective digital signal recorded with digital audio bits) that was developed by Philips to prevent the making of digital copies of a copy made from a CD, thereby helping to prevent bootlegging.

solo switch

A switch that activates the solo function, which allows only selected channels to be heard or to reach the output.

song position pointer

1. Short for *MIDI clock with song pointer*, ie the time data contained in the MIDI signal used to sync two sequencers together. The song position pointer advances one step each $1/_{24}$ of a beat, and also has a number signal for each measure or bar which indicates the number of measures or bars you are into the tune. 2. A type of MIDI data that tells a device how many 16th-notes have passed since the beginning of a song. An SPP message is generally sent in conjunction with a MIDI Continue message in order to start playback from the middle of a song.

sostenuto pedal

A pedal found on grand pianos and mimicked on some synthesisers, which only sustain notes if they are already being held down on the keyboard at the moment when the pedal is pressed.

sound

1. Moving pressure variations in air caused by something vibrating between 20 times and 20,000 times a second, or similar variations in other substances, like water. 2. Loosely, any audio signal, regardless of its energy form.

sound absorption

The same as *acoustical absorption*, ie the quality of a surface or substance which takes in a sound wave rather than reflecting it.

sound blanket

A thick blanket that can be put on floors or hung to help prevent sound from reflecting from hard surfaces.

sound card

A circuit board that is installed inside a computer (typically an IBM-compatible machine) providing new sound capabilities. These capabilities can include an FM or wavetable synthesiser and audio inputs and outputs. MIDI inputs and outputs are also normally included.

sound effects

Sounds such as door slams, wind, etc, which are added to film or video shots. Effectively, sounds other than dialogue, narration or music.

sound file (soundfile)

A digital-audio recording that can be stored in a computer or on a digital storage medium, such as a hard disk.

sound level

Abbreviation of *sound-pressure level*, ie a measurement of the amount of pressure created by a sound.

sound-level meter

A device that measures sound-pressure levels.

sound module

The signal-generator portion of a synthesiser or a sample playback unit that sends out an audio signal according to incoming MIDI messages and does not have keys with which to be played.

sound-pressure level (SPL)

A measure of the sound pressure present, measured in decibels above the threshold of hearing (.0002 microbars).

sound-pressure wave

Alternate compressions (compacting together) and rarefactions (spreading apart) of air particles moving away from something that is vibrating at between 20 and 20,000 times a second, or a similar occurrence in another substance, such as water.

sound quality

A characteristic of how well the diaphragm movement in a microphone matches the pressure changes of a sound wave reaching it, particularly sudden changes.

sound source

Something that vibrates between 20 and 20,000 times a second, producing a sound-pressure wave.

SoundTools

Digidesign's digital-audio-editing system.

soundtrack

An audio recording, especially on film or videotape.

sound wave

Abbreviation of *sound-pressure wave*, ie a wave of pressure changes moving away from something that is vibrating between 20 and 20,000 times a second.

source

Input mode on a tape machine/computer sequencer where the meters and the output of the machine's electronics will be the signal arriving at the input connector.

spaced cardioid pair

A far-distant miking technique of placing two cardioid microphones a distance apart (usually about six inches) and pointing away from each other by 90°.

spaced omni pair

Placing two microphones with omni-directional patterns between four and eight feet apart, so that one microphone picks up sound coming from the left and the other from the right.

spaced pair

Any two microphones spaced apart to obtain a stereo pick-up, especially using the spaced omni or spaced cardioid techniques.

space echo

An effect of repeating echoes of a sound.

SPDIF

Shortened from the first letters of Sony/Philips Digital Interface, a standard for sending and receiving digital audio signals using the common RCA connector.

speaker

A device that converts electrical signals into audible sound. Alternatively, a transducer that converts an electrical audio signal into a sound-pressure wave.

speaker out direct

Term used to refer to the practice of feeding the signal from a speaker output of an instrument amplifier to the recording console without using a microphone.

speed of sound

The wave velocity (ie the time it takes for one point of the waveform to travel a certain distance) of a sound-pressure wave (1,130 feet per second at 70° Fahrenheit).

spin control

A British term for *feedback control*, ie a control that determines the amount of delayed signal sent back to the input of a delay line, used to produce repeated echo effects.

SPL

Abbreviation of *sound-pressure level*, referring to a pressure of .0002 microbars, considered to be the threshold of hearing (ie the lowest level at which people begin to hear sound).

splice

1. To assemble previously cut pieces of recording tape with special tape stuck on the back side.
2. An edit performed in this way.

splicing block

A device that holds recording tape to facilitate the cutting of splices.

split keyboard

A single keyboard divided electronically so that it acts as if it were two or more separate keyboards. The output of each note range is routed into a separate signal path in the keyboard's internal sound-producing circuitr, or transmitted over one or more separate MIDI channels. Applications include playing a bass sound with the left hand while playing a piano sound with the right.

spring reverb

A device that simulates reverberation by driving a spring (in the same way that a loudspeaker cone is driven) and picking up the spring's vibrations with a contact microphone (a device that converts physical vibrations into audio signals).

square wave

A wave shape produced when voltage rises instantly to one level, stays at that level, instantly falls to another level and stays at that level, and finally rises back to its original level to complete the cycle.

stage

1. In reverberation effects devices, an echo added before the reverberation to simulate echoes that would come from a concert stage. 2. In amplifiers, one section of a component, having a particular function. 3. The partially enclosed or raised area where live musicians perform.

standard operating level

An operating level (ie the maximum average level that should not be exceeded in normal operation) that is widely used or widely referred to.

standing wave

An acoustic signal between two reflective surfaces with a distance that is an even multiple of half of the signal's frequency wavelength.

status byte

A MIDI byte that defines the meaning of the data bytes that follow it. MIDI status bytes always begin with a one (hex eight through to F), while data bytes always begin with a zero (hex zero through to seven).

step input

In sequencing, a technique that allows you to enter notes one step at a time, also called *step recording*. Common step values are 16th- and eighth-notes. After each entry, the sequencer's clock (ie its position in the sequence) will advance one step and then stop, awaiting new input. Recording while the clock is running is called *real-time input*.

step program/mode/time

To program a sequencer one note (or event) at a time in accordance with the rhythm to which the time value of one step is set.

stereo

A recording or reproduction of at least two channels where the positions of instrument sounds from left to right can be perceived.

stereo image

The perception of different sound sources being far left, far right or any place in between.

stereo miking

The positioning of two or more microphones in such a way that their outputs generate a stereo image.

stretched-string instruments

Instruments that use stretched strings to generate tones, such as guitars, violins and pianos.

strike

To put away equipment and clean up after a session.

stylus

The needle part of a phonograph cartridge that is in contact with the grooves of a disc.

subcode

Control information bits that are recorded along with digital audio and can be used for control of the playback deck, including functions such as program numbers, start IDs and skip IDs.

subframe

A unit smaller than one frame in SMPTE time code.

submaster

The fader that controls the level of sound from several channels (although not usually all channels) during mixdown or recording.

submaster assignment

The selection of which bus (and therefore which submaster) the console channel will feed into, usually accomplished by pressing a button in the switch matrix.

submix

A combination of audio signals treated as one or two channels (for a stereo image) in a mix.

subtractive synthesis

The generation of harmonically rich waveforms by various methods and then the filtering of these waveforms in order to remove unwanted harmonics and thus create sound. Alternatively, the technique of arriving at a desired tone colour by filtering waveforms rich in harmonics. Subtractive synthesis is the type generally used on analogue synthesisers.

sum

A signal comprising a combination of two stereo channels that are both equal in level and in phase.

sum and difference signals

When two stereo channels are mixed at equal levels and in phase, a sum signal is created. A difference signal is one where the mixture of the signals from the two channels has one channel phase-reversed so that any signal exactly the same in both channels will be cancelled.

super-cardioid pattern

A microphone pattern that has maximum sensitivity on axis and least sensitivity around 150° off axis.

surround sound

A technique of recording and playing back sound used in film, where the sound has a front-to-back quality as well as a side-to-side perspective.

sustain

1. A holding-out of the sounding of a pitch by an instrument. 2. The level at which a sound will continue to play when a synthesiser key is held down.

sustain pedal

The electronic equivalent of a piano's *sostenuto* (damper) pedal. In most synthesisers, the sustain pedal latches the envelopes of any currently playing or subsequently played notes at their sustain levels, even if the keys are lifted.

sweetening

Musical parts that are overdubbed in order to complete the music of a recording, especially the melodic instruments, such as strings and horns.

switch

A device that makes and/or breaks electrical connections.

switchable-pattern microphone

A microphone that has more than one directional pattern, depending on the position of the Pattern switch.

switch matrix

A series of switches – usually arranged in rows and columns of buttons – that allow any input module to be connected to any output bus.

sync

1. The circuits in a multitrack tape recorder which allow the record head to be used as a playback head for those tracks already recorded. 2. The same as *synchronisation*.

sync box

A device that takes several different kinds of sync signals and puts out several kinds of sync signal, allowing a device such as a sequencer to be driven by a sync signal that it doesn't recognise.

synchronisation

The running of two devices in time with each other so that the events generated by each of them will always fall into predicable time relationships.

sync word bits

A series of bits in SMPTE time code that identify the end of a frame.

synthesiser

A musical instrument that artificially generates signals (using oscillators) to simulate the sounds of real instruments or to create other sounds impossible to manufacture with "real" instruments and is designed according to certain principles developed by Robert Moog and others in the 1960s. A synthesiser is distinguished from an electronic piano or electronic organ by the fact that its sounds can be programmed by the user, and from a sampler by the fact that the sampler allows the user to make digital recordings of external sound sources.

system common

A type of MIDI data used to control certain aspects of the operation of an entire MIDI system. System-common messages include Song Position Pointer messages, as well as Song Select, Tune Request, and End Of System Exclusive messages.

system exclusive (sysex)

A type of MIDI data that allows messages to be sent over a MIDI cable, which will then be responded to only by devices of a specific type. Sysex data is used most commonly for sending patch parameter data to and from an editor/librarian program.

system-exclusive bulk dump

A system-exclusive bulk dump is the transmission of internal synthesiser settings as a manufacturer-specified system-exclusive file from a synth to a sequencer or from a sequencer to a synth.

system real time

A type of MIDI data used for timing references. Because of its timing-critical nature, a system real-time byte can be inserted into the middle of any multibyte MIDI message. System real-time messages include MIDI Clock, Start, Stop, Continue, Active Sensing, and System Reset messages.

take

A recording taken between one start and the following stop of a track.

take notation

The noting down of the takes of a tune on a take sheet or track log, along with comments.

take sheet

A sheet used to note the number of takes made on each tune, along with comments.

talkback

The system that allows an engineer to talk into a microphone in the control room and have his voice sound over the studio monitors and/or headphones so that he can talk to the musicians.

talk box

A guitar effects unit that allows a voice to modulate (control) a guitar signal. Operated by a vocalist talking with a tube in his mouth.

tap

A connection in the coil of a transformer.

tempo

The rate at which the music progresses, measured in beats per minute (ie the number of steady, even pulses that occur in each minute of the music).

tempo mapping

Programming a sequencer to follow the tempo variations of a recorded performance.

terminal

1. A point of connection between two wires, including a device on the end of a wire or cable that allows attachment and the accepting point on equipment casings. 2. A computer keyboard and monitor that allows access and entry of information into or from a computer.

terminate

To have an amplifier feed a resistance (usually via a resistor) that matches its output impedance.

THD

Abbreviation for *Total Harmonic Distortion*, an audio measurement specification used to determine the accuracy with which a device can reproduce an input signal at its output. THD describes the cumulative level of harmonic overtones that the device being tested adds to an input sine wave. THD + *n* is a specification that includes both harmonic distortion of the sine wave and non-harmonic noise.

thin sound

A sound that doesn't have all frequencies present. Especially refers to a sound that is deficient in low frequencies.

three-to-one rule

The rule which states that the distance between microphones must be at least three times the distance between either microphone and the sound source.

three-way speaker

A speaker system that has separate speakers to reproduce the bass, mid-range and treble frequencies.

threshold

The level at which a dynamics-processing unit begins to change gain.

threshold control

The control on a dynamics-processing device that adjusts the threshold level (ie the level at which it begins to change gain).

threshold of feeling

The sound-pressure level at which people experience discomfort for 50% of the time.

threshold of hearing

The sound-pressure level at which people can hear for only 50% of the time.

threshold of pain

The sound-pressure level at which people feel actual pain for 50% of the time.

throat

A small opening in a horn or driver through which a sound wave passes from the driver to the horn.

throw

In speakers and microphones, the amount of movement that the diaphragm can make (without restriction) in order to produce or pick up a sound wave.

thru box

A unit with one MIDI In port and several MIDI Out ports. Each MIDI Out port has the same signal as the MIDI In port, but with a delay of the signal (usually around 4ms).

thru port

A connector that puts out a MIDI signal identical to the input MIDI signal.

tie lines

Cables with connectors at both ends so that a signal can be sent or picked up from a remote location. Usually run through walls or floors.

tight (hyped) sound

The sound obtained by close-miking well-isolated instruments.

timbre

1. The timbre of the instrument is what makes it sound like that particular instrument and not like any other, even though the other instrument may be playing the same pitch. 2. One of the building blocks of a patch in a Roland synthesiser. Pronounced "tam-br".

time base

The number of pulses/advances per beat in a simple clock signal.

time code

Short for *SMPTE time code*, a standardised timing and sync signal specified by the Society of Motion Picture and Television Engineers. Alternatively, a type of signal that contains information about location in time and used for a synchronisation reference point when synchronising two or more machines together, such as sequencers, drum machines and tape decks.

time-code generator

A unit that generates SMPTE time-code signals.

time compression/expansion

The speeding up or slowing down of an audio recording without changing the pitch.

time constant

In a circuit that has reactance, the time it takes for the current or voltage to substantially stabilise in the circuit when the voltage or current is changing.

timing clock

1. An even pulse signal used for syncing purposes. 2. The same as MIDI Clock, ie time data in a MIDI signal that advances one step each $1/_{24}$ of a beat and can be used to sync two sequencers together.

timing tape

Plastic leader tape with marks every 7.5 inches along it. Used to edit silence between selections.

Tiny Telephone jack/plug

A smaller version of the phone jack/plug (ie .173 inches in diameter, rather than .25 inches) used in many patch bays.

tone

1. One of several single-frequency signals found at the beginning of a tape reel at the magnetic reference level that will be used to record a program. 2. Any single-frequency signal or sound. 3. The sound quality of an instrument's sound relative to the amount of energy present at different frequencies. 4. In some synthesisers, a term meaning the audio signal that will be put out by the unit which would be similar to the sound of an instrument.

touch sensitive

Used to describe a synthesiser keyboard's ability to generate a MIDI Velocity signal. Not all synthesiser keyboards are touch sensitive.

track

1. One audio recording made on a portion of the width of a multitrack tape. 2. One set of control commands in a sequencer recorded in a similar manner to an audio track and often controlling one synthesiser over one MIDI channel. 3. A term with the same meaning as the term *band track* (ie the part of a song without the lead vocal or without the lead and background vocals). 4. To be controlled by or to follow in some proportional relationship, such as when a filter's cut-off frequency tracks the keyboard, moving up or down depending on the note being played.

tracking

Recording the individual tracks of a multitrack recording.

transducer

A device that converts energy from one medium to another.

transfer curve

A graph of energy supplied versus energy stored by a storage medium (often magnetic tape).

transformer

An electrical device that has two magnetically coupled coils.

transformer matrix

A device that uses transformers to take two audio channel inputs and change them to a sum signal (ie a mix of the signals on the two channels) and a difference signal (ie the mixture of the two signals with the phase of one channel reversed so that any signal exactly the same in both channels will be cancelled).

transient

The initial high-energy peak that occurs at the beginning of a waveform, such as one caused by the percussive action of a pick or hammer hitting a string.

transient response

Response to signals with amplitudes which rise very quickly, such as drum beats and waveforms produced by percussive instruments.

transmit

In MIDI, to send a MIDI command to another device.

transposing

The act of changing the musical register of an entire piece of music by the space of an interval.

trap

A filter designed to reject audio signals at certain frequencies.

treble frequencies

Higher audio frequencies.

tremolo

An even, repeated change in volume of a musical tone. A periodic change in amplitude, usually controlled by an LFO, with a periodicity of less than 20Hz.

triangular wave

A waveform that looks triangular.

trigger

1. The signal or action of sending a signal to control the start of an event. 2. A device that emits a signal to control the start of an event, including a device that puts out such a signal when struck.

trim

1. Abbreviation of *trim control*. 2. To make a small adjustment to any control.

trim control

A device that reduces the strength of a signal produced by an amplifier, often over a restricted range.

trim status

Solid State Logic's Console Automation mode, which operates as follows: when a slide is at its trim point, the gain variations (fader movements) last programmed in the computer will be in effect; when the slide is moved from the trim point, gain or loss is added to or subtracted from the program.

troubleshooting

The act of locating the source of trouble in a malfunctioning device or system.

truncation

The editing of a sample playback so that only the desired portion of the sample is played. Effected by moving the start and end points of the sample playback.

TT

A trademark of Switchcraft, the same as *Tiny Telephone jack/plug*.

tube

An abbreviation of *vacuum tube*, ie an amplifying device that has elements to send and control current through a vacuum in a glass or metal tube.

tuned

A term used with reference to a circuit or device which is most sensitive to a certain frequency.

tuned cavity

A cavity which, because of its physical dimensions, will resonate at a particular frequency (ie it will tend to reinforce the energy at certain frequencies of vibration).

tuned pipe instrument

An instrument that uses a pipe of certain dimensions as a sound generator.

tuning fork

A metal fork that has two prongs which tend to vibrate and put out a fairly pure tone of one frequency.

turnover frequency

The same as *cut-off frequency*, ie the highest or lowest frequency in the pass band of a filter.

turntable

1. A device that supports and rotates a phonograph record during playback. 2. One of the round disc platters that holds a reel and reel lock and is driven by a reel motor (also known as a *deck*).

tweak

A slang term meaning to calibrate (ie to set all operating controls and adjustments in order to obtain a device's optimum performance), particularly in terms of very precise calibration.

tweeter

A speaker designed to reproduce only higher frequencies.

two-way speaker

A speaker system fitted with separate speakers – a woofer and a tweeter – in order to reproduce lower and higher frequencies respectively.

μ

1. The Greek letter *mu*, which is actually a forerunner of the English M, although lower-case *u* is often used in place of it, because of its similar appearance. 2. A symbol used to represent the prefix micro (ie one millionth).

unbalanced

Used to describe a method of interconnecting recorders, amplifiers and other electronic gear using twin-conductor cable.

undo

A command in some computer software that reverses the last command entered.

uni

A prefix meaning "one".

unidirectional

A pick-up pattern that's more sensitive to sound arriving from one direction than from any other.

unison

Several performers, instruments or sound sources sounding at the same time and with the same pitch.

unity gain

No increase or decrease in signal strength at the output of an amplifier or device when compared to the signal strength at the input.

update by absolute

Solid State Logic name for the action of rewriting the settings of an automated console control.

Update mode

A mode of console automation that allows the programming of a console channel to be modified so that, when the slide of the fader is at a predetermined point (usually the point marked "0"), the gain variations (fader movements) last programmed into the computer will be in effect, but when the engineer moves the slide up or down from this point, gain or loss is added to or subtracted from the programmed level.

vacuum tube

An amplifying device that has elements to send and control current through a vacuum in a glass or metal tube.

vacuum-tube voltmeter

A device that measures electrical voltage and uses a vacuum tube to drive its indicator so that testing the circuit does not load the circuit.

vamp

The repeated part of a tune at its end, usually the chorus or part of the chorus.

vamp and fade

A method of ending a recording of a tune where part of the music is repeated and the engineer reduces volume until the music fades out.

Variable-D

A patented invention of Electrovoice where several ports are inserted in the casing of a microphone. These ports are increasingly less sensitive to high frequencies, as they are further away from the diaphragm, reducing the proximity effect.

VCA

Abbreviation for *voltage-controlled amplifier*, ie an amplifier that will change gain according to the level of control voltage sent to it.

VCA automation

A system of channel gain (or other functions) controlled by a computer via the use of voltage-controlled amplifiers, which change gain according to the level of control voltages sent to them by the computer.

VCA fader

A fader with a VCA in its casing arranged so that, in manual operation, the slide of the fader controls how much control voltage is sent to the VCA and therefore controls the channel gain.

VCA group

Several VCA faders that are fed control voltages from a group master slide.

VCA master

A slider that feeds control voltages to several VCAs in order to control the gain in several audio channels.

VCA trim

A control in an audio system (such as a console) that can adjust the control voltage feeding all VCAs, usually with a limited range.

VCF

1. Abbreviation of *voltage-controlled filter*, the cut-off frequency of which can be changed by altering the amount of voltage being sent to its control input. 2. The digital equivalent of a VCF.

VCO

1. Abbreviation of *foltage-control oscillator*, which generates an AC control voltage, usually in the form of a low-frequency oscillator putting out a signal between .1Hz and 10Hz. 2. Abbreviation of *voltage-controlled oscillator*, which changes its frequency according to a control voltage fed to its control input.

velocity

In synthesisers and keyboard controllers, a MIDI message giving data on how hard a key is struck. Alternatively, a type of MIDI data (ranging between 1 and 127) usually used to indicate how quickly a key is pushed down (attack velocity) or allowed to rise (release velocity). (A Note-On message with a velocity value of zero is equivalent to a Note-Off message.)

velocity curve

A map that translates incoming velocity values into other velocities in order to alter the feel or response of a keyboard or tone module.

velocity microphone

Another name for *pressure-gradient microphone*, ie one whose diaphragm is exposed at the front and back and the movement of which is caused by small differences in pressure between the front and back of the diaphragm.

velocity sensitive

The same as *touch sensitive*, used to describe a synthesiser keyboard's ability to generate a

MIDI Velocity signal. Not all synthesiser keyboards are velocity sensitive.

vibrato

1. A smooth and repeated changing of pitch up and down from the regular musical pitch, often practised by singers. 2. A periodic change in frequency, often controlled by an LFO, with a periodicity of less than 20Hz.

virtual

Existing only in software.

virtual tracking

Having a MIDI sequencer operating in sync with a multitrack tape and controlling the playing of synthesisers along with recorded parts.

vocal booth

A isolation room used to record a vocal track so that other instruments in the studio don't leak into the vocal microphone. Also used to reduce ambience and reverberation in a vocal recording.

vocoder

An effects device that will modulate (control) one signal with another.

voice

1. In synthesisers, a pitch that can be played at the same time as other pitches. 2. In Yamaha synths, a term meaning the same thing as *sound patch*, ie a sound that can be created by the synth.

voice channel

A signal path containing (as a minimum) an oscillator and VCA, or their digital equivalent, and capable of producing a note. On a typical synthesiser, two or more voice channels – each with their own waveform and parameter settings – can be combined to form a single note.

voice stealing

A process by which a synthesiser that is being required to play more notes than it has available voices switches off some of the voices that are currently sounding (typically those that have been sounding the longest or are the lowest amplitude) in order to assign them to play new notes.

volatile memory

Computer memory that will be lost when the computer is turned off.

voltage

The electrical force that pushes electrons in order to obtain electrical current.

voltage controlled

Used to describe a device that will change its output according to the amount of control voltage sent to its control input.

voltage-controlled amplifier

The same as *VCA*, ie an amp that changes gain according to the level of control voltage sent to it.

voltage-controlled attenuator

Similar to a voltage-controlled amplifier, except that, with no control voltage sent to it, the amplifier will have no gain and no loss. As an increasing control voltage is sent to it, the amplifier reduces gain, causing a loss of signal strength.

voltage-controlled fader

The same as *VCA fader*, ie a fader with a VCA in its casing arranged so that, in manual operation, the slide of the fader controls how much control voltage is sent to the VCA and therefore controls the channel gain.

voltage-controlled filter

A filter (especially a low-pass filter) that will change its cut-off frequency according to the level of the control voltage being fed to its control input.

voltage-controlled oscillator

The same as definition 2 of *VCO*, ie an oscillator that changes its frequency according to a control voltage fed to its control input.

voltage-control oscillator

The same as *VCO* (definition 1), ie an oscillator that generates an AC control voltage, usually a low-frequency signal between .1Hz and 10Hz.

voltmeter

A meter that can test the level of voltage.

volume

1. A common, non-technical term equivalent to level of sound pressure and loosely applied to also mean audio voltage level. 2. Abbreviation of the term *volume control*.

volume control

An amplifier's gain control.

volume envelope

The way in which a note sounded by a musical instrument changes in volume over time.

volume pedal

A guitar pedal used to change the volume of an instrument or a similar device used with other instruments, such as an organ.

volume unit

A unit designed to measure perceived changes in loudness in audio material. The unit is basically the decibel change of the average level, as read by a volume unit (VU) meter. The movement of the VU meter is designed to approximately match the ear's response to changes in level.

vox

Latin for "voice", used on track logs to denote a vocal track.

VSO

Another term for a *vacuum-tube voltmeter*, ie a device that measures the electrical voltage and uses a vacuum tube to drive the indicator so that testing the circuit does not load the circuit.

VU

1. Abbreviation of the term *volume unit*, ie a unit designed to measure perceived changes in loudness in audio material. 2. A meter that reads levels of audio voltage fed into or out of a piece of equipment and is designed to match the ear's response to sudden changes in level.

wah/wah-wah

A changing filter that filters either more or less of an instrument's harmonics.

watt

Unit of electrical power.

WAV

The Windows audio file format. Typically encountered as "filename.wav".

wave

A continuous fluctuation in the amplitude of a quantity with respect to time.

wave flank

A term with the same meaning as *bank*, ie a collection of sound patches in computer memory.

waveform/waveshape

The shape made by fluctuations in a wave over a period over time.

wavelength

The length of one cycle (in feet, inches, etc) of a wave.

wavetable synthesis

A common method for generating sound electronically on a synthesiser or PC. Output is produced using a table of sound samples (actual recorded sounds) which are digitised and played back as needed. By continuously re-reading samples and looping them together at different pitches, highly complex tones can be generated from a minimum of stored data without overtaxing the processor.

wave velocity

The time it takes for one point of a waveform to travel a certain distance.

weber

A unit that describes a number of magnetic lines of force. Used in the measurement or statement of magnetic flux density (the strength of magnetism).

weighting

An equalisation curve used in audio tests that compensates for the Fletcher Munson effect at various levels.

wet

Having reverberation or ambience. Alternatively, consisting entirely of processed sound. The output of an effects device is 100% wet when only the output of the processor itself is being heard, with none of the dry (unprocessed) signal.

wheel

A controller used for pitch bending or modulation, normally mounted on the left-hand side of the keyboard and played with the left hand.

white noise

Random energy distributed so that the amount of energy is the same for each cycle, causing the noise level to increase with frequency.

wide-band noise

Noise that has energy over a wide range of frequencies.

width

Another term for *depth*, ie the amount of change in a controlled signal exerted by the control signal.

wild sound

Sound recordings that are taken completely separately from the master recording (or *picture recording*), and therefore can't be synced to the master recording.

windscreen

A device that reduces or eliminates wind noise from the microphone being moved or from blowing into the microphone on remote-location recordings.

wireless microphone

A microphone with an FM radio transmitter inside its casing that transmits a signal to an offstage FM receiver.

woodwind controller

A device that plays like a woodwind instrument, controlling a sound module by putting out a control voltage or MIDI command.

woofer

A speaker designed to reproduce only bass frequencies.

word

A shortening of the term *digital word*, ie a number of information bits that communicate one value.

workstation

A device that controls a variety of functions and is designed to be operated by one person, comprising a synthesiser or sampler in which several of the tasks usually associated with electronic music production – such as sequencing, effects processing, rhythm programming and storing data on disk – can all be performed by components found within a single physical device.

wow

A low pitch change that occurs because the speed of a recorder or playback machine fluctuates slowly.

wrap

The angle formed by the tape as it bends around the head.

write

To record digital data onto a digital recording or into computer memory.

write head

The device in a digital audio tape recorder that records the bits of digital information onto the storage medium.

Write mode

A mode of operation in an automated console where an engineer is in control of channel gain and the computer stores the changes in gain effected by the engineer over time.

XLR connector

1. A common three-pin connector used in balanced audio connections. 2. A microphone cable.

XY miking

A method of arranged two cardioid microphones for stereo pick-up, with the two mic heads positioned as close together as possible without touching, pointing 90° away from each other and 45° to the centre of the sound source.

Y-cord/lead

A cable fitted with three connectors, so that one output may be sent to two inputs.

zenith

The tilt of the tape head in the direction perpendicular to the travel of the tape.

zero-crossing point

The point at which a digitally encoded waveform crosses the centre of its amplitude range.